Zyklon

John Hazen

Black Rose Writing | Texas

The final approval for this literary material is granted by the author.

First printing

This is a work of fiction. Names, characters, businesses, places, events and incidents
are either the products of the author's imagination or used in a fictitious manner.
Any resemblance to actual persons, living or dead, or actual events is purely
coincidental.

ISBN: 978-1-68433-090-4
PUBLISHED BY BLACK ROSE WRITING
www.blackrosewriting.com

Printed in the United States of America
Suggested Retail Price (SRP) $19.95

Zyklon is printed in Cambria

This book is dedicated to our country's journalists, those members of a Free Press who doggedly search for truth every day.

Also by John Hazen

Fava

Journey of an American Son

Aceldama

Dear Dad

Zyklon

*The only thing necessary for the triumph of evil,
is for good men to do nothing.*
—Edmund Burke (1729-1797)

1

"Dave, have law enforcement officials been able to identify the three victims?" I asked our reporter, Dave Glass, who was on the scene in Brooklyn where a gang-style execution of three Hispanic men in their early twenties had taken place in the early morning hours.

"No, they haven't, Francine. I spoke to both NYPD and FBI officials before coming on the air and they are still trying to identify them. They have some leads but nothing solid at the moment."

"Thank you for your report. Keep us posted on any new developments."

The split screen shifted to me alone on the screen.

"That was Dave Glass reporting from the scene of a triple execution-style slaying in the Park Slope section of Brooklyn. We'll now leave you for a few messages from our sponsors and when we come back we'll get an update from Katrina Turow who's on the presidential trail with candidate Malcolm McKenzie. This is Francine Vega for Action 6 News."

I was rather wistful at that moment. Prior to my promotion to co-anchor for morning news on Action 6 News in New York, something like a triple murder in Brooklyn would have been my story. I would have been in the field, investigating stories, conducting interviews and following up on leads. That's my true love. Being an anchor was much better pay and higher exposure and I would have been a fool to turn it down a year and a half ago, but I longed in my heart to be back out there.

While Dave is an excellent, hard-working reporter, I would have had a leg up on this story. For example, I'd already learned from my husband, Special Agent Will Allen, that the FBI did know the identities of the three slain men (they were mules for the Diego cartel out of Mexico) but the authorities chose not to reveal that information to the public at this time for fear that it could hamper the investigation. Perhaps Dave had also been told this confidentially, but I doubted it.

After the commercial break, our viewers were welcomed back by my co-anchor, the white-haired news veteran John Gray.

"Let's head out to Battle Creek, Michigan where we'll find Katrina Turow, who will give us the latest on the improbable presidential campaign of Reverend Malcolm McKenzie. Thank you for joining us so early in the morning, Katrina. I know you must be exhausted, given that the Reverend's rally went until close to midnight last night."

"Sleep is highly overrated, John. I'll get plenty once the campaign is over."

Katrina Turow did seem to be indefatigable, on the tube at all hours of the day. In her low thirties, slightly older than I, she was a bright, pretty, perky blonde who was taking full advantage of the chance given her to make her name in this tough male-dominated business.

We both came to Action 6 News about seven years ago. She did much the same types of stories as I: mostly local events sprinkled with an occasional transit strike or other real news pieces. I would have liked to become friends with her but we were both young and ambitious. We weren't backstabbing or anything like that, but our competition kept us from getting close.

I was surprised and pleased, therefore, when Katrina gave me a warm hug and sincere congratulations after I was promoted to morning anchor. I did deserve it—I played a key role in thwarting a plot to destroy Mecca for which I was considered for a Pulitzer and was personally responsible for Action 6 News ratings rising from number 4 (that is, last) in New York to number 2—but that doesn't mean everyone welcomed me with open arms.

To his credit, my co-anchor, John Gray, has always been professional. He's never been especially warm towards me; he's not especially warm with anybody. But he wasn't antagonistic when I took over the chair beside him. Glenn Wilson, the morning meteorologist, on the other hand, was most definitely resentful. He's never done anything outwardly hostile but there were always little things he'd do to undermine me. Telling Frank McDermott, our station news director, that he'd let me know about a hastily scheduled programming meeting but then somehow forgetting to inform me so that I'd have to get a call asking me to join the meeting already in progress; things like that.

Word had gotten back to me that he's spread rumors that I'd gotten the anchor job not because of my abilities but because of my looks and my relationship with Frank. I wouldn't be surprised if he'd made comments that Frank and I were sleeping together. For the record, I have never slept with Frank or ever even thought of him that way. And the feeling is reciprocal. Frank is the most devoted husband and father I have ever known.

In regards to my looks, I can name at least ten other women I know personally—Katrina included—that I consider more beautiful than I am. As I'm doing a show I consciously refrain from looking at myself in the monitor. All I would see are the flaws in my appearance. This, in turn, would make me fixate on the relatively short shelf life accorded on-camera women in the news business.

I suppose there are some people that find me attractive since I was given the dubious distinction of being named New York Trends Magazine's Hottest NYC TV Reporter two years running. While I would rant about the sexism of the award, an inner part of me was flattered. I didn't make the cut this year, however. My guess is, now that I'm a mother, my desirability level has plunged significantly.

Granted, I was only twenty-eight when Frank approached me and advised me the anchor job was mine if I wanted it. I passed over a number of reporters who were much more seasoned than I when Willa Harrington, our former anchor, jumped to another station. But to imply that I hadn't earned my stripes was downright insulting especially after what I'd gone through.

I was nominated for a Pulitzer for a story that had international consequences. I say in all modesty that it was great journalism. It was my efforts that saved the city of Mecca from being destroyed and kept the world from plunging into world war. I worked closely with FBI Special Agent Will Allen (who would subsequently become my husband and the father of our daughter, Rosa) and Alan Westbrook, a brilliant but quite unstable genius/computer nerd. In the process, I was nearly killed a half dozen times. If that isn't "earning my stripes" I don't know what is.

I should have been a shoo-in for the Pulitzer but the federal government, which was profoundly embarrassed by complicity at the highest levels in the plot to destroy Mecca, did all they could to undermine—and even at times discredit—my efforts. Hence, the Pulitzer went elsewhere. Oh well.

Still, I never saw any advantage to confronting Glenn to see what his beef with me was. I always viewed weathermen as the defensive backs of TV news. My guess is that, when they were young boys, very few football players dreamed of someday being a defensive back. The glory positions are all on offense. Perhaps there are some meteorologists that see themselves doing that job from a young age. However, many ended up in that profession because they didn't have the stuff to be real news people. When Will and I would watch football and a defensive back would go up for an interception only to have the ball bounce off his hands, I'd remark, "That's why he's not a receiver." Weathermen like Glenn fit that bill.

Anyway, I digress. Earlier this year Katrina had been approached by the network and was offered the chance to go out on the presidential campaign trail with a candidate. The candidate they offered her was none other than my old friend, Reverend Malcolm McKenzie.

Reverend McKenzie, or simply "The Reverend" as he liked to be called, had been propelled to national prominence when he promoted the thing I was trying to thwart: a mad scheme to wipe Islam off the face of the earth by destroying Mecca. When I first became aware of the plot, I went to his brother, Edward, who worked for the State Department as an expert on Arab relations. Edward was extremely dismissive of my concerns but that did not stop him from conveying them to Malcolm, probably over a couple beers. The problem was that The Reverend did not think it ludicrous as he went on to make a nationally televised speech condemning Islam at one of those Southern mega-churches. He called it his own "Cross of Gold" speech that propelled him to such national prominence that he soon considered running for the Presidency.

Whenever he spouted this and other equally offensive ideas, the crowds would go wild. At first, he promoted his ideas as a holy war, Christianity vs. Islam, but as his message grew more vitriolic and gained more acceptance, he decided to enter the political realm.

After Katrina got the assignment to cover McKenzie, she invited me out to lunch since she knew I had a history with him. While she bemoaned being paired with such a minor candidate who would probably fizzle out after a month or two, she was determined to make the best of it. Another chance like this may not come along and she was a professional who wanted to make the most of the opportunity. She wanted to find out all she could about the man she was covering and the first step in that process was to pick my brain. She had already done a ton of research on him, including reading his autobiography, but she wanted to see if I had any personal insights on the man.

I described him as not an especially bright or inquisitive person but he was a master of latching onto what the people want to hear and exploiting that to his full advantage.

"The Reverend focuses on a large segment of the population—white males primarily—who feel society had left them behind. He offers them rationales as to why they aren't living in big fancy houses or driving the latest model Mercedes Benz. The reasons are always that "others"— immigrants, Mexicans, Muslims—had taken what was rightfully theirs. And in the process, these others had taken America away from them. Malcolm McKenzie makes it clear that he is the one person who can help them achieve the greatness denied them.

"Facts don't mean a lot to McKenzie. He's a master communicator and does it purely on an emotional level. As a man of the cloth, he cloaks his statements in religion, which the masses lap up.

"Katrina, watch your back. Reverend McKenzie definitely has a vindictive streak. I had done a couple of pieces on-air pointing out how fact-free his campaign was and how inconsistent many of his policies were and how dangerous the message he was spreading could be. He initiated a smear campaign against me after I got in his way. He probably thought it wiser not to go after Will, an FBI agent, but I was fair game. As a result, I received numerous death threats and protests from his followers. Those died down after a while."

I didn't think it wise to tell her that his vendetta only ceased after Will's two assistants, Agents Willoughby and Broderick, paid The Reverend a special late night visit.

Now, here we were four months later and instead of The Reverend's star plummeting from the sky, it instead was shining brighter than ever.

Katrina's tenure on the campaign trail, and not to mention her national visibility, therefore kept getting augmented and extended. Last time the campaign swung through New York, Katrina and I got together for lunch

"Katrina," I confided, "I am quite jealous of you."

"Of me? You're an anchor in the biggest market in the country. If anyone should be jealous, it should be me."

"I thought my girlhood urge for fame and notoriety had been sated but here I am wishing I was back out there again in the field, and on a national campaign no less."

"You'll just have to suffer through being a highly paid anchor with a happy marriage and kids you brag about all the time. Tough life you got there."

"When you put it that way, it does make me sound like quite a whiner, doesn't it?"

"I wasn't going to go that far, but..."

Two weeks later, Katrina began her live report from Michigan. During the commercial break, Katrina told us that a group—or more precisely a mob—of McKenzie supporters set upon the reporters during the rally. The Secret Service intervened and the altercation didn't last long enough for there to be footage although one competing network had secured a shaky smart phone video of the assault.

Katrina tried to downplay the incident but just looking at her made it obvious that it was more serious than she let on. The right side of her face looked swollen, as though she'd been beaten. Professional makeup had hidden most of the redness but it could not mask the swelling. Still, she soldiered on as if nothing had happened.

"During his remarks to a packed house at last night's rally," she noted, "Reverend McKenzie continued to hammer home his themes of better border protection and the need to punish Islam as a scourge on the face of the Earth. The crowds wherever he goes are receptive to these messages, and the reaction by the people in attendance on this night was no different.

"Reverend McKenzie has yet to hold a press conference," she stated, "but he has done several one-on-one interviews with Astra Broadcasting, including one he did yesterday just before his rally. Here is a short segment of that interview with Janine Tonelli."

The viewer then sees Reverend McKenzie and Astra Broadcasting host Tonelli sitting in heavily upholstered armchairs in front of shelves hosting an array of books on numerous subjects.

"Reverend McKenzie, can you give our viewers an explanation for your meteoric and improbable rise in politics to where you're now the leading candidate to take your party's nomination for President of the United States?"

"There's a hunger out there, Janine, a hunger for someone who hasn't been bought, for someone who tells is like it is and has spent a lifetime watching out for the forgotten people of this country. While my rise may be a surprise to many people, it sure isn't to me."

"What do you say to those who claim your campaign is built on hate and fear, especially against Muslims?"

"I hate no one. I have spent a life dedicated to loving my fellow man. But I know personally the insidious nature of Islam and find it contrary to everything this country stands for."

"Tell me about your personal experience."

"Most people know how close I am to my brother, Edward. We were extremely close growing up but then he married a Muslim woman who tore our family apart. Because of her, my brother and I didn't speak for over a decade. Then she tore his heart out by leaving him, taking their children and fleeing to Jordan. Now, my brother and I have reconciled and he is managing my campaign. I have nothing against Muslims. I just don't feel that they fit in well with the American way of life. That's just one example."

The viewer was switched back to Katrina.

"Last night, however, the Reverend added a new sector of society as being worthy of the public's enmity. I'm talking about the media. We as a group received special notice as being"

She looked down at her notes.

"in league with Satan aligned against America's interests. Later on in the rally, some people took his message to heart and decided they needed to attack Satan directly. Since all the reporters had been herded into a pen, we were an easily identifiable target."

She stopped cold. She appeared woozy and wobbled but then she steadied herself. One of her production assistants was obviously coming to help her but she waved them away as she composed herself.

"My apologies. Sometimes the weeks and months on the road can take its toll. Needless to say, Reverend McKenzie has, in his own words 'declared war on the dishonest media and will bring them to account for any lies that they spread.' "

She had another minute dedicated to her report but we could tell she was having trouble proceeding so I interjected before she finished.

"Katrina, thank you for your reports from the campaign. They are always fair and well-researched. You're doing exactly what a reporter should be doing. Keep it up."

She raised her head and looked directly into the camera. There was a determined smile on her lips.

"Thank you for those kind words, Francine. Don't worry about me. I'm in this to the end no matter what the candidate and his followers say or do. This is Katrina Turow reporting from Battle Creek, Michigan."

The report ended as the scene shifted to an adorable panda gnawing on some bamboo shoots. The director, Gary Freeman, indicated that we would go to commercial in fifteen seconds.

"We'll take a break now to pay some bills. When we come back we'll show you something else you can do this weekend as we join Stacy Wills at the Bronx Zoo with a report on Oscar the panda, the zoo's latest addition. I'm Francine Vega here with my good friend John Gray and you're watching Action 6 News."

We all fell silent.

It was later revealed that Katrina suffered two cracked ribs, a concussion and multiple contusions. Her staff had pleaded with her immediately after the incident to go to the hospital but she declined. After completing her report, she finally relented and went to the local hospital where she subsequently was admitted. Further examination revealed that her spleen had been lacerated when she was thrown against a chair. Suspecting internal bleeding, the doctors rushed her into surgery. If they hadn't operated, she could have died within hours.

Just before we were to return from commercial break, I heard Station News Director Frank McDermott coming through on my earpiece. The panda would have to wait. Gary indicated we were about to go live: three, two, one. I began to speak while across the bottom of the screen were the words: Breaking News.

"We have just received word that Aaron Kaplow, the so-called Zyklon Killer, has been executed by the State of Texas. His death was confirmed at 6:23 this morning. Mr. Kaplow was convicted of murdering Lawrence Heinz, a resident of Austin, Texas."

An old mug shot of Aaron Kaplow, a brown-haired unshaven man in his mid-forties, displayed on the screen beside me.

"Three years ago Mr. Kaplow incapacitated Mr. Heinz and tied him to chair in a hotel room that had been completely sealed with duct tape. Kaplow then released Zyklon B, the infamous gas used by the Nazis to exterminate Jews and others at concentration camps, most notably Auschwitz, into the room, killing Heinz within minutes.

"The case received national attention not only because of the gruesome method in which Kaplow murdered his victims but because Mr. Heinz was the great-grandson of Albrecht Himmel, a barbaric SS officer who oversaw many executions at the Auschwitz Concentration Camp. The police and FBI had also determined that at least five other people, also descendants of Nazi officials, were known to have been killed in the same manner over the period of ten years in multiple cities. Two of these victims lived here in New York City.

"In each of the murders, Kaplow left a note highlighting the victim's Nazi lineage and providing a warning to any future SS-type officers from coming forward, knowing that their sins could be visited on future generations.

"After Aaron Kaplow was captured and tried in Texas, the State of New York requested that he be extradited to New York to stand trial for the murder of Frieda Horzapfel and Wendy Smith to give the families of those victims some level of justice. The State of Texas refused to release Kaplow from its jurisdiction and proceeded with the execution this morning. This has placed a significant strain on the relations between the two states for well over a year.

"For more on the execution, we turn to Gene Chebra from our sister station in Austin. Gene, this is Francine Vega in New York. I understand you've been following this case from the beginning."

Gene took it from there, rehashing much of the information I had just provided the viewer, but adding additional insights. For example, he pointed out how hostile the relations between the two states had become. He also talked about the notes left by each of the bodies noting that the person themselves may be innocent but they still had blood on their hands put there by their notorious relatives. The notes went on to state that the Jews who were gassed at Auschwitz and other camps were similarly innocent.

The killings, which took place over the course of ten years in five different cities—Austin; New York; Chicago; Norfolk, Virginia; and Paris, France—went unsolved until the Austin police received an anonymous tip and raided the apartment in which Aaron Kaplow was residing. There they found the pellets from which the gas could be produced, rolls of duct tape and anti-Nazi scribblings. These pieces of evidence, combined with his history of mental illness and his being the descendant of Jews who had survived the camps, made for an open and shut case. The final nail in the coffin was that he was in Paris at the same time the victim there was murdered.

The defense argued that Kaplow was being framed, that all the evidence was planted. Even the trip to Paris, his lawyer claimed, came about when Kaplow was notified that he was the winner of a contest he couldn't remember entering. All these claims fell on deaf ears and the jury rendered its guilty verdict in less than an hour. The claims, as well as a finding that he may not have been competent to stand trial, were discounted all the way up to the Supreme Court.

Most executions in Texas don't merit Breaking News status on New York stations but this one was different. Aaron Kaplow was implicated in at least two similar murders here and there was the ongoing dispute between our two states over jurisdiction. But even if there weren't these commonalities, I made it crystal clear to Frank that I would never forgive him if he didn't notify me as soon as the execution happened. Call it closure or justice or whatever, but I owed it to Wendy Smith to break into whatever story we were covering at the time to announce to the world that her killer had been removed from this earth.

2

Six years earlier

I had just arrived at work for the day when Frank called me into his office, telling me there was a story he wanted me to cover.

"Francine, We just got word over the wire that the Zyklon Killer struck again, out in Queens this time. The victim was a Wendy Smith. I want you to cover it."

"Isn't the Zyklon Killer George Zimmerly's story?"

"Yeah, but I want you to cover this one."

George had been on the outs for the past few months when he botched a report on a milk price fixing scheme that resulted in the station paying out a couple million dollars to settle a lawsuit. I felt sorry for George. He was a good reporter who made a costly mistake. But my sympathy for him didn't stop me from wanting a substantive story that I could sink my teeth into.

"Sure Frank, I'll run with it," I replied, trying to conceal my excitement.

There wasn't a lot on Wendy Smith in the announcement of police notice. She was in her mid-twenties, a Vassar graduate and had just started working for a midtown public relations firm, Alderson & Valenti. I figured that was the place to start. Our office was only about ten blocks away so I hurried over rather than call.

The young receptionist, a woman in her mid-twenties named Julie, had obviously been crying. My guess was that she had recently been told about her co-worker's murder and that they had been close. I introduced myself and told her I was there to ask about Wendy Smith. Fresh tears appeared in her eyes.

"Wendy and I were very close. She was engaged to be married next spring. I was going to be in her wedding party. I dare you find a single person who can say a negative thing about Wendy. She was active at a soup kitchen in Queens. She didn't have to do that, you know, but she did it."

Julie went on another ten minutes, extoling the virtues of Wendy in between bouts of crying her eyes out. I thought to myself that, if I died, would there be anyone who would carry on like this?

"Why would anybody kill Wendy?" she asked. "Why?"

I spoke with a couple more of her colleagues, each of whom painted the same picture but added no more information to the puzzle. As I was leaving, Julie called out to me.

"Ms. Vega, here is the number for her grandmother. She was Wendy's only family. Can you let me know if you find out anything?"

"I will, Julie. Thanks."

I dialed the number for her grandmother, Lena Smith, who lived on Long Island. I wasn't the first reporter to call Mrs. Smith, but since she hadn't yet been deluged, she answered my call. She later credited my courteous manner as the reason she granted an interview with me instead of any other reporter. The previous reporters that had called her dived right in with their questions about the murder and her reactions to it, some even before they identified themselves.

I would like to claim I was more courteous than the average reporter, but it was purely a case of my inexperience that came off as courtesy. When she answered, I momentarily froze. What I had rehearsed in my mind suddenly seemed crass. I said the first thing that came to my mind.

"Mrs. Smith, I'm so sorry for your loss. I can't even imagine losing a loved one like this, especially a granddaughter with her whole future ahead of her."

"Thank you. Who is this?"

"I'm sorry. This is Francine Vega from Action 6 News. I wanted to talk to you about your granddaughter but I understand if you're not in any mood to talk now. It was wrong of me to call to get your reaction to her death right now. I feel like such a vulture."

"It comes with your profession, I'm afraid. Would you like to come to my house this evening so we can talk? I want the world to know what an exceptional woman my granddaughter was. Now they only know her as the descendant of a butcher, but she was so much more. I need someone to tell her story. I think you are that person."

Three hours later I rang the doorbell at a well kept, split-level home in Bethpage, New York, a modest, relatively affluent suburb not too far out of the city on Long Island. Lena Smith greeted me at the door and invited me in. She was a slim and trim woman with pulled back gray hair. I estimated her to be in her mid-seventies. She poured Cokes for both of us and we sat down in her living room.

"Tell me about Wendy, Mrs. Smith."

"Please, call me Lena and I'll call you Francine, if that's okay," she responded in precisely enunciated English with touches of the German and Spanish she spoke in her youth.

"That sounds fine."

"I know it may sound biased but Wendy was the finest person I've ever known. She was lively, intelligent and personable. She would drop anything to help a person in need, even people she didn't know. She was in her junior year at NYU majoring in public administration when she read an article about the Peace Corps. Next thing I know, I get a call from her telling me she'd taken a leave of absence from school and would be heading to Nepal in three weeks as a Peace Corps volunteer. She was there as a grade school teacher but she helped out in many projects in the village, including constructing a viaduct to bring in fresh water from the neighboring hills.

"That's just one example of the person she was. Her parents died in an auto accident when she was young and she lived with me from then on so I knew her the best of anyone on earth. Here, let me show you some things she did."

She left the room and came back with a box of memorabilia. I got to see all of the awards Wendy won and all the essays she wrote. In other words, I saw all the keepsakes that any doting grandmother would pull out to brag about her beautiful granddaughter. While I didn't want to press her, I did want to get to the point of the visit. Otherwise, journalistically this would have been a total waste of time.

She was nearing the bottom of the box when she pulled yet another award and a tear came to her eye.

"This is a certificate of merit Wendy earned in high school for her proficiency in French. When it came time for her to select a language in junior high, she told me she was going to learn both German and Spanish. She knew I spoke both languages although I never spoke either of them once I stepped foot onto American soil. She wanted to share knowing those languages with me. Instead of being pleased, I exploded. 'You may learn Spanish if you so choose, but I forbid you to speak one word of the language of those foul people in this house. Do you understand me?'

"It came out with such venom and hatred that the poor child was petrified. I had never so much as raised my voice to this beautiful girl her entire life, but in one sentence I had rendered her petrified. I said something inane to lighten the mood, but it was a lame attempt. She didn't ask me why I didn't want her to study German but she reassured me that she wouldn't.

"I should have told her right then and there the entire story about my father, the great-grandfather she had never met, but I was too ashamed of myself. I would tell her when she was older and could better understand—no, understand isn't the right word, no one could ever understand a person acting the way my father had acted—let's just say absorb what I would tell her. There would be time later, I told myself. Little did I know there would be no time."

"Can you tell me about your father?"

"Let me go back to the beginning, if you don't mind and have the time."

"I don't mind. Please, take your time."

"I was born and raised in Buenos Aires, Argentina. My mother died when I was very young; I don't remember much about her. My father was known as Johann Schäfer. He was a kindly, quiet man who worked in a local paper mill. We lived in an upscale section of the city and I attended the finest private school in the city. We lived in circumstances far beyond what a factory job should have provided, but it all seemed natural to me and I never asked any questions.

"When I was eighteen and had just started studying at the University of Buenos Aires, I met a tall, dark and incredibly handsome American, Mark Smith, who worked at the American embassy. Despite the fact that he was ten years older than me, we dated and fell in love.

"My father did not like Mark at all, but he never gave me any specific reasons. He tried to say it was the age difference, but I pointed out that he was fifteen years older than my mother when they married. There were plenty of good solid Argentine boys I should be dating, not some American playboy, he'd say. Undeterred, I continued to see Mark, but I no longer brought him to my house.

"Mark and I had been going together for a year when one evening he picked me up at my dormitory to go to dinner at El Gaucho, our favorite restaurant. He seemed distracted and upset. I asked him what was wrong. He claimed it was nothing but as the evening progressed, his mood got even more preoccupied and distressed. I begged him to please tell me what was wrong. He paused initially and then he started to slowly explain.

"He started by telling me he loved me so much he could not stand it. 'And that makes you sad?' I asked, trying to lighten the mood. He said he loved me so much that he had planned to ask me to marry him that night. I told that if he did ask, my answer would be yes so I still did not see the problem.

"He then said that, after he told me what he needed to tell me, I might not be so quick to agree to marry him. 'What did you do, kill a man?' I joked. He paused and then responded. 'No, I didn't but your father did.' I asked him what he was talking about. He then told me that just before he came here, his superiors told me that my father's name was not Johann Schäfer but was actually Michael Strauss, an ex-Nazi who was an officer at the Buchenwald concentration camp. He was directly connected with the murder of at least thirty people while at that camp. I accused him of spreading lies. He had seen the evidence, sworn affidavits from dozens of witnesses. I countered that eyewitnesses identify the wrong suspects all the time.

"Then he told me there was forensic evidence as well. One witness, who was a policeman before he was arrested and interred, was able to get fingerprints from the officer who he saw shoot his wife in the head for some minor infraction. He preserved the fingerprint, knowing he might be able to use it if he ever got out of that hellhole. Authorities were able to lift your father's fingerprint and it's an identical match.

"Mark apologized but I would not hear of it. I told him he was a beast for even believing such a thing. I told him I hated him and then I stormed out.

"I fled the restaurant and ran the three miles back home, tears streaming down my face. When I arrived there, Father's things had been cleaned out and he was nowhere to be found. The network of ex-Nazis throughout Argentina was strong in those days and Michael Strauss had already been alerted that his identity had been uncovered. They took Strauss out of Buenos Aires and put him into hiding elsewhere.

"All I found was a short note he had penned just before he left telling me he loved me and that I would be hearing many lies about him over the coming days that I shouldn't believe. I needed to be strong in the face of these lies. The note went on to say that, because these lies had strong forces behind them, he had to get out of the city until the hysteria died down. He would let me know where he was settled as soon as he could safely do so. He also told me about a bank account he had created for me that I could access to continue my schooling and pay my living expenses. He finished by again saying he loved me and hoped we could be together again someday soon.

"I read the note over and over again, trying to believe that what Mark told me were lies, that my father was the gentle Johann Schäfer and not the brutal beast they were portraying him to be. Father's hasty departure did not do much to dispel my fears.

"My father's job at the paper mill was relatively low level and as I got older, I did begin to wonder how we could afford the nice things we had. I made an off-hand comment one day and Father claimed that it was family money. His father had been a wealthy banker who'd been killed during the war but had been able to get his money out of Germany prior to the war.

"He said no more and I did not pursue the issue any further, but questions lingered in my mind. If nothing else, why was Father so uneducated? When I was young, he could read and write but was so uninformed about the world. It wasn't that he was stupid or simple. As the years went on, he educated himself but if he had grown up rich, wouldn't he have received a proper education back in Germany?

"I also recalled the day that Adolf Eichmann was captured by the Israelis in the early sixties and taken back to Israel to stand trial. I was doing my homework on the kitchen table when two men showed up at our door. They had a brief discussion with father that I could only partially hear and then they left. Father was sullen and frightful for days after that. At one point, he grabbed a glass paperweight and hurled it against the wall, shattering it in pieces, all the while hurling invectives about the "fucking Jews." He immediately remembered I was in the room and apologized for his outburst and he returned to his former self.

"All these pieces fit together into the picture Mark painted of my father, but I persisted in believing the best of the man I knew and loved. Holding out hope that this nightmare would resolve itself, I left school and moved back home, waiting for Father to walk through the door, a vindicated man.

It was three months later when there was a knock on the door. I opened the door and standing there was one of the men who had come to our home some years ago.

"'Fraulein,' he said, 'I have a letter from your father.'

"He handed me the letter, bowed slightly, turned on his heels and walked away. I still gave my father the benefit of the doubt but I wondered why he didn't simply drop the letter in the mail rather than have this man serve as his messenger. I chided myself for overanalyzing everything and tore open the letter, hoping for some news, any news, about Father.

"The letter did not provide much in the way of anything new but there was a new dimension. It was rambling and somewhat unhinged.

"He still felt it was unsafe for him to reveal where he was located but hoped to reunite with me soon. It was the last two sentences in the letter that really unsettled me: 'The dirty Jews will stop at nothing to spread their lies. Don't believe them, my dearest Lena.' Other than that line and the previous unguarded outburst, I had never, ever heard him speak like this. He had never expressed a thought, either good or bad, about Jews, but now this.

"Just as I was feeling the most totally alone in the world I had ever felt, the doorbell rang again. I opened it and it was Mark. I alternated between being overjoyed to see him again and slamming the door in his face. I flew into his arms. I then asked to see the documentation against my father. He replied that, if he could get access to it, he would show it to me.'

"Three days later, Mark called me and asked if I could come to the embassy. We entered a sealed room with a Marine sentry posted outside. A thick folder was already placed on a conference table. I sat down in front of it, almost afraid to touch it for fear the words and images inside would burn my fingers. Mark started to walk away to give me some privacy when I grabbed his arm and asked if he would sit down beside me as I went through the material.

"There were twenty-five affidavits of witnesses to and victims of the crimes of Michael Strauss. There was some limited forensic evidence such as the fingerprints but no pictures of him as an officer in the SS, so I still held out a sliver of hope that this was the wrong man, that it was a terrible misunderstanding.

"Sitting with Mark, I read each affidavit through thoroughly, no matter how gruesome and graphic the description was. While each successive word of each account made the truth abundantly clear, it was the last affidavit that damned my father. Even though it was so devastating—or perhaps because it was so devastating—I pleaded with Mark to make me a copy of the affidavit. It was strictly against the rules. He objected, but ultimately, he relented."

Lena got up and went to the desk in the next room and brought back a sheaf of yellowing papers. She proceeded to read it aloud to me, translating from German to English as she read.

3

My name is Miriam Berger. I was born and raised in Munich but am presently a resident of Haifa, Israel. The date of this deposition is Friday, June 7, 1968.

Late in the evening of November 9, 1938, or what has become known as Kristallnacht, there was a knock on the door of the apartment where I lived with my parents, Ruth and Samuel Abramowitz, and my young brother, Isaak. I was thirteen years old at the time.

My father looked through the peephole and then opened the door. It was our dear friend, Hans Werner, who had worked with my father at an auction house for years until my father was forced out of his job under the Law on the Profession of Auctioneer that was enacted in February 1938. Between then and November, we were able to live on the money my parents had saved over the years, or periodically selling some of our belongings and on the kindness of the Werners.

The Werners had been guests at our house a number of times so I knew them rather well. They were always nice to Isaak and me.

When Mr. Werner arrived at our door, my father and he had an intense discussion. I could not overhear what they were talking about. Immediately after that, my father took me to my room where together we packed up my few belongings into an old cardboard valise we had. Then he knelt down and gave me a big hug. When he released me, there were tears in his eyes. Seeing him like this and sensing something was terribly wrong but not knowing exactly what it was, a tear escaped from my eye. He reached up and brushed it away from my face.

"My little sparrow," he always called me that because I was always singing and he joked that I was going to be the next Piaf, "you are going to go and live with Mr. and Mrs. Werner for a short time. You have always been such a good girl who would listen to your mother and me. I want you to listen to the Werners in just the same way. Do you understand?"

I was too emotional to say anything so my father pressed me again.

"It is important that you understand what I am saying. You must obey the Werners and do everything they say. Okay?"

"Yes, papa."

"Your brother is going to live with another family we know in Augsburg. We will all be together again soon, but in the meantime, you are never to mention us to anyone. Starting tonight, you will be known as Berta Werner. You grew up in Hamburg. Your parents were Klaus and Ilsa Werner but after your father died in an automobile accident and your mother died of tuberculosis, you came to live with your aunt and uncle, Hans and Giselle Werner. Your home is located at 156 Romanstrasse, here in Munich."

My father made me repeat this information back to him at least ten times until he was satisfied that I knew it by heart. He then led me back out to the living room where my mother, Isaak and Mr. Werner were waiting.

"Give your mother and Isaak big hugs," my father said. I did and then he leaned back down to me and likewise gave me a huge bear hug.

"We'll be together again soon, my little sparrow," he whispered in my ear. He then stood back up, handed the valise to Mr. Werner. Mr. Werner held the valise in his left hand and took my hand with his right. He nodded to my parents and we departed.

It was the last time I ever saw my parents or Isaak. I don't know if the other family ever came to get Isaak or whether they were among the thousands that were taken into custody that terrible night.

Mr. Werner had me hunch down on the floor in the back seat of his car and he put a dark blanket over me. He told me that it was extremely important that I not say a word or move the entire ride back to his home over three miles away. A simple muscle twitch could have been the difference between life and death for both him and me.

He drove slowly to his apartment building, but not so slowly as to be noticeable. During the trip we could periodically hear shouting and swear words, and at one point he had to pull over and someone shined a flashlight into the car. I could make out the bright light through the blanket, but I was doing exactly what Mr. Werner told me to do and did not so much as breathe for as long as I could.

The light moved on and I could hear a man demanding to see Mr. Werner's papers, which I assume he produced since, after a few more inquiries, we were allowed to proceed.

I tried to keep track of the turns Mr. Werner was making but it was useless trying to determine where I was. Soon after we were stopped, Mr. Werner made a turn and the inside of the car was brightly illuminated, but it was not by a flashlight. This was a yellowish, not white, light that filtered through my blanket. It also became uncomfortably hot and stifling in the car. I was almost to the point where I was desperate enough to throw off the blanket to get some air when Mr. Werner whispered back to me.

"Lie still, my dear Berta, we'll be past this in a minute or so."

True to his word, the unbearable heat inside the car soon dissipated and the illumination was gone, leaving me once more in darkness. After that, we drove the remaining couple of miles in peace and quiet. Three blocks from his home, Mr. Werner pulled over to the side of the road and told me to get up from the floor and to come around and get into the passenger seat beside him. We then drove on to his apartment building. He pulled into his parking spot and we entered the building. As we were waiting for the elevator, another man walked into the lobby. I immediately stiffened but Mr. Werner remained calm.

"Ernst, how are you?"

"As well as might be expected, Hans. Have you heard what's happening?"

"Heard it? I drove through it! This is my niece, Berta. I had to pick her up at the train station and we couldn't help but go right through the middle of it. You know the big synagogue on Nymphenburger Strasse? It was entirely engulfed in flame. People were roaming the streets, destroying anything they could find."

"Well, we're lucky we don't have many of them in our neighborhood. There wasn't much looting or destruction around here. You're lucky you weren't attacked in the frenzy."

"We did get asked for our papers at one point. Luckily, everything was in order and they let us pass on. Oh, where are my manners? As I mentioned, this is Berta Werner. Berta, this is Ernst Flick. He lives on our floor."

"So, are you here for a visit, Ms. Werner?"

"Unfortunately, Berta's parents, my brother and his wife, both passed away and Berta has come to live with us from Hamburg."

"I am so sorry for your loss, Fräulein Werner, but welcome to our fair city. I assume you participated in the Hitler Youth in Hamburg. We'll have to get you enrolled in the local chapter once you get settled."

"I would look forward to that, Herr Flick. Thank you."

"A respectful and courteous young woman. I like that."

The elevator finally came and we rode up together, exchanging small talk until we arrived at the 5th floor. When we got off, Mr. Flick said his goodbyes and went to the right. We went to the left.

As soon as we entered the apartment, Mrs. Werner ran from the other room to her husband.

"Thank goodness you're fine. I was beside myself with fear. The devil is on the loose tonight."

Then she turned to me and reached out to give me a hug.

"And I am so relieved you are alright, too, my dear. Berta, welcome to our home."

"Thank you, ma'am."

"Stop the ma'am right now. I am your Aunt Giselle and from henceforward I am taking place of your mother, although I am a poor substitute. But if you hesitate or appear to be not familiar with us, it could cost us all our lives."

"Now, now, my dear. Our Berta has already passed her first test. We rode the elevator up with Ernst Flick and our "daughter" handled herself quite well."

Mrs. Werner took my hands in hers and looked me in the eyes.

"I'm sorry, but this is new to all of us. I'm nervous but I forgot how terrified you must be. We must all learn how to behave differently, and we must learn quickly."

In the realm of behaving differently, I was under strict orders not to ask about my family, even in private.

"The walls have ears," Papa Hans would say.

I doubted that anyone could actually hear me in our own apartment, but the wisdom of my new parents' advice was that I needed to establish new habits. If I asked questions or even reminisced about my family in private, there would be an increased chance that I would slip when I was out in public. Still, that did not stop me from occasionally talking about them.

One time, I was sitting in my room staring out the window. I must have looked especially forlorn and sad because Papa Hans and Aunt Giselle (I tried calling her Mama once and she just shook her head, saying that Aunt fit her better) walked in and sat down beside me.

"You probably wonder how we know your parents and why we took you in. Well, your father saved Aunt Giselle's life. This was five years ago. At the time, I didn't even know your father worked at the same firm as me. We were vacationing at Großer Brombachsee, a large reservoir in the Franconia Lake District of Bavaria. I was snoozing in the sand on the beach they had built up when this man ran close to me, kicking sand all over my face and body.

"I sat up, brushing away the sand that was now in my eyes and swearing at this inconsiderate lout. When I could see again, this man was diving in the water and he started to swim furiously out into the lake. I was angry and was about to shout out to him again when I noticed what he was swimming towards. It was your Aunt Giselle. She was a fine swimmer but she had gone out too far and a motorboat had hit her. Whether the boater had done it on purpose or by mistake we will never know.

"Your aunt was unconscious, floating face down in the water. In another minute or so, she would be dead. It was hard to believe but the only person on the entire beach to see her get hit was your father and he did not hesitate to rush to her rescue. I bet you don't know how strong a swimmer he is, do you?"

I shook my head no. If we'd ever gone anywhere to swim, I didn't remember it.

"He got to her and turned her over and started to drag her over to a raft about fifty feet from where they were. I thought about going to help but unfortunately I am a weak swimmer. I pulled out a pair of binoculars we had in our bag to get a better view. He lifted her up onto the raft. I was paralyzed with fear. I don't think I breathed until I saw her body involuntarily convulse as she started to breathe again.

"It was at that moment that I think both of us noticed the blood. The propeller of the boat had made a deep gash in her shoulder. All your father was wearing were his bathing trunks. Without hesitation, he took those off and stuffed them into the wound to slow down the bleeding. By this time, other vacationers had dived in and were swimming toward the raft to assist. He looked up from your aunt for the first time and saw them. It was at that point that I got a good look at his face. Your father is rather a handsome man, but I don't think I'm telling you anything you don't know."

I smiled.

"Anyway, once he saw people swimming toward him he secured the bathing suit around her shoulder with the ties and then dove into the water, stark naked. He swam away as furiously as he had before. I followed him only for a little bit but soon I returned my view to my wife. By now two other men were on the raft, attending to her. She seemed conscious now, but I could tell how disoriented she was. To this day, I feel shame that I did nothing but sit and watch."

Aunt Giselle reached over and squeezed his hand. I imagined she had done this gesture hundreds of times over the years when he expressed his guilt.

"Soon a boat had gone out to pick up your aunt to bring her to shore. By the time they carried her off the boat, an ambulance had shown up. They loaded her in the back and I climbed in beside her. She was in the hospital for two days to repair her shoulder. It took over sixty stitches. The doctors confirmed that if it were not for the quick action of the disappearing man, Aunt Giselle would be dead.

"Back at the resort, I tried to locate the man to thank him but he was nowhere to be found. The hotel front desk said that he and his wife checked out right after the accident. They were registered as Mr. and Mrs. Schmidt.

"The auction house I work for is the largest in all of Bavaria and I did not know at the time that your father worked there, too. It was three weeks after the accident when I was walking down the hallway and there he was. He noticed me and started to turn around to walk away, acting like he had forgotten something.

"'Aren't you the man at Großer Brombachsee?' I called out.

"'You must have me mistaken for somebody else,' he replied.

"'But I want to thank you. That was my wife you saved.'

He stopped. After a few moments he responded, but he would not turn back to me.

"'You're welcome.'

"'What's your name?' I asked.

Another pause.

"'Samuel, Samuel Abramowitz,' he replied.

"It all became clear at that moment," Papa Hans continued." This was 1933 and the first of the anti-Jewish laws had been passed. Your parents probably would not have been allowed at that resort even before the laws, but now they faced imprisonment if they were caught. That's why they registered as the Schmidts.

"Not only did he jeopardize his own health and safety by rushing to save your aunt but then he sealed his fate by taking off his swimming trunks to stop the bleeding. It would be impossible at that point for everyone not to see that he was Jewish. That was why he swam away and hastily departed the resort."

Papa Hans stopped for a second, obviously embarrassed to broach a delicate subject like circumcision, even obliquely. I indicated I understood what he was referring to and that he shouldn't be embarrassed.

"I went over to your father and gently turned him so he could face me. I looked him in the eyes and thanked him again. I was so filled with emotion that I could not help but to give him a big hug, which I think surprised him. I then asked if he and your mother could come over for dinner one evening so your aunt could properly thank him as well. He reluctantly agreed. It was getting tougher for Jews and non-Jews to associate, even at that time.

"We got together and found that the four of us had much in common and became fast friends. As you remember, we came to your apartment a number of times and got to know you and your brother."

I had always known my father was a good man but he never appeared to be the hero type to me. I guess I might have said something to that effect when Aunt Giselle slowly unbuttoned her blouse so that she could lower it to expose her left shoulder. I shuddered at the sight. The gash and scars were the worst I had ever seen.

"Everything your Papa Hans told you is true. I would not be here today if it were not for your father's quick actions."

Aunt Giselle and Papa Hans let that sink in for a few moments before he continued.

"Unfortunately, the situation has gotten so much worse as the years have gone on. In fact, it became extremely dangerous for your parents and us to get together socially. I would come up with reasons to schedule meetings with your father at work even though we had no projects or clients in common. It was the only way we could talk. It was at one of these meetings that he asked if we would be able to help you and your brother. He wanted to get you out of the country. I checked with those clients that I could trust in France, Holland, Switzerland and other countries, but none could help us.

"After your father was let go, I went to him and offered our home to shelter you and your brother. At first he thought it was too dangerous, but soon he realized that there were no other alternatives. But he thought it was too dangerous for both you and Isaak to come here. It would be harder to explain. Also, we both had to admit that Isaak looks more Jewish than you do. Your father thought it wiser to get your brother out of Munich. Anti-Semitism is much more virulent in the city.

"We originally decided we would have you come live here around Christmas. But then, when Kristallnacht happened, we accelerated our plans. He and your mother had hoped to sit down with you beforehand, but they never had the chance.

"So there you have it. I hope your family is safe right now but there is no way I can check without jeopardizing them or us. I'm sorry."

"I understand, Papa Hans."

And I did understand. It was obvious he was as grief-struck with worry as I was, and I loved him for it.

I poured my heart and soul into being the best Berta Werner I could be. Papa Hans was able to get me some identification papers attesting to this new identity. They enrolled me in the local school. I was registered in the local chapter of the Hitler Youth, although they did get me exempted from many of the meetings because of a doctor's note documenting an asthma condition I did not have. No one seemed to question my new identity or background. I was able to maintain the charade for nearly five years.

The war broke out officially in September 1939, but we were relatively unscathed. Basic provisions were rationed, but we got by. Work at the auction house progressively scaled back, but Papa Hans was able to keep his position.

It was not until 1943 that life began to fall apart. First, in March of that year, Papa Hans was conscripted into the army. He was in his mid-forties and thought he was exempt but after defeats in Russia and Africa, the net was cast much wider for men to serve. He left us for the western front on March 18. It would be the last I would ever see him.

Aunt Giselle did her best to provide for us, but without marketable skills, her abilities were limited.

On September 3, 1943, at 4:03 in the afternoon there was a knock on the door. Aunt Giselle was out on errands. I had so assumed the identity of Berta Werner that I answered the door. Two men in suits were there.

"Miriam Abramowitz, you are to come with us. We have a warrant for your arrest."

How they knew my true identity, I will never know. I tried to protest but they grabbed both my arms and dragged me out into the hallway, not allowing me to gather up any of my belongings. As they escorted me away, I could swear I saw Herr Flick's door close.

When I mentioned I wanted to talk to Aunt Giselle, they responded that she had already been arrested for harboring a Jew. They would not let me see her or talk with her.

It was on that day that I became a walking corpse. Someday, my body will catch up with the rest of me.

I fully realize that I have gone on for a long time in this statement without getting to the purpose, namely providing any information on the crimes I witnessed committed by Michael Strauss. There are two reasons for this.

First, I use any forum I can to tell the story of the Werners, my Papa Hans and Aunt Giselle. They sacrificed their lives to save me in a bestial time. I have recorded their heroics at Yad Vashem and they are now counted among the Righteous Among the Nations. I think about them every day and for many years I held out hope against hope that suddenly there would be a knock on my door and there would be one or both of them, *holding their arms out to me. This dream faded with the years.*

I did find out about my parents and Isaak. They all ultimately perished at Auschwitz.

I also talk about the happier times of my life as an introduction in an attempt to put me in a better mind before I talk about the likes of Michael Strauss. It never works, though. It is my lot in life that the beasts—Michael Strauss, Herr Flick and all the others—and not Mama, Papa, Isaak, Papa Hans and Aunt Giselle, are the ones who populate my dreams, rendering each one a nightmare.

I won't go into a lot of detail about my condition or treatment or things I witnessed over the next year and a half. There have been many, many accounts that tell the story far better than I can. Let me give you a brief summary of, for lack of a better word, my travels.

After my capture, I was placed in a holding cell at the local jail where I had no food or water for three days. Frankly, I think they forgot I was there. When they finally came for me, the place reeked because I was also not provided toilet facilities. That was when I received the first beating I had ever received in my life. In their minds, I should have been forced to clean up after myself but there was no time since the orders were to transfer me immediately to the Flossenbürg Concentration Camp. The man whose job it became to wipe up my wastes made sure to make time to beat me unconscious, however. I don't even remember the lorry ride to my new home.

I was a resident of Flossenbürg for six months, where I worked as a slave laborer in the armament plant there. It is with great pride that I can state my certainty that not one of the shells I had any part in producing ever exploded on the battlefield.

After that, I was transferred to Buchenwald. I was never told the reason for being sent there, but from what I understand, I was one of the lucky ones as most of the remaining residents of Flossenbürg were subsequently executed or sent on a death march to Dachau.

I encountered Michael Strauss on my first day at Buchenwald, December 12, 1944. It was sunny but bitterly cold. We got off of our transports and were forced to stand at attention for nearly an hour. There were about three dozen of us, about evenly split between men and women.

Eventually, Obersturmfürer Strauss, along with one other SS officer, Untersturmfürer Weber, came out of the building where their offices were located. Strauss walked along our ranks, inspecting us. Occasionally he shook his head at the decrepit condition of the man or woman in front of him. Once he leaned over to Weber and whispered something after which they shared a laugh. A number of us were shivering uncontrollably in the cold since none of us had been issued coats. Our shivering only increased his disdain for us.

He came to me and stopped directly in front of me. I had long ago learned that, unless directed otherwise, I was to direct my gaze to the ground and not make eye contact. A haughty attitude, or even the perception of haughtiness, could result in severe punishment, decreased rations and, in at least one instance, I observed summary execution.

Strauss stopped in front of me and took his pistol from his holster. Putting his pistol under my chin, he raised my head so that he could see my face. 'My but you're a pretty one,' he said. Then, without warning, he took the pistol away from me, aimed it at the middle-aged man to my left and pulled the trigger. The bullet tore through his throat, causing him to go down but he did not die immediately. The man lay there for over a minute in pure agony, trying to cry out but unable because of the damage the bullet had caused to his throat and larynx. The whole time, Strauss kept looking at me, smiling. I stared back, expressionless.

Eventually, the gurgling and other noises from this poor man ended as he died. It was at this point that Strauss noticed that his bullet had passed through the man and had struck a woman who was standing on the other side. She tried not to let on that she had been hit in the shoulder, but the blood flowed down her sleeve and she could not hide her pain.

"Untersturmfürer Weber," Strauss commanded, his eyes still focused on mine, "attend to that woman."

With that, Weber took out his Luger and calmly shot the woman in the head, killing her instantly. At least that is what I assumed happened since my eyes did not dare leave their fixed focus on Strauss' face. But since I heard the gunshot and was later assigned to help carry the woman's body over to the crematorium, I think my assumption is on pretty solid footing.

After the woman was shot, Strauss smiled again.

"Our rations are in short supply. There, I have ensured that you will have more food to eat. What do you say, Fräulein?"

"Thank you, Herr Obersturmfürer."

"And what about my hard-working assistant?"

"Thank you, Herr Untersturmfürer."

"I don't think he could hear you, standing all the way over there."

"Thank you, Herr Untersturmfürer," I said again, only much louder.

"That is much better. What a proper, courteous young woman. I'm certain you will get along fine here."

We were dismissed.

Once in the barracks, I made the acquaintance of a Polish Jewish woman about my age named Adrianna Berkowitz. She was a lovely creature who spoke fluent German. Her story was much like mine. Her father was an attorney who tried to hide her with friends in Czechoslovakia but she was eventually found out and was bounced from camp to camp. She was a talented seamstress whose skills were put to use wherever she was sent.

She was the only person I felt I could truly talk to about my former life, about the good times. We would stay up long after curfew, whispering and acting like schoolgirls again.

We were walking back to our barracks when Obersturmfürer Strauss stepped in our way. We halted and our eyes immediately cast downward. As before, Strauss pulled out his pistol and raised my chin up.

"My but you're a pretty one."

"Thank you, Obersturmfürer Strauss," I responded.

He then did the same thing to Adrianna and she gave the same response.

"I really don't know which one is prettier."

He repeated the pistol under the chin back and forth between us three more times. Then, on the third time putting the muzzle under Adrianna's chin, he pulled the trigger, putting a bullet in her brain, killing her instantly.

"That decides it. You're prettier."

He walked away as calmly as he had approached us, leaving me wishing I had that bullet lodged in my brain instead.

Within another two weeks, we could hear the war getting closer and closer. Many in the camp despaired that the Allied bombs might come too close and hit our camp; others of us were wishing that they did. As the war drew close, the brutality of the guards increased but it was not because of orders they received from Obersturmfürer Strauss or Untersturmfürer Weber. Three weeks before the Americans liberated our camp, these two officers along with most of the rest of the SS deserted the camp and the war. The lowly guards, fearing an uprising, stepped up their cruelty but soon even they had to abandon us.

When an American soldier, Private James Sanders, came upon me, I was battling typhus. I weighed only 83 pounds. At the time, he didn't realize that there were hundreds or even thousands in as bad or worse shape than I and he dived in to try and save me. He shared some of his rations with me, but I threw them up immediately. I alternated between a semi-conscious state and delirium. At one point, I looked up at his face and told him that at one point in my life someone had told me I was pretty. He simply smiled in return.

Private Sanders carried me over a mile to an Army medical hospital, where I was treated. I understand that he got in some trouble for his efforts since he risked opening an unstoppable floodgate, but they did not turn me away. Like Papa Hans and Aunt Giselle, Private Sanders was a stranger who helped me in my darkest time of need, but unlike my two adoptive parents, I now alternate between blessing the Private and cursing him for finding me and keeping me alive.

It has been many years since the war and one may rightly question my ability to recognize Michael Strauss from a grainy picture taken in Argentina of a man identified as Johann Schäfer. It is not really hard to understand. When I go to bed at night and when I wake up each morning, Michael Strauss's face is what I see. I have tried hard to replace that terrible visage with that of my wonderful husband and beautiful children, but it can't be done. I would know that beast's face at any time, in any place.

More practically, however, I can recognize Michael Strauss simply from the deep scar that runs the length of his right eyebrow. It would make him stand out in any crowd.

Yes, that picture is most definitely of the man I knew as Michael Strauss.

4

Lena put the paper down. Her eyes were welled up. I waited for her to compose herself.

"I really didn't have to read this all the way to the end about the scar—a mark on my father's face I've known my entire life—to know what Miriam had said was true. When I was young and something was bothering me, my father would come up to me and put his hand under my chin to raise my head so that he was looking directly into my eyes. Then he would tell me, 'my but you're a pretty one.' I would feel instantly better. That's a distinct power a father can have over a daughter, isn't it?"

I thought best not to mention that I wouldn't know because my father had abandoned me when I was a baby. She continued.

"After finishing reviewing the file, I squeezed Mark's hand and asked him if he still wanted to marry me. With all his heart he wanted to marry me, he replied. We were wed and then we moved to New York. Shortly after that, my daughter, Mary, was born. When she was eighteen she married a wonderful man, Gil Smith. I joked with her at the time that she was lazy and only picked Gil because he had the same last name. I, on the other hand, had to work hard making the change from Schäfer to Smith."

She smiled at the memory.

"They had Wendy a year and a half after they were married. Two years later, a trucker who fell asleep on the L.I.E. ran into Mary and Gil's car, killing them both. I was given custody of Wendy. Now, she's gone, too. All because she had some leftover DNA from a monster. Who would do something like that, Francine?"

"I don't know, Lena. But I will be sure your granddaughter's story gets out, at least as much as I am able."

"Thank you."

I was the most introspective I'd ever been in my life on the ride back to Manhattan. I was surprised at how affected I was by Lena and through her, Wendy. Even though they touched me personally, I was still viewing them through a journalist's eyes. I thought of all the opportunities I missed for follow-up questions. I was also kicking myself for not having Jonas along to film the interview. I had thought a chat with a grieving grandmother would be background at best, but I missed some lines and reactions that would have made for great television. Then again, she may not have opened up as much in front of the camera.

I got back to the office and briefed Frank. He told me to write it up and I could have some time on that evening's show. I was so excited; it was one of my first real pieces at the station. It would be something that would show my worth. More real assignments would come my way. I had about four hours to pull it all together. I had already composed the segment in my mind, so that should not be a problem. There was one more thing I wanted to do.

I went online to see if I could contact Miriam Berger. She would have been around eighty years old at that point, so I wasn't even sure she'd still be alive. I wasn't quite sure what I'd accomplish contacting her to dredge up her past, but it seemed like a solid journalistic thing to do, at least at the time. Getting a quote from her to insert into the story could really give it depth. I didn't even know if she spoke English so I could be totally wasting my time.

She lived in Haifa at the time she gave her statement nearly forty years earlier, so I thought I would start there. I went online to search the various Haifa phone directories, but I could not find any Miriam Bergers. Next, I would try contacting the newspapers and TV stations in Haifa to see if they had any information on her.

I called a general number for the Haifa Post and a young woman answered, first in Hebrew but she switched to English once I identified myself. The woman seemed excited to be talking to a New York City television reporter. I didn't let her know that I worked for the station that was rated fourth out of four in the City.

I told her what I was looking for and she immediately checked the newspaper's database for information on an eighty year-old Miriam Berger. I could hear the clicking on the other end of the line.

"I think I may have something," she excitedly pronounced.

"I just found a short article from our paper in June of 1984 saying that a Miriam Berger stepped in front of a bus the day before. She was killed instantly. She was a Holocaust survivor. 59 years old. The article says that despite many efforts by the government to offer counseling and psychiatric assistance, there was a high rate of survivor suicides. It says here she left a note that she could not go on after learning nothing was going to be done to bring an SS officer to justice for the war crimes he had committed and against whom she had provided detailed testimony some years earlier. She was survived by her husband, two grown children and one grandchild. I hope that helps."

"It does, thank you," I lifelessly intoned.

"I can't do this."

"Can't do what?" Frank responded.

"This piece. This job. I don't have the stuff, Frank. I feel like such a lousy human being right now. I'm berating myself because I didn't dig further into a grandmother's grief; because I didn't have a cameraman there to capture her angst. Then when I was done with her, I attempt to contact a Holocaust survivor to get her insights on the murder of a descendant of her tormentor. Let's reopen those wounds, can't I? And then, to top it off, I find out that she committed suicide nearly twenty years ago. And do you know what my reaction was? Relief! News of her suicide brought me to my senses and I feel relieved that someone else didn't witness the monster I've become."

He let me talk myself out.

"Francine, this is a profession where if you don't feel like an absolute bastard once in awhile, you're not doing your job. You're young and still learning, but I've seen you connect with people. Do you really think Lena Smith would have opened up to the type of person and reporter you're saying you are? Do you think she would have confided in you at all? You dug up some truths here. That's what we do. There's nothing more anyone can ask of a journalist. I'm not sure if it's good or bad, but your skin will toughen up as time goes by.

"My admiration for you is only increased because of the feelings you just expressed. I would have been disappointed if you'd been just a stock reporter and not have invested yourself in a story as gruesome as this. As time goes on, you'll learn how to steel yourself, but I hope not too much. Our industry needs more of the emotions you're expressing today."

Frank's pep talk did a lot to buoy my spirits. I at least wasn't going to quit right then and there, but I was still unconvinced. I needed to turn to one last place: my mother. I gave her a call.

My mother told me pretty much exactly the same thing Frank did, but with more passion and in less precise English. She would have no daughter of hers quit like this. In short, she told me to suck it up and tell the story that needed to be told.

I felt like new.

I grabbed Jonas and we headed down to the 7th Precinct on the Lower East Side of Manhattan. I asked to speak with Detective Edward Martino, the officer who was dispatched to the crime scene at Wendy Smith's apartment on the corner of Clinton and Broome Streets once it was determined that she was the victim of the Zyklon Killer. He agreed to an interview on camera.

We conducted the interview and then hurried back to the station to edit the interview and get it ready for insertion into my final report. Jonas and I then headed back down to the Lower East Side for a live report from in front of Wendy Smith's apartment building. There were still two police cars there, which helped to enhance the visual effect.

We got our spots, Jonas adjusted his camera and sound equipment and we went through a couple dry runs. Then we waited.

At about ten minutes into the evening news, I could hear the evening anchor, Vance Johnson, over my earpiece.

"And now we go live to Francine Vega who is reporting live from the Lower East Side on the latest news on the Zyklon Killer."

"Thank you, Vance. We in the news industry like to come up with phrases that will catch the public's attention. Whether it's Son of Sam or throwing 'gate' onto any scandal, we have a tendency to boil a story down so that we can capture it in a short, pithy phrase. Zyklon Killer is such a slogan, but if I were to use it here, I would also be shortchanging the victim, Wendy Smith.

"I learned a lot about Wendy today. She was bright and alive, the type of person who illuminated any room she walked into. She took a year of her life when she could be partying or learning how to make money and joined the Peace Corps to help others. She was to be married next year and had so much to offer the world when a madman cut her life short.

"A short while ago I spoke with Detective Edward Martino of the NYPD. Let's play a portion of that interview."

The tape of the interview then played.

"I'm here with NYPD Detective Edward Martino. What can you tell us about the murder of Wendy Smith?"

"Ms. Smith is the third known victim of the serial killer known as the Zyklon Killer, the second in New York. The Zyklon Killer's pretext for selecting his victim is that he or she is descended from a Nazi War Criminal. The killer has been so named because the method used to kill the victim is by sealing off a room and then pumping in the deadly gas Zyklon B, which was used by the Nazis at various concentration camps to exterminate inmates. It is an especially horrific way to die.

"Ms. Smith was reported to be the great-granddaughter of Michael Strauss, an Officer at the Buchenwald Concentration Camp."

"The killer makes no allowance for the innocence of the victim?"

"Notes left with several of the victims, including Ms. Smith, indicate that innocence is not considered in the selection process. Only the relation to the war criminal is considered. The notes indicate that there were tens of millions of victims in World War II who were also completely innocent."

"Thank you, Detective Martino. Do you have any leads as to the identity of the Zyklon Killer?"

"I cannot comment on an ongoing investigation. Let's just say it is a top priority for the NYPD to apprehend this killer. We are collecting and comparing evidence from both New York cases and we are working closely with the FBI and multiple national and international law enforcement agencies to track him or her down"

The tape ended and the report returned to me.

"It is my job as a professional journalist to remain impartial and uninvolved in the story I'm reporting. However, today I'm afraid I'm not acting professional. I would have liked to know Wendy Smith as a friend, but that can never be. This murderer ensured I would never know her because he embraced a concept of visiting the sins of the fathers onto their offspring; a concept that we, as a modern society, gave up centuries ago. He must be found before he can kill again. If you have any information on the whereabouts of this deranged individual, please call the number at the bottom of the screen.

"This is Francine Vega, reporting live from the Lower East Side for Action 6 News."

I was just getting over Wendy Smith when three weeks later a video of her murder appeared on VisionNet, one of the lesser Internet sites on which people can post their videos. VisionNet quickly took it down, but in the fifteen minutes it was on the Internet, the video went viral. As a journalist covering this story, I was compelled to watch it, but I wish I hadn't. I won't go into detail about the effects of the gas on this poor woman I felt I had come to know, but it is a sight I will remember in my nightmares the rest of my life.

The FBI attempted to track down the killer through the video but it was untraceable. The feed appeared to emanate from Des Moines, Iowa, but that led nowhere. The computer skills were reminiscent of those displayed by Alan Westbrook, the man who set the 'destroy Mecca' movement in motion but who ultimately helped to thwart it; this person was that good. The defense attorney for Mr. Kaplow attempted to argue that his client did not have such skills but the jury was unmoved. They were persuaded, rather, by the video itself.

The police had apprehended Aaron Kaplow in a small motel on the outskirts of Waco, Texas. In putting together their case, the prosecution discovered that a George Kraml lived in Waco. He was a descendant of Fritz Kraml, a murderous and sadistic Waffen SS officer assigned to the Sobibor Concentration Camp where thousands of Jews perished. The prosecution was able to link some writings they found in Kaplow's apartment to Fritz Kraml and convinced the jury that a new attack was being planned, with Mr. Kraml as the next victim.

I thought it strange not only how easily they caught Aaron Kaplow, but the reports I read indicated he had been extremely sloppy, leaving copious amounts of evidence seemingly out in the open. In New York and the other cities where he committed his crimes, on the other hand, he scrupulously covered his tracks. I passed it off as his getting cocky or perhaps his mental condition had deteriorated to the point where he could no longer adequately cover his tracks. Or maybe he was just tired of it all and wanted to get caught.

The New York cops were mum about what evidence they had that linked him to the New York crimes, but the general feeling was that they also had a strong case here. When Texas refused to grant extradition, uproars of protest erupted from the beat cop all the way up to the Governor.

Despite any misgivings or questions that remained in my mind about the case, I moved on and really did not give it much thought until the day I reported that the execution had taken place.

5

I jumped on the E train heading home to Queens. I missed being able to walk home like I used to when I had my Manhattan apartment, but it didn't make sense keeping it after Will and I married. He had his all-paid-for house and sent his kids to an excellent school two blocks away. Having grown up and lived in Manhattan my entire life, I was quite biased towards that borough and thought of Queens as one of the suburbs, and a rather boring one at that.

I noticed a dark-haired, relatively tall man in a navy blue suit get on the subway car the same time I did. He took a seat directly across from me. As we trundled along, it seemed whenever I looked up he was staring at me. Perhaps he recognized me or most likely, he thought I looked familiar but couldn't quite place me. I probably should have paid him more mind, but I was tired and I was looking forward to seeing my little Rosa again. And as a TV personality, I constantly get those 'I know you from TV but I can't quite place you' stares all the time.

Will had always told me to be careful walking the streets. Being a celebrity, albeit a relatively minor one, I had to be careful. There were numerous certified wackos out there. But I had too much of my mother in me. She would wander around the worst areas of Harlem—doing tenant organizing or some other advocacy work—at all hours without giving it a second thought. Like her, I had a tendency to be oblivious to any dangers that could be around the next corner.

The subway pulled into my station. The man in the suit got up the same time I did. As I was heading up the stairs to the street, he caught up to me. He grabbed my left arm from behind with his left hand while I felt his right hand—or most likely the gun that he was carrying in that hand—in the small of my back.

"Don't say a word and you won't get hurt," he promised.

I had trouble believing this was happening to me. He yanked my bag from my shoulder, which made me hope this was simply a mugging; that I would be lucky and he would take my cash and credit cards and then let me go on my way without hurting me. He rifled through my bag, extracting the pepper spray I always carried, and handed the bag back to me. I sensed the worst. He was leading me somewhere.

I had previously been kidnapped when I had gotten too close on the Mecca story. I should have been murdered but I survived only because Alan Westbrook had a schoolboy crush on me and he would not allow Colonel Jacob Lawson to issue the final order for my execution. Instead, I was dumped in the middle of the Meadowlands marshes in New Jersey. I didn't feel I was going to be as lucky this time.

We walked a block and arrived at a large black town car with blacked out windows. He opened the rear passenger side door.

"Get in," he ordered in a voice whose tone indicated there was no negotiating the matter.

It wasn't until I was already in the car that I saw another man sitting there. My skin crawled.

"Lawson," I lifelessly intoned. I was in the presence of Jacob Lawson, a man—a monster—that I had met only once in my life, and that was for all of at most three minutes. And yet I loathed him and all he stood for. This was the person who was involved, directly or indirectly, in at least five attempts on my life. If it weren't for dumb luck, the skill of my FBI agent/future husband and an irrational infatuation of a brilliant but highly unstable man, I would have been dead a long time ago.

He was also a man who, as a rogue Army Colonel, had nearly set the wheels in motion for World War III to erupt. He had been convicted in absentia of treason by a court martial and was one of the world's most wanted men. Yet here he was, sitting serenely in the back of a car on a street in Queens.

"It's a pleasure to see you again, Ms. Vega. Or do you go by Mrs. Allen now?"

"Call me whatever you like. I'm just a loose end you need to tidy up, is that it?"

"Now, now. Is that any way to talk, Francine? I'm not into vendettas. You bested me, fair and square. I've moved on, on to new things."

"What sort of new things can you be into these day? I imagine having a price on your head rather cramps your style."

Goading this psychopath, a man who once again had my life in his hands, was probably not the smartest approach but I was attempting to occupy his attention while I slowly (and I hoped stealthily) slid my hand into my coat pocket to activate my phone and contact Will. I obviously did not succeed.

"I wouldn't do that."

"What?"

"Reach for your phone so your agent husband can rush in, like the cavalry. It won't do any good."

He held up a small black electric device with a red blinking light.

"This is a jammer. Any cell or smartphone within one hundred feet is rendered totally useless. Before you arrived, I was having fun activating it whenever anybody walked by talking or texting. The looks on their faces and the occasional expletive as their calls were dropped mid-sentence were priceless."

I moved my hand back away from my coat pocket.

"You seem to be adept at amusing yourself. What do you need me for? If I take you at your word, they're not going to find my lifeless body in a dumpster somewhere a week from now. You also don't strike me as the nostalgic type so I don't think I'm here to reminisce about the good times we've had. So why exactly am I here? I should get home."

"Ah, direct and to the point. I've always liked that in you. Yes, yes. Little Rosa. A year and half now, isn't she? I bet she's getting big. And what's the babysitter's name again? Emma. That's it."

The hair on the back of my neck was standing on end. He knew my life like a book.

"Yes, it's Emma."

He stared right through me. Then he spoke.

"I hear they executed the person reputed to be the Zyklon Killer."

"You keep up with current events. That's commendable, especially for a man without a country."

That last dig had an impact as he blanched.

"Oh, Ms. Vega, I have a country. At the moment it does not have me but someday that will be remedied, I assure you. To return to my original point, the man reputed to be the Zyklon Killer was executed today."

"You said 'reputed to be' twice now. You don't believe he was the Zyklon Killer?"

"You catch on quickly. As a matter of fact, I can assure you he was not and you're going to find out who the real killer is. If you do it before he—or she—strikes again is immaterial to me, but you will do it."

"How are you so certain they killed the wrong man? And even if they did, what makes you think I have the time or interest in tracking down whoever the real Zyklon Killer is?"

"Regarding your first question, Aaron Kaplow was my cousin. I've known him since childhood. He was incapable of committing these murders. Such a gentle soul."

"People change. Just because you knew him as a kid doesn't mean he wasn't capable of doing something unspeakable when he grew up. Our airwaves are full of stories about people who snap and shoot up a school or a crowded theater. Afterwards, his neighbors, friends and relatives remark about how quiet a man he was, how he 'seemed so nice' and they have trouble conceiving he could have been capable of such a heinous act."

Lawson was somewhat taken aback. I sensed he was not used to anyone ever challenging anything he said. When he made a pronouncement, it was almost always the final word. But his silence only lasted the briefest of moments.

"I knew him; he was incapable of such deeds."

Again, it was meant to be a pronouncement not to be challenged.

"Do you think he was aware of *your* deeds? Of any of the people you mowed down who got in your way over the years?"

"As a matter of fact, yes. I told him. He was somewhat of a confessor for me."

I was stunned at the nonchalance with which he admitted his crimes. He continued.

"In regards to your second question, there are several reasons why you will willingly pursue this. First, your interest is piqued. I see you many mornings on the news, Ms. Vega, and it is so obvious that you detest spouting lines written for you by others. Don't get me wrong. You're an excellent anchor but you long to be back out in the field, hunting down stories, being an investigative journalist. You need another 'destroy Mecca' story, even as a part-time venture. You crave it; you need it."

Before I could protest, he cut me off.

"But, being an anchor is a far more prestigious—and not to mention lucrative—profession that you won't jeopardize to go off half-cocked to please a psychotic arch enemy. I need a more personal inducement to convince you."

"And that is?"

"Alan."

"Alan? Alan Westbrook? You've been in contact with him? Is he okay?"

My mind raced back to my dealings with the troubled, tortured genius that was Alan Westbrook. I thought of his irrational attraction for me, his desire to avenge his brother's death on 9/11 by hatching a plot with Lawson to launch a nuclear strike that would wipe Mecca off the face of the earth. He eventually teamed with Will and me to foil this plan once he realized that his brother did not die as a result of the terrorist attacks but rather at the hands of Lawson.

The last I'd heard from Alan was a year and a half ago when he sent text messages to Will and me congratulating us on the birth of Rosa. I'd tried numerous times since then to contact him, all with no success. If nothing else, Will and I each had ten million dollars we wanted to return to him, money from Alan's lottery jackpot winnings that Lawson had deposited into our accounts in an effort to frame us with implications that we were working with Iran to attack Israel. We didn't want or need this money; it belonged to Alan.

However, as he had after his brother was killed, Alan fell off the face of the earth.

"Last I had heard, Mr. Westbrook was doing fine. He is living down in Texas, just outside Houston. He leads a meager, pathetic life, but he's getting along. That all can change depending on your answer."

"Why would you want to hurt Alan?"

"He betrayed me. Unlike you, he owed allegiance to me and then he turned. He's lucky I haven't hurt him already. But I can't entirely blame him, he's such damaged goods."

"Allegiance to you? Who are you, the Führer?"

He ignored my dig but simply carried on.

"I am not asking that much of you, Ms. Vega. A little of the intensive investigative journalism that you've become famous for, that's all. In return, you save a man's life, a man I know you have some affection for. Your answer, please?"

I still wasn't ready to commit myself to helping this monster.

"Why come to me? I'm sure there must be others more qualified to investigate this than I am."

"Believe me, I tried private investigators to try and save my cousin's life. They were all worthless. In my present state, I can hardly go to the authorities to dig out the truth. Even if I could, now that Aaron is dead, they are not going to want to pursue an inquiry that says: Whoops, we killed an innocent man. You get results, Ms. Vega. Plus you have backdoor access to the FBI. It's a no-brainer as far as I'm concerned. Your answer?"

I could see that offering any further arguments was futile.

"Okay, I'll look into it for you. I'll see what I can find out."

"There, that wasn't so hard, was it?"

There was an accordion file of papers on the seat beside him that he handed over to me.

"These are some documents that will help you get started. You'll also find instructions on how to contact me. I expect progress reports every two weeks at a minimum. I've been assured it's all untraceable in case your FBI husband wants to try and track me down."

I moved to exit the car but he had one more thing.

"So, what do you think Malcolm McKenzie's chances are?"

"You want to talk presidential politics, now?"

"Well, we both have ties to the former reverend. He was useful in getting the public into a dither about destroying Mecca. I thought that since you had a connection, maybe you had an opinion on his miraculous rise to become a leading presidential candidate."

It was true that I did have a connection. I had first discussed the theory that there was a plot to destroy Mecca with Reverend McKenzie's brother, Edward, who worked in the State Department. To be honest, the plot sounded so far-fetched at the time that I don't really blame the Under Secretary for telling his brother about the plot. The next thing I knew The Reverend was promoting the plan to rain fire-and-brimstone down on Mecca to punish or even destroy Islam. He started local but it did not take long before he had a national audience.

I assumed that Reverend Malcolm McKenzie had achieved his fifteen minutes of fame and would retreat back to his quiet life as a pastor in small-town Upstate New York. Instead, his popularity only increased as he appealed to the country's basest human nature. It wasn't long until he took a leave from his ministerial duties to enter politics. Instead of getting his feet wet with some local council or mayoral position, however, he went for it all and announced his candidacy for the presidency. Soon, despite pundit predictions that his appeal was short-lived and he would fade away, the other candidates were the ones who dropped out one by one. Now, Malcolm McKenzie was standing alone as his party's standard-bearer.

I was about to give Lawson my opinion of McKenzie and his political chances but then Lawson abruptly lost interest in me.

"You are free to go now. You're dismissed."

He shifted his gaze to look out the window. It was as if I was no longer in the car.

6

I walked the three blocks home in a confused and frightened stupor. What had I just agreed to? What bombshells was I holding in the folders he'd given me? What if I had said no? Would I be dead right now?

I grabbed the mail in the box as I walked in the house. Since the door was unlocked, I expected that Emma, our housekeeper/nanny, would still be there with Rosa. The usual routine was that I arrive home around noon at which point Emma would leave to go to her other job and I would watch Rosa. Rosa and I would then nap together.

Albert and Stella, Will's children by his previous marriage, would still be in school and wouldn't be home for another three hours. Will would get in around six. We'd have a couple hours together until I had to get to bed to get a decent night's sleep before waking at 3:30 to get to the station in time for the 5:30 show.

"Emma, I'm home," I called out.

"Fava, we're up here. No Emma, just little ole me," I heard Will call out from our bedroom. I ran up the stairs to find him playing peekaboo on the bed with Rosa. She was squealing with delight, which only intensified when I walked into the room. I can barely control my emotions whenever my year and a half old daughter raises her arms up to me. I picked her up and swung her around, producing more squeals.

"This is a pleasant surprise. I thought you were in court all day."

"Well, Willoughby and I were sitting in the room adjacent to the courtroom waiting for our turns to testify when the door opens and a guard leads the jurors through and into the courtroom. They were supposed to enter through another door and when the judge realized the jurors saw us in advance, he was livid. First, he lit into me but I wasn't having any of it and told him I was only sitting where the bailiff told me to sit. Then he got on the poor guard's case for using the alternate route that may have tainted the jurors.

"It probably would have been okay but since this is such a high-profile RICO case, the judge didn't want anything that could even hint that the verdict could be appealed or overturned and he declared a mistrial. In his defense, I understand why he was so angry. Although this was only the first day of the trial, they'd already gone through twelve days of jury selection that they'll have to do all over again.

"Anyway, after that, I said screw it and I told Willoughby I was taking the rest of the day to be with my lovely wife and daughter. Maybe I'll surprise the kids by picking them up at school. So, how was your day?"

I paused a second, trying to figure out how to phrase what I had to tell him. I contemplated not telling him. He looked so happy, even joyous, playing with our daughter. Why ruin that mood? I could work quietly behind the scenes, then tell him about my encounter.

On the other hand, he had a right to know. Colonel—make that former Colonel—Jacob Lawson was as much Will's mortal enemy as he was mine. Lawson may have attempted to kill me a few more times than he did Will, but Lawson also had Will's four-year old daughter kidnapped and held as a hostage. That one act can never be forgiven.

My mind was made up for me as Will noticed my hesitation, recognizing that I was troubled about something.

"What is it, Fava? Is something wrong?"

"I had a visitor today."

"Really? Who?"

I hesitated once more.

"Who was it, Fava? You're scaring me."

"Lawson."

Will's face immediately contorted into a mixture of pain and disbelief.

"Where? Why didn't you call me?"

"Here, in Queens, three blocks from here. I was forced into his car. He jammed my cellphone."

"Are you okay?"

"Yes, all we did was talk. He asked me for help."

"What? Why on earth should you help him?"

Will's vehemence came through, scaring Rosa and she started to cry.

We both calmed down and then soothed her as well as each other. I related the entire encounter and Lawson's request—or more correctly demand—that I help hunt down the real Zyklon Killer and exonerate his cousin.

"I got the plate number. They were Oregon plates. It was a black Chrysler town car."

"We'll run the number and ask the New York cops to keep an eye out, but you as well as I realize it won't be much help. My guess is that the tags are fake or they've been replaced or the car abandoned down by the docks. The man is meticulous. And remember, he had—or rather has—connections inside the FBI that we still haven't tracked down. He's back in the wind."

He paused for a second before continuing.

"You believe him?"

"I can't think of any reason he would lie about this."

"Even if Texas executed an innocent man—and I'm sure it's not the first nor will it be the last time they did so—I can't think of a reason you would help this monster. The only thing that traitor deserves is to be at the receiving end of a firing squad."

"Will, he'll hurt Alan if I don't help him."

"Alan? He knows where he is? I've tried tracking Alan down using FBI resources but it always comes up dead end after dead end. Alan's like Lawson; if he doesn't want to be found, he won't be."

"Well, Lawson says he knows where he is, in Texas somewhere. Alan betrayed him and he'd have no qualms about killing him. He may be bluffing. Maybe he has no idea where Alan is, but he was pretty convincing. Will, Lawson's still a powerful man. He has connections everywhere and over $200 million of Alan's money. I wouldn't discount his threat. In any case, I don't think it's a bluff I want to call. In a short span of time, we both got pretty close to Alan and wouldn't want anything to happen to him."

Will considered this quietly. We both looked down at Rosa who was now sleeping soundly on the bed.

"Can you imagine anything more beautiful than that?" he asked.

I looked down at her, then up at him and finally at the both of them.

"No. No I can't."

"Fava, Lawson must have some ulterior motive. There's got to be something else going on here. He uses people until they're expendable and then he throws them away."

"I don't trust him either, Will, but I don't see what harm there can be to making some inquiries and digging into this story some."

"I still don't like it."

"Will, there's one other thing. It was an observation Lawson made. About me. It struck close to home."

"And that is?"

"He's seen my broadcasts and, while I was good at being an anchor, he could see I was not happy reading news someone else gave me. It was obvious I was happier doing my own reporting and investigation."

"I thought you loved your job."

"I do. But the more I thought about it, I never remember being more alive, more energized than when we were working together on the 'destroy Mecca' story. This story has the potential to be big, too, especially if Lawson is right."

"Whatever you decide, you know I'm here for you. How would you handle it with Frank?"

"I'll probably take a leave of absence, six months or so. If he wants to take me back as anchor, fine. If not, that's fine, too. Worst comes to worst, I think I'd be snapped up anywhere."

Will put his arms around me and pulled me close.

"You think that, do you?"

"You bet."

I could tell what was on his mind. Since he didn't have to pick up the kids for another hour and a half, we put Rosa in her crib and turned on the monitor. He led me to the bedroom, stripping off our clothes as we walked on.

7

The next day I finished the show and, while I was putting in a couple of hours wrapping a few things up and preparing for the following day's show, my cell phone rang. I looked at the display and saw that it was Alexander Kent, son of New York Governor—and currently his party's leading presidential candidate—Peter Kent.

Four years ago, I had interviewed the younger Kent regarding a charitable foundation he was heading to combat youth depression and mental illness. He was nice in a nebbish kind of way. He was smart and well-read with an Ivy League education and all the right contacts.

We went out for drinks a few times after that. During one of our dates, I received a text that Aaron Kaplow had been apprehended. My mood immediately went dark and he asked me what was wrong. We had gotten close enough at that point that I told him about Wendy Smith and how much the Zyklon Killer case affected me. He was supportive and it greatly improved my mood having someone there to talk with.

I think he wanted our relationship to become something more serious and we went out a few more times after that but it never went any further. He got involved in his father's political campaign and I was immersed in my career, so we drifted apart. That was fine with me especially since Will entered my life at that time.

I looked at my phone and was both surprised and pleased to see it was Alexander. I answered the phone.

"Hello. Alexander? What a pleasant surprise to hear from you after all this time. How long's it been?"

"Hello, Francine. It has been some time. I think I last called you maybe a year and a half ago. I saw your piece yesterday morning on the execution of the Zyklon Killer and I remembered how much it affected you when you were reporting on the case years ago. I just wanted to check and make sure you're okay."

"That's sweet of you to think of me and my well-being after all this time, Alexander. I'm doing fine."

"I'm glad to hear that. It must be a relief that this monster has finally been brought to justice."

"Well, I'm not so sure about that."

"Ah, right. Your super-liberal tendencies don't let you believe in the death penalty as a form of justice. I've always liked that about you."

"No, it's not that. I'm not sure what I believe in a case like this. As you correctly remembered, I am against the death penalty. But this case was so horrific, so outside of anything I'd ever encountered that it shook me to my core. I don't think that the death penalty for a person like this is necessarily the worst thing that could happen."

"So what aren't you sure about?"

"I'm not so sure they executed the right man."

"What? The evidence seemed extremely solid, even ironclad."

"Yes, maybe too ironclad. I'd always had my doubts on how neatly sewn up it was. Then something happened yesterday that further convinced me as to Aaron Kaplow's innocence."

"Really? What was that?"

"I'm not at liberty to divulge that, but I'm going to investigate a bit and see what I can find out."

"Well, knowing you, you won't stop until you get to the truth."

"Thanks, Alexander. We'll see. So how's your father's campaign coming along?"

"Virtually sewing up the nomination this early can be both a blessing and a curse. It's so easy to get complacent and start coasting. But on the other hand, we can start honing our attacks on The Reverend."

"I still am finding it hard to believe that McKenzie has gotten this far and will be your opponent in November. I feel guilty that I'm the one who gave him his initial push, inadvertent as it was."

"He is definitely a unique phenomenon. He's tapped into a meanness and fear in the American people I never thought we had. People are so tired of Washington politics and self-serving politicians that they feel we need an outsider to shake things up. It's obvious they'll latch onto anybody."

"Well, your father's never served in Washington and he's got a squeaky clean and exemplary record. Those should all work in his favor, shouldn't they?"

"Yes, but he's been in politics so the taint is there. Anyway, once the mudslinging starts, nobody is left clean. Hopefully the early polls that show Dad with a double digit lead in a head to head confrontation with McKenzie will hold up through the rest of the primaries and into the election."

"Let's hope so. Well, I've got to run. I'm so glad you called. Maybe we can get together for drinks sometime, if your father can go without you for that long."

"He's quite possessive, that man. I'll let you know next time I'm in town and I'll sneak away without telling him. Keep me posted on Zyklon. I'd be curious to know what you find out."

"Will do. Be well, Alexander."

After I hung up, I headed over to see Frank. Jonas Clarke, my old cameraman, friend and lifesaver was chatting with Frank when I arrived. Because I wasn't in the field any more, I hadn't worked with Jonas for well over a year. Between anchoring and motherhood, I'd been so busy I hadn't so much as seen him in over a month, and even then I was late for a meeting and couldn't stop to chat.

Over the past couple of years I'd been so stressed I didn't have time for anything. Raising Rosa, being a good wife to Will and helping to take care of Albert and Stella took up all my spare time. Jonas's and my schedules did not overlap so there were no natural times we'd get together. Every time I thought to call him, something else would come up. Then it got to the point where I was too embarrassed to call.

As I walked in, Jonas looked in my direction.

"Frank, there's somebody to see you."

With that he got up and walked past me. In the past, I'd get one of his toothy grins and a bear hug that would totally envelop me in his massive six-foot four frame. Today, nothing. He was obviously hurting from the fact that I'd been such a terrible friend. Actually, I hadn't been a friend at all, and to a man who had taken a bullet saving my life. I felt mortified as I walked into Frank's office.

"Got a minute, Frank?"

"Sure, Francine. As a matter of fact, we were just talking about you."

"About what a lousy friend I've been?"

Frank could only shrug and smile in return.

"What did you want to see me about?"

"I'm going to need a leave of absence. Six months should do it."

"What? Is this a health thing? Everything okay with Rosa? Will?"

"Everything's fine on that front."

"Well?"

"Frank, I had a visitor yesterday."

"Oh? Who was that?"

"Lawson."

Frank was another person whose life had been adversely affected by the former colonel. His reaction was quite similar to Will's.

"He wants me to investigate the Zyklon Killer. He claims that Texas executed the wrong man. Aaron Kaplow was his cousin and Lawson is convinced he could not have been the killer. He claimed Kaplow was framed. If I don't help him, Lawson will hurt or kill Alan Westbrook. I just need some time to sort this out. I don't think I can refuse, but I can't do it while I'm doing my anchor duties."

"You know, Francine, we've been riding on your back ever since Destroy Mecca. Our news rating went from fourth in the city to second because of you. The suits here, me included, like to pretend our brilliant moves have been responsible for our success but everyone from the network president on down knows that it's because of you and you alone. If you leave, even for a short period, we'll revert back to what we were. For that reason, I can't authorize a leave of absence."

I was hoping it wouldn't come to this. I really loved working at Action 6 News, and I loved working for Frank, but this was something I really had to do. I regretted it, but I would have to give Frank my resignation. I was about to do so but when I looked at Frank, he was smiling.

"You're trying to phrase your resignation, aren't you?"

"Yes, I am."

"Before you wrack your brain any further trying to figure out just the right thing to say so as not to offend me too much, let me finish my thought first. No, I won't approve a leave of absence. What I will approve is for you to move back to being a reporter."

I was dumbfounded and utterly confused.

"Francine, after Mecca, you could have written your ticket to do anything you wanted wherever you wanted. You could be the next Christiane Amanpour or Richard Engel, ferreting out stories in the darkest corners of the world. Yet, you chose to stay here, and I greatly appreciate it. Maybe the other suits don't reward loyalty but I do.

"But I can tell you're not happy. You do good work as an anchor. No, let me amend that; you do great work as an anchor. But it's obvious that this is not where your heart is. You need to be out in the field."

"That's exactly what Lawson told me."

"Well, he may be a monster but I've never heard anyone say that he wasn't brilliant, too. One of these days, you're going to walk into my office and tell me you've gotten an offer from one of the networks that's too good to pass up. On that day you'll hand me your resignation, we'll have a teary farewell over a few drinks and I'll wish you Godspeed. Until then, I'm going to do my damnedest to keep you and to keep you wanting to come to work."

"How you going to explain this to management? One day I'm at the desk and the next day I'm not. They don't like to appear that they made a wrong decision, do they?"

"I'm going to try a radical approach around here: honesty. I'll tell them this is the only way to keep you. If that falls flat, I'll resort to lying and tell them that you got another offer.

"Now, if Lawson is correct, Zyklon does sound like it could be a hell of a story. I'm just trying to imagine the roadblocks that will be thrown in your way. Texas will pull out all the stops to keep you from proving they executed an innocent man. But before you dive too heavily into that story I need to give you something that will get your feet wet back in the field of reporting. It's not unusual for an anchor to do an occasional field piece so nobody would think twice about it until we come up with a more permanent shift. At the same time we'll correct an unfortunate situation."

"And that is?"

"You and Jonas. Give me a half hour and I'll come up with something for you to work on together."

"Thanks, Frank. For everything."

True to his word, Frank came back to me with a story he wanted me to cover. Councilman Theodore Evans had hastily put together a press conference to address new allegations of corruption and undue pressure being put on city agencies to award contracts to a construction firm owned by his brother-in-law. He put the word out at 1:45 in the afternoon that the briefing would be held at 2:30. We supposed that he was hoping the limited notice would keep media attendance down. This way he could claim he was being transparent but at the same time minimize the damage a full-scale media assault could do.

I'd been following the councilman's predicament so it wasn't as if I was walking into this absolutely cold. The reporter that had been covering the councilman story, Bill Waters, was out at the far edge of Brooklyn covering a train derailment so the short notice worked perfectly for Frank and me. He could claim that he needed someone who could get to the Upper West Side immediately and, since Bill was out of pocket, I had to be drafted into duty. Otherwise, who knew what feelings had to be soothed and what egos stroked as I stepped in on someone else's story.

Frank gave me the assignment and I flew over to Jonas's workstation. He was sitting there, brooding, still bothered by our previous interaction.

"C'mon J. Grab your camera. We have to get uptown in twenty minutes! Let's go."

I shocked him out of his reverie such that he jumped up, grabbed his camera and ran out after me as if he were acting on instinct. We made our way down to the C Train and one was there within minutes.

As we rode the train uptown, Jonas reverted to sulking. I needed to figure out a way to bring him back.

The weather had been quite warm and Jonas was wearing his ever-present T-shirt under a military-style vest with all sorts of pockets to hold his equipment. The scar on the triceps of his left arm was readily visible. I pointed at it.

"Jonas, it's not every woman who can point at a scar on a man and say 'he took a bullet for me.' "

"Nope, I bet they can't."

We were silent for a few more minutes. I could tell something was forming in his mind and it would spill out any moment now. I knew I would not like what he said, mostly because I deserved it.

"Frannie, you know I've only seen Rosa once, when you were in the hospital. That was, what, a year and a half ago?"

"You know you'd be welcome at our home anytime, Jonas."

"It doesn't seem like it. You've been a different person. It's almost like I'm a person from a former life that you're ashamed of as you've moved on."

"Oh, Jonas, it's not that way at all."

"It sure feels like it."

"J, let me tell you what it was."

"Please do."

"I felt like I was a fraud, an imposter. I'd excelled at everything I've ever tried in my life yet I felt so inadequate as an anchor."

"What you talkin' about? You're fantastic, far better than that airhead Willa you replaced."

"Not in my eyes. Each morning after I finished, I could only see the flaws, the flubs I'd made the previous three hours. I felt like a fraud. There are so many other reporters more qualified then I am. I stumbled onto a great story that vaulted me over them, probably unfairly. You know me better than anybody, J. I've confided so many things to you over the years that you know me maybe better than my own husband does. Because of that, a part of me figured that you'd be as ashamed of me as I was."

"Never, Frannie. But I was hurt, very hurt."

"J, I suck at being a friend. You remember there was only one woman in my wedding entourage, my college roommate. But on the men's side were you, Frank and Will's colleagues. The only reason I had the one woman is because she was the one who maintained the friendship. She was the one who kept in contact over the years, not me. If it were left up to me, she would have been cast aside, just like I did with you. I am so sorry. You are the best person I know, and I treated you like shit."

"So what now?"

"Well, I won't have the pressure of being an anchor anymore. I'll need a cameraman."

"What! What happened?"

"It was my choice. I worked it out with Frank. I'm going back to reporting. I have a big piece I'm going to be working on and I'll need your help. That is if you still want to work with me."

"You know I do, Frannie."

"Good, we get off at the next stop. Let's do this report and then I'll call Will and tell him to stop and get some steaks to throw on the grill. You, sir, are coming home with me to get acquainted with my daughter!"

8

It felt great having Jonas back in my life. Before we piled into his clunker he tossed me his keys and asked if I could drive. He was subject to periodic migraines and had taken some medication when he felt one coming on. He could drive but it would probably be safer for me to drive. I thought that was a dubious assumption, but I agreed.

We headed for Queens. The 1989 Dodge Aries was a wreck the last time I rode in it over two years ago; it had gone significantly downhill since then. At least before it didn't spew a steady stream of black smoke out of its tailpipe like it did now.

"It's a good thing I'm such a slow driver, Jonas. I doubt we can get this heap over thirty-five anyway. I tell you what. I'm going to take up a collection so we can put this thing out of its misery and give it a proper funeral."

"You mustn't say things like that. That's not how you treat an old friend."

I knew he didn't mean anything by it, but I took his jibe to heart.

"Unfortunately, I do."

"Now, now Frannie, that's all behind us, you hear? You lost your way for a bit but you've come to your senses. That's all I ever want to hear about it, okay?"

"Okay. J., there is one thing I want you to do for me, but only if you want to."

"You name it."

"You've probably heard Will call me Fava. It was a nickname he came up with when we were devising a scheme to smoke out Alan Westbrook a lifetime ago. As soon as he said it my eyes welled up because it was the endearment my mother would use for me when she was alive. She was the only one who'd ever called me Fava. Will immediately apologized for stumbling on something so personal and offered to come up with another name. It was that moment that I realized I was falling in love and told him that it was not just okay for him to call me Fava but it felt right, too.

"What I'm trying to say is that I'd only accept that nickname from people I love and it would be more than right for you to call me Fava as well. I make it sound like I'm bestowing some sort of honor here, but you know what I mean."

"Yeah, I do. Appreciate it, but I'll probably just stick with Frannie. Old dog, new tricks, ya know?"

"Yeah, I know, J."

The car complained with a groan as I accelerated to get onto the FDR. I probably pushed it a little more than I should have, but there was enough of a gap for the car in the right lane to adjust. The same wasn't true for the car that entered the highway right behind us. He stayed on our tail, not yielding for an instant, as he forced the oncoming car to screech his brakes and lean on the horn.

"Jesus H.," Jonas said as he turned around. "What an asshole. We're lucky he didn't go right through us!"

After that the trip was uneventful, for a while anyway. As we were proceeding along I worried about how the kids would react to Jonas. The first impression this six foot four, two hundred seventy pound man often made on people could be one of trepidation and fear. I knew that Will had raised his kids to respect people of all races, but you never knew with kids how they'd react to someone so different than they were used to. I was sure I was worrying needlessly. In any case, Jonas' charm and sense of humor could win over anybody of any age.

We proceeded to the Triboro Bridge and onto the Grand Central. Just after LaGuardia Airport, we got off to weave through the local streets. I noticed that Jonas was continually turning around with a concerned look on his face.

"What's up?" I asked.

"That same asshole, the Audi, that got onto the FDR with us is still behind us. Seems a little strange."

I glanced in the rearview.

"You're right, it is. Is he following us?"

"Seems as though."

I started to slow as a light changed to yellow and then gunned it (well, I gunned it as much as the decrepit Aries would allow me) through the light as it turned red. We could hear horns blaring as we departed the intersection.

"Damn," he exclaimed, "He's still following us."

I pulled out my phone and called Will. Unfortunately I got his voicemail. I left a frantic message.

We came to another intersection and I made a hard right turn, just missing a mother carrying a small child. The Audi was still on our tail, steadily closing the gap until they actually bumped us from behind. I went as fast as traffic would allow, which at midday was barely above a crawl. At one point, we pulled up behind a car that was stopped in the right lane at a red light. When the Audi pulled up behind us, the man in the passenger seat jumped out and ran to my side and banged hard on the window. He hit it with such force that the window cracked. He shouted something but I couldn't make it out. It sounded like 'Loss'.

At that moment, the light changed. As soon as the car in front of us moved up, I put my foot to the floor, cut to the right, going even faster as then I swerved back in front of that car. More blaring horns. The man who had just been shouting at us jumped back into the Audi and they continued in pursuit.

I was going to turn onto the Boulevard, which would have afforded us more lanes and more maneuverability but in retrospect I probably was wise to stay on the narrower side streets. After all, it was a case of a beat up old Aries versus a modern Audi. It would have been no contest out on the open road.

My adroit move at the intersection at least put a car between them and us, but we knew it wouldn't be long before they caught up again. Jonas' determined look on his face quickly transformed to a smile as he told me to pull into an open spot by a fire hydrant.

"What? We have to keep moving!"

"Just do it."

I complied. It was then that I noticed that Jonas had had me pull in front of a police precinct.

Jonas didn't say anything but instead he reached over and leaned on the horn. He kept it blaring until a police officer came racing out of the precinct. Within a few seconds the Audi came by. The two men glared into our car but proceeded on.

The cop wanted to give us a ticket but when I showed him the card Will had given me for such situations, he backed off.

My phone rang. It was Will.

"Are you okay? Where are you?"

I explained the situation, telling him we were safe.

"I'll see you at home," I offered.

"No, stay where you are. You're relatively safe there but they may be waiting for you to drive on. I'll be there in twenty minutes. I'll bring Willoughby along. He'll drive Jonas's car."

True to his word, Will and Agent Willoughby arrived twenty minutes later. A different local cop did happen by during that time and advised us that we couldn't park where we were because it was in front of a hydrant. Rather than getting into the details of what actually happened, I told him we'd broken down and that my husband was on his way. Looking at Jonas's car, the story was entirely plausible.

I ran to Will and hugged him tight.

"Hi, Agent Willoughby. I hope you're well."

"Hello, Ms. Vega, Mr. Clarke."

Ever the uptight bureaucrat, Agent Bernard Willoughby was as formal as ever. He wasn't exactly the type person you'd invite to liven up a party. But you couldn't ask for a more loyal person. His devotion to Will bordered on the fanatical and that devotion had saved our lives on a couple of occasions so I could put up with him being officious. I did get a kick out of the look of disdain on his face when he saw the car he was to drive.

We piled into Will's car and proceeded toward home. We kept a sharp eye out for the Audi but it was long gone and we drove on, arriving home without incident. We invited Willoughby to join us for dinner but he claimed he had other plans. I doubted he had anything else going on; he was just uncomfortable in social settings.

In regards to how the kids reacted to Jonas, I needed not to have worried one bit. His huge smile and gregarious personality won them over immediately. It wasn't long before he was down on the floor, playing Twister with them. The sight of this behemoth interwoven with the diminutive Albert and the tiny Stella brought squeals of delight out of all of us. Will was somewhat concerned that Jonas could lose his balance and crush one of the kids, but I was fully confident that he'd thought this through and he'd take the necessary steps to keep this from ever happening.

When Jonas held Rosa in his arms, I felt especially ashamed that I had ignored him for the past year and a half. Looking on them and the obvious bond they immediately felt for each other as he lifted her up high over and over again to her utter delight further deepened the shame. What was I thinking? Was focusing on my career and on being a new mother so all-consuming that I couldn't spare a few minutes over that time for this dear, wonderful man, a man who had saved my life, no less. And who knows, his quick thinking may have just saved my life again. What a terrible person I am!

The kids had their dinner and then went off and did their thing as we sat down to our meal. One of Will's many talents is that he's a master at the barbecue. He brought the steaks in and we sat down to eat and discuss the day's events.

"So you have no idea what these guys were after?" Will asked.

"Not a clue. He yelled something but I couldn't make it out. It sounded like he was saying 'Loss'."

"Well, in the morning you'll sit down with our sketch artist to see if we can get a hit on the guy who ran up to you. Jonas, you didn't see either of the men, did you?"

"Not clearly. No. I'm sorry."

"That's quite understandable."

"Hey," I interjected, "we were both just trying to stay alive, right J? Just like old times."

I reached over and held his hand. Will then asked the obvious.

"You think he could have been saying 'Lawson'?"

"Maybe, but why? It's only been a day since I saw him so he can't expect me to have come up with anything yet, could he? Then again, the man is an unstable sociopath. Maybe after our chat he changed his mind and decided I was more of a liability than an asset. Who knows what goes through his mind? I don't know. I really don't."

We finished our meals and hung around a little while longer but both Jonas and I had early morning assignments. About a half hour before Jonas was to leave Will stepped away. I saw him talking to somebody on his phone.

"J, I'm so glad we did this. I'm so sorry for being such a jerk."

"Water under the bridge; water under the bridge. We'll just have to make up for time missed, won't we?"

He flashed his biggest smile.

"Yes we will. Next time I doubt you'll let Albert win at Twister."

"He beat me fair and square! But I'll work on it so I'll give him more of a battle next time."

"You do that."

As I was giving him a big hug there was a knock on the door. I opened it to find Agent Willoughby standing there. Will spoke up.

"I don't know if that Audi's still out there so I asked Agent Willoughby to come back. He'll follow you home."

"I'm sure I'll be fine," Jonas half-heartedly protested but it was obvious he appreciated the escort.

"See you tomorrow, Frannie?"

"You bet!"

After one more hug, Jonas was on his way. I was glad Will thought of calling Willoughby to tail Jonas.

We got ready for bed. We'd only just turned off the lights when Will's phone rang. I turned the lights back on as he grabbed his phone off the end table and looked at the display.

"It's Willoughby. Knowing him, he's probably calling to let me know the package has been delivered," Will joked. He pressed Answer.

"Hey Bernie."

There was a pause as Will's face shifted to concern and then to horror.

"Oh no. Oh no."

He listened silently for a minute.

"Can you assist the locals until I get there? I'll be there in fifteen minutes or so. Good, see you then."

Will hung up and then looked at me with love and concern, obviously mulling over how to phrase his next utterance.

"Fava, something's happened."

"Jonas. Is he okay?"

"Jonas pulled onto the FDR from the Triboro. Bernie got separated a couple of cars from Jonas in traffic and then there was a fender bender that kept him from pulling out. Bernie lost sight of Jonas as he went around a curve. Seconds later Bernie heard a loud explosion. He jumped out of his car and ran up the FDR and found Jonas's car engulfed in flames. I'm sorry, Fava."

I couldn't stand any more.

"I'm going to head there now."

I was about ready to tell him there was no way I wasn't coming as well but then I remembered the kids. Someone had to stay with them.

"I'm so sorry, Fava. I'll call you when I get there. I called Agent Broderick and asked him to come over. He should be here in about half an hour. Until then, do not let anyone in. Here, take this."

He wasn't convincing himself, let alone me. He handed me his spare pistol.

"You remember me showing you how to use one of these when we were in Israel? The safety is here. Aim and squeeze. Keep a tight grip, but not excessive tight. Don't shoot yourself or any of the kids. You can give it to Rick when he arrives."

I was going to protest that I didn't need Agent Broderick or the gun; I would be perfectly fine. Will's tone, however, was not one that welcomed discussion. Besides, we both knew full well that I was still in danger. And so were the kids.

Will called when he arrived at the scene but he didn't have any updates. The car was still engulfed in flames as the fire department had just gotten there. Two hours later he called back.

"Well, the car fire is out but it's still smoldering. We have to get the car to the lab but preliminarily our best guess is that it was an explosive device, and a pretty powerful one at that. We haven't found Jonas's remains yet but that's not that unusual given the intensity of the explosion and the fire that followed."

Will stopped as he realized that his clinical analysis of the situation might have appeared cold and aloof.

"I'm sorry, Fava, giving you a report like this."

"That's okay. You're doing your job. I know you're not insensitive in the least."

"I'm going to be here a couple more hours while the CSU sifts through the wreckage. I'll call you again in a bit. I love you, Fava."

"I love you, too."

The only emotion that exceeded my fear was profound sorrow, especially in the dark house. It wasn't long before I was reduced to sobs as I lay on my bed.

9

Sleep had only just overtaken me when my cellphone rang, jarring me awake. At first I was disoriented but then reality flooded back in as I reached over to answer. It was Will.

"Will, any news?"

"Fava, there were no human remains in the car! None whatsoever. Jonas may still be alive."

"Where is he?"

"We have no idea. My men are scouring the neighborhood and the hospitals."

"Do you think they took him as a hostage?"

"Let's not jump to any conclusions and get ourselves worried over what might have happened."

Where was Jonas? My mind was racing all over. I was relieved that there was a possibility he survived, but what happened to him? Could the men in the Audi have kidnapped him before blowing up the car? Why? Perhaps he had only been injured and wandered off. My dark mind went back to a story I'd covered some years ago about a dog that was found dead at a hazardous waste site. The State spent tens of thousands of dollars performing a necropsy (it was pointed out to me by a veterinarian once that this was what you called an autopsy on an animal) to figure out what chemicals had killed the dog only to find out that it had been hit by a car and crawled into the building, looking for a place to die. I hoped this wasn't the case with Jonas.

I went back to bed to try and get some sleep. I contemplated not going to work; Frank would have totally understood. In fact, he probably expected as much but I wasn't going to give anyone even the littlest bit of satisfaction that they had beaten me. I probably wasn't going to give my 'A Game' today, but I was determined to be there, delivering the news for all to see.

As I anticipated, Frank was surprised to see me when I walked into the studio. He tried to convince me to go back home, but he saw the look in my eye and relented. He did lighten the mood by noting that I looked like death warmed over but that Martha Brooks, our makeup artist, could do wonders.

The broadcast went without incident. Jonas's car explosion was our lead story. We were in our last commercial break after which we would hand it over to the national show when one of the interns, Kathy Lucy, handed me a note there was a call for me. I told Kathy to keep whoever it was on the line for the few minutes it took to do our closing. As soon as we were done, I picked up the phone.

"Francine Vega? This is Dr. Fred Madden from Lenox Hill Hospital. Do you know a Jonas Clarke?"

"Yes. Is he there? Is he okay?"

My heart was about to beat out of my chest.

"Well, he's gone through a lot of trauma and has some head injuries but he seems to be resting comfortably now. We're checking him out and will keep him for a few days.

"He was found stumbling around in the neighborhood about two blocks from here. A local resident saw him fall down and at first thought he was a drunken homeless person but then she saw blood on his shirt. He was semi-conscious and semi-coherent so she guided him over here.

"We tried asking him some questions. He had no idea what happened to him. He even had trouble remembering basic things like his name, where he lived or what happened to him. But when we asked him if he had any family, he responded: 'Only Francine, Francine Vega.' Then he lost consciousness. When I looked in his wallet, I saw his work I.D. and I figured you must be the Francine Vega he was talking about."

"I am. Thank you so much for calling me."

"Do you know what happened to him?"

"His car exploded on the FDR. I don't know anything beyond that. Have you gotten in touch with the police or the FBI yet? They've been looking for Jonas."

"I just came on duty a half hour ago, right when Mr. Clarke walked in. I didn't know they were looking for him."

"I'll be there in twenty minutes or so."

"You're family?"

He obviously was familiar with me and was trying to figure out how I could possibly be family with this dark Black man.

"Yes, yes I am most definitely family."

Not knowing how long I was going to be there, I grabbed my workbag as well as my purse. When I stuck my head in Frank's office to tell him where I was heading, he said he was going as well.

Frank and I jumped in a cab and headed uptown to the hospital. By the time we arrived, Will was outside Jonas' room along with Agent Broderick. With them was a dark-haired, attractive woman in her mid-forties wearing a tan pantsuit.

"Fava, Frank," Will started. "Jonas is still out. They decided to put him in a medically-induced coma to give him time to recover. His brain took quite a pounding from the explosion. It's wait and see. Willoughby didn't let on that he was also hurt when he tried to assist. He approached the car several times to try and help Jonas. On one of his approaches there was a secondary explosion. He's in surgery so they can remove some metal shards. His prognosis is pretty good."

He paused to let it sink in. I looked over at the woman.

"Oh, this is NYPD Detective Jane Kelly. Because of the nature of the explosion, this is going to be a joint FBI/NYPD investigation. Because of my relationship with you and Jonas, I'll be acting in a support capacity. Agent Broderick will be the FBI lead. Detective Kelly will coordinate the investigation for the NYPD."

Will was definitely not pleased, but I couldn't tell whether it was because of his subordinate role, having to work with the local police or both.

"Can we go somewhere to talk?" asked the detective. At the moment, the waiting room on the floor was empty so Detective Kelly, Broderick, Will and I went there. Frank remained outside of Jonas's room. We all sat down. Broderick spoke up first.

"The car's at the FBI crime lab. It was most definitely an explosive device affixed to the bottom of the car. We won't know for a day or so whether it was on a timer or detonated remotely. I understand that two men in a silver gray Audi had accosted you and Mr. Clarke on the way to your home. Is that correct?"

"Yes."

Broderick knew all this but I assumed he was making sure Detective Kelly was up to speed. She indicated she was fully informed by her next question.

"I understand the men in the Audi yelled something at you, Ms. Vega?"

"Yes, but through the closed window I had no idea what they were saying. It sounded like 'Loss' but I didn't stick around to ask. Ultimately, we pulled in front of a police precinct not far from my home. The Audi drove on by. I had no idea they'd go after Jonas."

"Did you happen to get the license plate?"

"Yes, New Jersey YES245 but the FBI ran it already and it was stolen."

"I thought as much. Did Mr. Clarke have any enemies? Anybody who'd want to do him harm? Any financial issues? Any exes or jilted lovers that you knew of?"

"Jonas? Everybody loved him. I don't think he had any money problems. He and his ex-girlfriend, Eunice, get along better now than when they were seeing each other. No, I cannot envision anyone on earth wanting to harm J."

"And what about you? Could they have assumed it was your car they were sabotaging?"

I almost blurted out that I sure hope no one would ever assume that junk was mine, but now was not the time for levity.

"I hadn't thought about it. I guess there could be people holding a grudge against me for a variety of reasons."

I was about to mention Lawson and our meeting but I caught Will's eye as he warned me against saying anything more.

"Were you about to say something, Ms. Vega?" the detective asked.

"No, thoughts were just running through my mind as I try to figure this out."

"I understand. Do you think you could come down to the precinct later today to talk some more and to give a description to our sketch artist? Let's say around 4?"

I nodded yes as she gave me her card.

With that she rose.

"I have to get back to the station. I'll see you then."

"If it's okay, I'll go with you," Broderick offered. "Maybe we can lay out our plan for the investigation. Will, you want to join us and then we can go over to the lab and see if they've found anything in the car?"

"Sure, I'll join you in a few."

Will and I walked back to Jonas's room. Frank had to get back to work, making it clear that I was to take at least the next day off, or even more if I needed it. He gave me a hug and left, leaving Will and me alone.

"Why didn't you want me to mention Lawson and the folder he gave me?" I asked them as soon as everybody left.

"I don't know. This Detective Kelly was just foisted on me when I got here. She seems okay but as you know with Mecca, we've been burned too many times to be overly trusting. I'd like to find out more about her before divulging too much. Plus, once we mention the folder, it's no longer ours. I want to determine if Lawson's threat to Alan is real before we give it up."

"You okay with the joint investigation and with you not being the federal lead?"

"Oh, I'm the lead. Don't you worry about that. Rick and I have it all worked out. I have full confidence that Rick would conduct this case properly and keep me in the loop but he would be the first to admit that he doesn't want the responsibility of leadership. He came to me with the proposal that he'd be in charge in name only but I'd really be calling the shots. He knows how much this means to me."

"I'm going to go in and sit with Jonas for awhile. Did you know when he came in here semiconscious the doctor asked him if he had any family his answer was me?"

Will smiled.

"I wouldn't doubt it. You take as long as you need. I'll look after the kids. Oh, and I asked Detective Kelly if she could post a uniform out here for a couple days. I don't want to take any chances that they may try again."

He kissed me goodbye and headed over to the precinct.

I went in and gave Jonas a kiss on the cheek. Even though there were bandages on various spots on his head and face and much of his skin had a purplish hue of black and blue marks, he looked serene. I pulled a chair beside his bed and held his hand as I recited a silent prayer for his recovery.

After fifteen minutes or so I dug out my workbag figuring I should try and be productive while I was sitting here. I pulled out the folder Lawson had given me. A chill ran through me as I thought that something in here could be the reason Jonas was lying here in a hospital bed.

I also thought about Will's reticence in divulging the existence of the file or acknowledging that it could provide clues as to who did this to Jonas. Given that officials in his own department were complicit with the plot to destroy Mecca—and in turn were willing to sacrifice Will and me to that cause—was enough to keep him from completely trusting anyone, especially someone he didn't know. I put all these thoughts to the back of my mind as I opened the file.

Knowing how buttoned-up military Lawson was, I expected the files to be organized and catalogued. Instead, I found a hodgepodge of newspaper clippings, handwritten scribbling and Internet printouts. There were pieces on his cousin, Aaron Kaplow, and how exemplary a youth he was. He won spelling bees and fishing derbies and was MVP on his Babe Ruth baseball team. At the same time, there were report cards and such indicating how middling a student he had been. I supposed these were included to highlight that Mr. Kaplow was probably not capable of carrying out the intricate plans developed by the Zyklon Killer.

In the folder there were numerous pieces about the history of Zyklon B, how it is produced and handled and how it was used during the war for extermination. I had done research on the gas back when I was originally covering the story, so these sheets lent nothing new to me.

I had pretty much gone through the entire file and was about to conclude that the information contained in it was worthless when a stray newspaper clipping fell to the floor. I picked it up and glanced at it. It was from the Tel Aviv Journal newspaper and was dated July 3, 1961. The headline was: Forensic experts confirm corpse is not Hans Steiner. It read:

In a stunning setback to famed Nazi hunter Efrain Friedman's efforts to bring the most notorious Nazi officials to justice for crimes against humanity, forensic coroners have conclusively determined that the corpse of the body previously identified as the infamous SS Officer Hans Georg Steiner, is in fact not Steiner.

Friedman had hoped to duplicate the success of efforts last year by Mossad in extricating Adolf Eichmann from Argentina and bringing him to Israel to face trial. Acting on what he thought was confirmed evidence of the location of Steiner in Argentina, Friedman and several of his men attempted to capture Steiner. However, in the battle that erupted, the man believed to be Steiner was killed.

Friedman smuggled the body out of Argentina and transported it to Israel to verify to the world that they had indeed killed the notorious Nazi Obersturmbannführer who was directly responsible for over two thousand deaths of innocent Jews during the war and indirectly connected to thousands more. Now, forensic evidence has proven that Friedman killed the wrong man. The identity of the deceased is unknown.

Relations between Argentina and Israel, which were already tense by the Eichmann seizure, have been further strained. The South American country is demanding not only that the remains be returned for identification but also that Friedman be arrested to potentially face trial for the murder of one of its citizens. Since there is no extradition treaty between the two nations, it is unclear what future actions, if any, will be taken.

The one question on the mind of Jews in Israel and around the world: Is Hans Georg Steiner still alive and, if so, where is he?

I pulled out my computer and typed in 'Hans Steiner' into the search engine. I only needed a general overview of him so I clicked on his name in the Internet encyclopedia.

Hans Georg Steiner (b. May 13, 1907; d. ?) was born and raised in Bavaria west of Munich with his father (Rudolf Steiner), mother (Gretchen Rupp Steiner), and four sisters (Inga, Marta, Katrina and Eva). Rudolf Steiner was a successful farmer in the area and was able to send his son to private school and to the University of Würzburg. At university, Hans entered into a course of study to become an architect but in his second year *he left school to work for the Nazi Party in Munich.*

In 1930, his efforts came to the attention of Heinrich Himmler, who had the previous year been appointed by Adolf Hitler as Reichsführer of the Schutzstaffel or SS. Steiner joined the SS with the rank of Hauptsturmführer, the equivalent of a captain. Within two years, he was elevated to the rank of Obersturmbannführer, or lieutenant colonel, the position he would hold until the end of the war.

Steiner reported directly to Himmler and was responsible for touring the network of concentration camps where mass executions were carried out. His role was to examine the various techniques for killing employed at each camp and to suggest ways to improve effectiveness and efficiency while reducing cost.

Steiner was known facetiously as "Herr Qualitätskontrolle" or "Mr. Quality Control". However, this somewhat humorous moniker belied how feared he was throughout the concentration camp system as he was known to order prison officers to report to the Eastern Front or even their executions if he felt that they were not diligently performing their duties.

In early 1945, Steiner was believed to have escaped from Germany just prior to the Allied advance and was thought to have fled to Argentina. It was speculated that he was able to bring with him millions of dollars in gold bullion and a number of priceless artworks, including several paintings by Rembrandt, Picasso and Vermeer.

The rest of the article was a rehash of the newspaper article about the botched capture that I only skimmed.

I read a lot about the Holocaust when I was covering the Zyklon Killer story but it's not something I'll ever comprehend. Every time I learn new information about a monster such as Hans Georg Steiner, my skin crawls anew. How can any human being do such things? I'll never understand it.

How does Steiner relate to the Zyklon Killer? He obviously had a connection to the gas Zyklon and its use at the camps, but that was a long time ago. There's no way he's still alive. What relevance would he have to today's user of that poisonous gas? There had to be more, pieces of the puzzle that I would have to ferret out and put together. But that would have to wait for another day. I was exhausted and needed to close my eyes for a bit.

I placed the newspaper clipping back in the folder. Despite my exhaustion, I decided to finish glancing through the remaining few pages left in the folder. There was more useless info on Zyklon gas. The last page was a printout about the upcoming presidential election and the two candidates: Malcolm McKenzie and New York Governor Peter Kent. This article was totally unrelated to everything else in the folder. It struck me as odd that it was included here but I was too tired to give it much thought as I put my head back on my chair and closed my eyes.

10

When I next opened my eyes, sunlight was just starting to filter through the blinds. I had slept the entire night in that chair, and my back felt it. I looked up to see Jonas sitting up in bed, smiling at me.

"You look terrible, Frannie."

I jumped out of the chair and rushed over to give him a big hug.

"And you look wonderful, J!"

"I somehow doubt it, but it's great to be alive."

"Do you remember anything about what happened?"

"Not much. I remember my car stalling on the FDR and getting out to see what's wrong. After that, nothing until I woke up here and saw you sittin' there."

I relaxed and sat back in my chair but then nearly jumped back out of it when I noticed someone else in the room, sitting in the shadows behind all the machinery connected to J. He was asleep; his head was down so I couldn't make out his face.

I slowly reached for my purse to extract my phone to call 911. I contemplated yelling out for the cop who was supposedly outside the door but I figured that this man had slipped by the cop, or worse, so calling 911 was my best option. When I activated the phone, it beeped and the man looked up. I couldn't believe my eyes.

"Alan?"

"Hi, Francine. Mr. Clarke. I'm glad to see you're doing better."

Jonas only nodded in return, unsure of what to make of my former comrade, Alan Westbrook, who helped set off the 'destroy Mecca' movement but then was instrumental in helping to thwart the plot, as he calmly sat in Jonas's hospital room. I would have gone over to give him a hug but because it all seemed so surreal, I didn't move toward him.

"Alan," I asked, "it's great to see you again. I think about you often, wondering how you're doing."

"I've been fine, Francine."

"So, what are you doing here? And how'd you get by the police officer stationed outside this door?"

"Well, as to getting by Officer Kenner, I sent him a text message advising him that he needed to get back to the precinct immediately. I do hope you'll explain to his superiors and to your husband that the text was my doing so that the officer won't get into trouble."

I'd almost forgotten how much of a genius Alan was, especially with computers. He could easily do something like hacking into someone's cellphone. He was, after all, able to send me text messages indicating his calls were originating from Antarctica.

"In regards to your first question, I'm here because I heard the news of the attempt on Mr. Clarke's life."

He said this as though Jonas wasn't in the room with us but then he turned to Jonas.

"By the way, Mr. Clarke, I've arranged it so that you will not pay a dime out of pocket for your stay here. It's the least I could do, if not to you then to Ms. Vega here."

Jonas thanked him in a bit of disbelief. Alan turned back to me and continued.

"I also understand you had a visit from our mutual friend, Jacob Lawson."

It was hard not to note the level of contempt in his voice when he mentioned his former mentor's name.

"I don't believe the two events—Jake's chat with you and the explosion—are unrelated."

"Lawson ordered the bombing?"

"No, I don't believe so. Rather, I think the explosion was related to the story Jake has you working on, clearing his cousin's name."

"Alan, I thought you were somewhere down in Texas."

"That's what Jake believes. Obviously, he's mistaken."

Alan gave me one of his off-center smiles that showed that he had done something to lead Lawson astray and keep him off-balance.

"Lawson also said you were somewhat down and out, but you appear to be fine. In fact, you look better than I remember you looking when we last parted a couple of years ago."

"Well, having a couple hundred million dollars at one's disposal tends to improve one's appearance and lifestyle."

"Hold on. Now I'm totally confused. I thought you had turned your entire lottery fortune over to Lawson back when you were"

I paused to come up with the correct word.

"Back when I was crazy?"

"That wasn't exactly where I was going, but yeah, that about sums it up."

Alan smiled again, but it was a softer smile.

"Yes I did. At one point I turned over my entire $475 million to Jake, believing he would know best what to do with it. He used about $200 million getting the atomic bomb and deploying it to destroy Mecca. We were lucky there, weren't we?"

"Yes, we were. But I still don't understand how you got the money back."

"It's simple. Jake's sloppy when it comes to computer management skills. It was a breeze hacking in, getting his account numbers and passwords and reclaiming the money. The hard part was doing it in such a way that he still thinks he has the money. But I finally figured out a way to do it. As long as he only draws down small amounts, he'll never realize it's not in his account. If he embarks on something that requires a significant outlay, then he'll know."

Alan seemed proud of himself.

"So you say you're keeping track of Lawson and his online activity?

"Yes."

"And that's how you know he wasn't responsible for Jonas's car blowing up?"

"Yes. I could tell he was surprised by the news when he heard about it last night."

"But you think there's some sort of connection there."

"Yes, Jake was on to something big but, given his persona non-grata status, he could only go so far in his investigation. That's why he recruited you to help him. It not only has to do with clearing his cousin's name but something much bigger. In this case, he's been careful and all his emails and messages are coded in a way I can't figure out. It has something to do with national security. Remember, Jacob Lawson may be a sociopathic killer but, in his heart, he's also a super-patriot or at least his version of one."

"Do you know that he used a threat against you to convince me that I needed to help him?"

"I figured as much, and I'm touched that it would be an inducement for you."

"We went through a lot together, Alan."

"Yes, yes we did."

"So, knowing that you're safe and out of his reach, I don't see any reason to help him out."

"Oh, you'll do it. I know you will."

"Why are you so sure?"

"First, you're an old school journalist. Never mind the potential of a bigger story, knowing that you can develop a story that will conclusively prove that an innocent man was put to death has way too much of a pull on you. But second, if the other story is as big as I believe it is and can have national or even international consequences, you're duty bound to follow it wherever it may lead. The same way that you could not resist the pull of 'Destroy Mecca', you can't resist this.

"Lastly, don't worry about me. I'll be able to take care of myself. But even if I can't and Jake takes me out, remember that he killed a good part of me when he killed Freddy on 9/11. He'd just be completing the job."

Alan's face took on a somber aspect at the mention of his twin brother, Frederick.

There was not much to say after that. I asked Alan if he wanted to come stay with us but he declined. He thought he still needed to stay under the radar and could help more underground. As he was leaving, I had one last question for him.

"Alan, do you know anything about Hans Steiner? He was a Nazi war criminal."

"Not any more than what's in that folder there."

He gave me a sheepish look.

"I took the liberty of reading through the file while you slept. Jake gave you this material, right?"

I nodded.

"Well, the one thing you should assume is that every scrap of paper is in there for a purpose. Jake wouldn't include it if he didn't think it was pertinent in some way."

With that he walked out the door. After that, Jonas practically ordered me out, telling me I needed to get back to my family and my job.

11

I still wasn't sure how Frank was going to finesse my leaving the anchor seat but it turned out fate intervened. When I went to see him the next morning, an attractive, a 40ish year-old woman with pulled-back auburn hair and wearing an expensive tailored suit was waiting for me. When she turned around to greet me I recognized her immediately.

"Francine, this is Janet Kahn, President of Allied Broadcasting."

We shook hands.

"Ms. Kahn, it's a pleasure to meet you."

"And I you. You've made quite a name for yourself here in New York and throughout the country and the world itself. I wanted to thank you for staying with the Allied Broadcasting family."

"Well, this industry is famous for terrible, self-serving bosses so when you find a great one such as Frank here, it's best to stay where you are for as long as you can."

I looked over and Frank was blushing a bit.

"Be that as it may, your reputation has spread far beyond the New York market. But I always find that it's best not to judge people purely on their reputations but to get some first-hand experience as to the character of the person, don't you agree?

"Yes, sometimes reputations can be constructed on misinformation and misunderstandings."

Ms. Kahn eyed me for the briefest of seconds, probably wondering if I was judging her character as well. She herself knew full well that her reputation was as a hard-nosed, take-no-prisoners executive who was known for jettisoning people as soon as they were of no use to her. In a male-dominated business, it was difficult to determine whether this reputation was grounded in fact or whether it was the creation of rumors, innuendo and minds willing to believe the lies.

"It is much better to meet people face-to-face so they can draw their own judgments about each other. But we can perhaps continue this philosophical discussion another time so I can get to the reason I am here.

"As you know, Katrina Turow has developed some complications after her surgery on her ruptured spleen. She'll have to remain in the hospital for at least another week. Then it will probably be another couple weeks after that before she'll be able to resume a grueling campaign schedule. Now, we have a couple national correspondents who would love to step in but I thought that, given your national reputation," she used air quotation marks and gave me the slightest of smiles when she used this word, "and also your past history with Reverend McKenzie, I thought it a natural fit for you to take Katrina's place in reporting on the campaign."

She let it hang there for a moment.

"Frank and I discussed your leave of absence from your anchoring duties and Frank is sure he could fill in without too much difficulty. The way I see it, this is a win-win for both you and the network. What do you say?"

The journalist part of me screamed for joy at this big break. But then the human side poked me in the ribs to remind me that I had a year and a half old baby at home. How could I leave Rosa—and Will and Albert and Stella—for such long stretches of time?

"Can I get back to you after I discuss this with my husband? I do have an infant and two young kids at home."

"That's perfectly understandable but it can't be any later than tomorrow morning. Otherwise, we have to move on to someone else. The Reverend is going to hold a rally in two days at the Red Bull stadium in Harrison, New Jersey, which is just outside Newark, and I need someone there. Here's my card with my cell phone number on it."

"Oh, I do have two conditions that must be met before I'll agree."

Kahn eyed me skeptically, not knowing what my demands were going to be.

"And they are?"

"Jonas Clarke, my cameraman must come along with me when he's able. He's recovering rapidly. He might not be ready to join me by

Thursday's rally, but should be ready shortly after that."

She looked relieved.

"That should be no problem. Frank expected you would probably make such a demand. And the other?"

"That Katrina Turow get her job back as soon she is able, whether it's to help me or me to help her."

At this demand, Kahn looked a bit more troubled.

"Well, we'll see."

Frank interjected himself here.

"You know, growing up whenever my brother or I would ask my mom for something and she responded 'we'll see', we knew that the answer was no."

"If that's the case, then I am going to have to respectfully decline your offer."

I could tell that Janet Kahn was not at all happy about Frank taking my side, but she knew she was going to have to relent.

"Yes, Katrina can have her job back when she's able."

"Great. I'll get back to you with a final decision today. Thank you, Ms. Kahn."

Will was on a case so I wasn't able to get in touch with him until mid-afternoon. When I finally reached him, he couldn't understand why I hesitated.

"Fava, we'll get by here. This is a dream assignment that you can't turn down. You'll kick yourself forever if you say no."

"But I have responsibilities here. To you. To the kids. I can't just up and leave you in the lurch."

"I don't even know where the lurch is. I've probably been there before and didn't even know it."

"Don't kid."

"I'm sorry, but I feel the main thing we need to give our kids is our all, and that means doing the best we can at the things we do best. The lesson we pass on to our kids is that they need to keep doing, keep striving to be their best. We all have to make compromises in life, but when an opportunity like this presents itself, I want our kids to know that we made the best of it and that we expect the same of them when they get their chances. You may be having second thoughts for all the right reasons, but I think it may backfire in the long run. I don't want Albert and Stella and Rosa to grow up afraid to try new experiences."

"Won't they think I'm being selfish, doing something I want to do rather than thinking about them?"

"No one could ever think that about you, ever."

"So, you want to get rid of me that bad, huh?"

"Don't let the door hit you on the way out, okay?"

I laughed and gave him a lame retort.

I called Janet Kahn back to tell her I'd do it.

"Great. I'll messenger your credentials and pass for the rally over to you in the morning. Thank you, Francine."

Next I called Katrina in the hospital. I'd called her once to see how she was doing but this time I called to give her the word directly about me filling in for her. Knowing how these things are usually handled, corporate management would forget or neglect to advise the one person most affected by a decision they made: Katrina Turow. I wanted her to know from me that the job was hers when she was ready. Otherwise, I could only imagine what she would think if she discovered it by turning on the TV and there I was.

"Thank you so much for calling, Francine. I appreciate you filling me in. And no, as you guessed, nobody from the network has contacted me yet."

"So are you feeling better?"

"I'm getting there, but I'm still pretty weak. It's going to be a week or two before I'll be able to be back at full strength."

"Anything new on The Reverend you can tell me? It's been a while since I last dealt with him."

"There's not much to report on him that isn't well known. He's pretty much an open book. You know The Reverend's style, his self-aggrandizement, his fire and brimstone, wrath of God approach. He's a master at whipping his followers into a frenzy. I'm living evidence of that. Every now and then he'll try and inject some policy initiatives into his speeches, but after a few minutes, he knows that's not what his followers came to see. You can literally feel the energy level in the room plummet so he reverts back to the evangelical bombast and the energy shoots right back up.

"He's a master of painting the darkest picture of this country imaginable and casting blame for all of our ills on convenient scapegoats. You know the usual suspects: Muslims, immigrants, foreigners, infidels, you know, others. His message is that the poor condition of the general American public is not in any way their fault but is because of these other groups.

"Even when he's discussing policy or issues, there's not a lot of substance in what he says. He's surrounded himself with some decent campaign staff but nobody who has any depth on any subject."

"Has he been accessible to the press?"

"Yes and no. He'll hold press availability sessions but then only allow for a limited number of questions. And even then, he'll only call on those reporters he knows will give him favorable coverage. I never fell into that category. He did call me a couple days ago, though."

"He did? Why?"

"He feels guilty."

"The Reverend? Feeling guilty?"

"That's the weird thing. I've watched the footage of when I was being assaulted and he was definitely standing there smirking, acting like I deserved it. But then he called me to apologize. I really believe he was contrite. His apology was real, not put on. He's like two different people. I've heard this from numerous sources who've been burned by him in public but then are charmed by him when alone with him. He's one way when he's in front of his adoring masses but he changes into a decent human being when he's one on one. In any case, at least for the moment he feels guilty about how I was accosted. We'll see how long that lasts."

"I know what you mean about the two different faces of Reverend Malcolm McKenzie. In one breath, he acknowledged that if it weren't for me he'd still be a small-town preacher, attending church suppers and officiating at the occasional baptism, wedding and funeral but in the next he'll rail about how I stood in God's way to mete out punishment to the lowest infidels ever to inhabit this earth. It was only when he received some FBI persuasion did he stop attacking me."

That evening I went to the office to view some recent clips of The Reverend so I could get a better feel for the man before I attended the rally. I called up the tape of his first debate. He was one of ten men contending for the party nomination. He was the ultimate outsider in this group. There were five Senators, two Congressmen and two corporate CEOs. The CEOs tried to portray themselves also as from "outside the Beltway" but their act fooled few people since they were well known for many years as political contributors and operatives.

Prior to the debate, while the pundits were giving the pronouncements and predictions, the candidates were gathered in various cliques, chatting with each other about the other candidates. Only Reverend McKenzie stood alone as he read over his notes. It would have been natural for him to be intimidated in such a setting, but his standing apart was not an indication of a reticence to do battle. He would not be cowed by anyone. From the second the red lights went on, indicating the cameras were on, he was on the attack. And what an attack it was.

He knew that he had to come up with a line, one that could capture the media's attention to be used over and over again. And it had to be his opening line; it couldn't be buried deep in his statement.

As determined by a lottery, McKenzie was the sixth to give an opening statement. The first five were of little note, offering the canned thank yous to the moderator, to the crowd in attendance, to the university hosting the debate, etc. before they launched into the unconvincing reasons why they would make the best presidents. Then it was The Reverend's turn. He stared into the camera for fifteen seconds, saying nothing. Then he began.

"What we have here is a pack of chicken hawks, waiting to swoop down and feast upon a tender young squirrel. As they get closer in their dive, they're going to find that their prey is not some naive little thing but a bear, ready to tear them to shreds with its mighty claws. It's ironic that, of the ten men standing up here, only one—the meek backwoods pastor—did his duty when his country called. You elect any of these other men, these chicken hawks, you're going to get someone who has not seen war, has not had a close friend die in their arms. These men would think nothing about sending your sons and daughters off to die in a foreign land. It will all just be a game to them. Your sons and daughters would be indistinguishable pawns in that game. To me, they will remain your sons and daughters."

His 'chicken hawk' attack worked. The Reverend's service record was unassailable. Malcolm received his Master's degree from Drew University's Divinity School and had just been ordained a minister in the Methodist Church in 1991 when President George H. W. Bush announced that U.S. troops had just invaded Iraq initiating Operation Desert Storm. Recalling his father's passion for service in the armed forces, he soon enlisted to become an army chaplain and it wasn't long before Lieutenant Malcolm McKenzie found himself stationed in Diyala Province, Iraq, administering to the spiritual needs of the troops.

As the American forces rolled towards Baghdad, Chaplain McKenzie was right beside them. If ever there was a "praise the Lord and pass the ammunition" type, it was he. He was involved in all aspects of his fellow soldiers' lives, even taking up arms on more than one occasion. He detested taking the life of another human being but protecting his friends was a sacred duty.

These other men never expected such a direct attack and they were off-balance for the rest of the debate. This set the tone for the campaign in general. Reverend Malcolm McKenzie had made his mark and would continue making it all the way up to the nomination.

12

The next day I received my credentials and two days later I found myself herded along with about twenty other journalists into an upper deck section, far away from the stage but also far away from the masses. Despite the isolation and the distance, I didn't think that The Reverend would have much difficulty making himself heard in any part of the arena.

As I hadn't participated in a presidential campaign before, I didn't personally know any of the other journalists crammed into the pen with me, although I was familiar with some of their reporting. I did get a number of inquiries about Katrina's health but, other than that, they stayed in their own cliques and didn't interact with me that much, which was fine with me.

The crowd was filing in, filling seats close to the stage and spreading out from there. There were folding seats on the playing field as well as the permanent seats in the stand. From my vantage point, by 8:00, the lower seats were filled. The media was by itself in the upper deck, which seemed a trifle surreal.

At 8:03 the lights all dimmed and the crowd went quiet as they awaited their hero's entrance onto the stage. After a minute or so, a choir of forty singers, twenty men and twenty women, streamed out and took their places. They each wore a robe that was red, white or blue so that when they were seated they gave a rough impression of an American flag.

They sat still for a few moments. The crowd was likewise still, as if in breathless anticipation. The choir then rose as one and once they were all standing, orchestral music started to pour out the stadium's loudspeakers. The crowd stood as well when the choir began singing "God Bless America". It wasn't long before the entire stadium was singing along. We in our isolated press box didn't know exactly what to do but we didn't want to antagonize the crowd so we stood up, too. But I didn't notice too many of us singing along.

I had to admit that the choir was good, providing interesting harmonies throughout the old favorite. Neither did they disappoint when they switched to the National Anthem. I noticed that more of my colleagues were singing at this point.

Once the Star Spangled Banner concluded, silence again descended on the stadium. A minute or so later, twelve men in military uniforms (it was difficult from our distance to determine what if any branch they represented) emerged on the stage, six on each side. As one, they lifted trumpets to their respective lips and blew a fanfare. If anyone may have been dozing, they were wide-awake now.

The fanfare then transformed into an introduction to a song everyone in the audience immediately recognized. The crowd went wild as the choir launched into a full-throated rendition of "Onward Christian Soldiers", the trademark theme announcing the entry of The Reverend himself.

Knowing how to fully milk the crowd, The Reverend let the choir get into the song before the grand entrance so that he came in on the refrain "Onward Christian Soldiers, Marching as to war, with the cross of Jesus, Leading on before."

As he walked onto the stage, a huge screen behind the stage that had been dark came to life with The Reverend's smiling and joyful face in front of a waving flag. The full theater was only warming up.

He was in full glory as he waved to the crowd and accepted their homage. Two men in suits that I did not immediately recognize accompanied him. I asked one of my colleagues who advised me that they were legislators, two Assemblymen to be exact, from the northwest and most conservative part of New Jersey. They were regaling in the adoration, although my guess is that probably three-quarters of the people there had absolutely no idea who they were.

The Reverend let the cheering go on for a full five minutes, after which he held up his hand and the crowd noise died down almost instantaneously. He stepped up to the microphone.

"My good friends of New Jersey, I thank you for this kind and enthusiastic welcome to your fair state. Some of my advisors told me: don't bother going to New Jersey; focus on states where you have a chance. You'll never win in New Jersey. But I was determined to come here. They then told me to go to the part of the state where they knew I'd get a strong reception. The people are hostile to you here in the urban northeast, they said. But I responded by asking whether Daniel refused to go into the lion's den, whether David would go somewhere else than where Goliath was or whether Jesus himself told God: You take on the devil, I'm too scared.

"Well, here I am. I was born and raised in this fair state and I wasn't going to ignore it. And I can bear witness that there are no devils here; just good, hard-working people who want a better life, a more Christian life, for them and their families who know that I'm the candidate who can best help them in this regard."

The crowd responded enthusiastically, but the Reverend was only getting started.

"Now, I'm not worthy to carry Jesus's sandals, but perhaps I'm the one who can pick up his work and head down to Washington and throw the money-changers out of our sacred temples of government. This country needs people who have not been bought and sold to lead us. We need an outsider who can instill strong Christian values that have been sorely lacking for far too long in public life.

"Hmm, do you happen to know anybody with those qualifications?"

The crowd then responded with what had become a trademark of his rallies as they shouted as one: "The Reverend!"

He showed the crowd some mock surprise, which drew the requisite laughs and applause. He raised his hand to quiet them back down as quickly as he had jacked them up.

"I do have to amend my earlier statement. When I look out on all your faces, I certainly see no devils among the audience here. I see strong faces, kind faces, American faces. But all I have to do is raise my gaze slightly and there in the rafters I find a pack of jackals, waiting to do the devil's bidding and pounce on the masses to tear them apart with self-serving lies. Of course, I am referring to the men and women of the written and televised media.

"Many of them slithered across the Hudson from Gomorrah, some are home-grown but they all do the work of the devil, whatever hole they crawled out of.

"I do note that we have a special guest hiding amongst these heathen. Despite working for a minor network, she is well-known to many of you here in the metropolitan area. I have met her myself, and while she seemed like a nice enough person, she has committed the unforgivable sin that all too many of our journalists make. She has made herself the story, forgetting that she is merely a reporter, not a part of the story she's reporting on.

"Be that as it may, I have a surprise for her in welcoming her to our campaign."

With that, three words replaced his gigantic face on the screen behind the stage: NO CHEEKS LEFT!

I could almost feel the other reporters distancing themselves from me. While The Reverend had previously castigated and disparaged the media in general, I was the first journalist to be specifically named by him. Katrina was a victim, collateral damage; I was a target.

My colleagues were looking to be as far away from me as they could get. Every eye in the stadium was on me. I was tempted to stand up and take a big bow or give him the finger or run out of the stands or some combination thereof. Instead, I simply nodded in The Reverend's direction. He smiled in return. He then looked up at his slogan on the screen.

"This slogan came from a discussion I had in my first meeting with Ms. Vega and she thought I was being too vengeful in my attitudes towards Muslims. She asked if we shouldn't be living according to Jesus's admonition that we should 'turn the other cheek' in how we deal with our enemies? My response was that we as a country have turned the other cheek so many times that our full face is a scarlet red. We have no more cheeks to turn, I told her at the time. Now it's time that the United States show some tough love toward the adherents of this blasphemy.

"I stop short of labeling this collection of foul beliefs that have plagued the earth for over a millennium as being a religion. And when I become president, I will make sure that the United States will rise back up to its predominant place in the world and the nations whose soul has been poisoned by Islam will be sent back to the Dark Ages."

The Reverend would go on in a similar vein for another forty-five minutes, but my report was already crystalized in my mind. I listened in case he happened to make any salient points, but I knew he wouldn't say anything of substance. He had two purposes for this rally. First, he sought to speak to his base, to stir them up. Second, he wanted to attack me personally. He was hugely successful on both counts.

As soon as he was finished, I headed out to my cameraperson, Judy Serrano, who was all set up and ready to go in the vestibule. While Judy is extremely competent at her job, she had somewhat of a personality deficit. I was so looking forward to Jonas coming back to work, probably within the next week.

I found my mark and put an earpiece in my ear. Judy got me in focus and we waited for the network anchor, Jeff Climpson, to introduce me. After about two minutes, I heard Jeff coming through.

"Now we have Francine Vega reporting from the Reverend McKenzie campaign. The Reverend has just concluded a rally in Harrison, New Jersey. This was your first such rally, wasn't it, Francine?"

"Yes, it was, Jeff. And it was quite eye opening."

"Tell us about it."

"First of all, let me clarify for our viewers exactly why I'm here. I'm here as a result of Reverend McKenzie's attack on the media, which in turn resulted in a physical attack on one of our own, Katrina Turow. Katrina was seriously harmed at his rally and is still in the hospital. Please get well soon, Katrina.

"At tonight's rally, McKenzie continued his vicious attack on the media, and highlighted me specifically. In the context of the media, he even referred to New York as a modern day Gomorrah.

"The Reverend announced no major initiatives or policies to report. He stuck with his usual themes of fear of others—Muslims, immigrants, Mexicans—and blaming them for various real and imaginary ills plaguing the country.

"He alternated between whipping the crowd into a frenzy and being their calming, soothing father figure. Immediately after the rally concluded, I was able to interview Patrick Michaels, a conservative Assemblyman from Warren County in the northeast, who was here at the rally. Here's an excerpt from that interview.

"Assemblyman Michaels, what did you think of Reverend McKenzie's performance this evening."

"That's one of the problems with you folks in the media. You rate everything as a "performance," looking for your sound bites to make your job easy. Well, his performance was great but even more so, any casual observer can see that this great man is talking to the soul of America. In fact, he is the soul of America."

"You're not concerned about the lack of substance or details he is offering to address problems facing this country?"

"Reverend McKenzie has a vision of greatness for this county. He's not going to bog us down with wonkish details that take our focus away from that vision. This presidential campaign is a holy war. You members of the media need to decide on which side you will come down. Will you be for this great country, or against it?"

The viewer was switched back to my live report.

"It may be speculation on my part, but I sensed that tonight's rally was a test of sorts. I think that Reverend McKenzie, whose message plays extremely well in places such as the Midwest and Deep South, wanted to gauge the reaction he would get in a heavily blue part of the country. Overall, I think he got what he wanted.

"The crowd did not fill the small stadium. But the crowd, small as it was, was enthusiastic and filled with the spirit. The Reverend looked pleased that his word seemed to be accepted even in this part of the country.

"Back to you, Jeff."

"Where's the campaign off to now, Francine?"

"Madison, Wisconsin. That state's primary is next week but he has the nomination sewn up and he is not looking to the primary. Instead, The Reverend will be holding what would be his eighth rally in that state with an eye towards November."

"Thank you Francine. Have a safe trip."

"Thanks, Jeff. This is Francine Vega, reporting from the McKenzie presidential campaign in Harrison, New Jersey."

After I finished, I walked to the stadium offices, hoping to find someone for some follow-up interviews but the place had cleared out completely. Judy and I had traveled together in a company car but she had family in nearby Union and her sister was going to pick her up for her to stay in New Jersey. I told her no problem; I'd drive myself back to the City.

I made my walk to the press parking lot adjacent to the stadium. At one point I thought I heard a noise behind me and I turned around. I saw a maintenance man off in the distance doing some cleanup. I felt relieved.

I got to my car, which was the only one in the lot, when a man reached around me and grabbed my arm as I was about to unlock the door. He spun me around. He wasn't a tall man, but he was wide. My guess was that he pushed the scales to about 270 pounds.

His breath reeked of alcohol, cheap alcohol I reckoned, and I was about to get a full dose of it as he started to tell me what he thought of me when out of the dark an arm went around the neck of my accoster. His left arm was twisted behind him and two moves later, the slob found himself on the ground. He was able to gather himself and run off. Neither my rescuer nor I thought it important enough to run after him.

I looked and there was Agent Broderick.

"Agent Broderick? What are you doing here?"

"Miss Vega. I'm here exercising my rights as a citizen, attending a political rally of a candidate of my choice."

I almost had to laugh at this prim and proper FBI agent's lame attempt at humor.

"Will had you tail me, didn't he?"

Broderick fidgeted like a schoolboy who'd been caught throwing eggs at cars.

"Did he have you tail me?"

"He was concerned, and rightfully so it turns out."

Without another word I climbed into my car and drove away. Forty-five minutes later I walked into our bedroom, where Will was waiting for me.

"You think I can't take care of myself?"

"I know you can."

"Then why have one of your agents tail me?"

"Just backup, that's all."

"If nothing else, being a bodyguard for me is outside the jurisdiction of the FBI, isn't it? How can you explain this improper use of bureau resources?"

"Rick was doing this off the books. We were talking about your new assignment, he volunteered and I accepted his offer."

"You had no right to do this without discussing it with me."

"Listen, if you're going to be pissed at me for worrying about you and doing whatever I can to be sure you're safe, then we'd both better get used to you being pissed off."

I was about to offer a sarcastic retort but then I smiled and shook my head.

"Yeah, I guess we should get used to it."

13

The next morning, as I was putting my makeup on and Will was in the shower, the phone rang.

"Hello."

"Ms. Vega? This is Detective Kelly. We met last week."

"Of course. How are you detective?"

"Is Special Agent Allen there?"

"He is, but he can't come to the phone right now."

I've always been reticent to reveal that someone else is in the midst of performing something personal such as showering or going to the bathroom.

"I was wondering if he could come down to the precinct this morning. I think I may have found something relating to the bombing of Mr. Clarke's car."

"Shouldn't you be working through Agent Broderick?"

"Oh, I already spoke to him and he'll be there at ten, but we all know who's in charge here, don't we?"

I had to laugh. This detective was pretty sharp.

"Yes, we do. Is there any specific message I can give him?"

She paused for a second and then decided to tell me.

"You're pretty involved in this case anyway so there's no harm in filling you in. We found the detonator that was used on the car and it's unique. It's obviously homemade, but by somebody schooled in such gadgets, probably military. But the big news is that I recognized the workmanship. I had evidence retrieved from a previous bombing and the detonators matched perfectly. I don't believe in coincidences. The two bombs were made by the same person."

"Wow, that is big. I'll be sure to tell him that. I'm sure Will can be there at ten."

"Agent Broderick is already looking through FBI files regarding the previous bomb, but let me give you the date and place in case Special Agent Allen has his own files. Our records show that he worked on the case years ago."

I grabbed a pen and paper.

"Okay, shoot. When and where was it?

"February 6, 2010 in Greenpoint, Brooklyn."

"Did you say February 6, 2010?"

"Yes, why?"

"I don't believe in coincidences either. We'll both be at the precinct at ten."

When we arrived at Detective Kelly's office at five minutes to ten, we were ushered into a conference room where Agent Broderick was already seated.

"Hey Will, Ms. Vega. Detective Kelly should be here shortly. She's interrogating a suspect in a different case that they just hauled in. We all know how that is."

I was about to tell him that after all we'd been through together, he could call me Francine but I realized it wouldn't make a difference. Agent Broderick lived by a certain code that embraced formality and eschewed familiarity. In his eyes, I would always be Ms. Vega and likewise he'd prefer that I call him Agent Broderick.

"Agent Broderick," I responded, "I never thanked you for coming to my assistance last night. That was rude of me, so I'm thanking you now."

"You're welcome, Ms. Vega. Glad to have been of assistance."

Detective Kelly walked in. She was in an extremely good mood.

"I hope you weren't waiting long, but technically I'm perfectly on time. Boy, I wish all my cases were like this. There was literally a smoking gun in the suspect's hand as he stood over the body. Then, he not only was guilty but he had a conscience and waived any need for a lawyer as he fully admitted his guilt. I expected I'd have to keep you folks waiting for hours but it was in and out in fifteen minutes."

"I could use a case like that every once in awhile," Will responded. "So, Francine tells me you connected this bomb to one that was detonated over a decade ago."

"Yes, it was a case you worked on, I believe, in Greenpoint, Brooklyn on February 6, 2010. The blast was in a remote industrial park on a Sunday morning so there were no injuries. Other than the car itself, which was an old unregistered junk heap, there was no damage to property. I was a beat cop in the 94th Precinct at the time. My job was to keep the crowds away, but I was pretty nosey and involved myself in the investigation. It was my first bombing so I learned everything I could."

"And I was involved," Will noted, "because we monitor every bombing, especially after 9/11 but since no one was hurt and or property damaged, the case faded away, unsolved."

"The only thing we deduced," continued the detective, "was that it was a professional, military-style job. The detonator I saw yesterday triggered my memory and, after comparing the two, I concluded they could only have been made by the same person. I showed them to one of my techs and he agreed. Will, could you have the FBI lab examine them and see if they come to the same conclusion?"

I bristled involuntarily at this comely detective who was far closer in age to Will that I called my husband by his first name.

"Of course."

"Going on the assumption that the bombs were constructed by the same person, the question is, how are the two events related? Maybe they're not related; maybe the same guy was hired to do two completely unrelated jobs. But we should start looking into any links between the two events."

"Which is why Fava, I mean Francine, is here," Will told her.

Detective Kelly looked in my direction. Prior to this, I might not have even been in the room. To her credit, the detective did not raise any objections to me, a civilian, being present at what should have been exclusively an inter-agency law enforcement get-together. I suppose she thought that if Will had brought me, I must have some purpose. She would patiently wait until that purpose made itself known.

"Detective, as we discussed over the phone, there are few real coincidences in life. But something else happened on the date of this bomb blast, February 6, 2010."

"And that was?"

"That was the exact same date and time that the Zyklon Killer murdered Wendy Smith, in Queens, not far away from the explosion."

"Um, that actually does sound like a coincidence."

"I would have thought so except for one thing."

"That is?"

"The Zyklon Killer may still be alive."

"Run that by me one more time. Didn't they just execute him in Texas?"

"They executed the man convicted of the crime, but I have reason to believe he was innocent. The Zyklon Killer is still out there and may somehow be related to both explosions."

"Why don't you start at the beginning."

I was reluctant to explain further, but it didn't seem like I had much choice anymore. Looking over at Will, he nodded his agreement. I brought her up to date on my history with Colonel Jacob Lawson, his belief that Aaron Kaplow was not the Zyklon Killer and how he threatened Alan Westbrook as inducement for me to prove his cousin's innocence.

"So, the car bombing and the killing of Wendy Smith happening on the same day in New York City? Probably a coincidence. But then for the same device to be used not only on that day but also years later at the same time I learn that the Zyklon Killer may still be alive? Now we're moving into the realm of cause and effect."

"Since this Lawson fellow seems to be such a nemesis, why didn't you tell me about him when we first spoke?" The detective was angry that we withheld information from her.

Will responded. "Don't get an attitude, detective. Lawson didn't seem relevant at the time. First, it was Jonas's car that was blown up so the focus was on him. Knowing Jonas the way we do, it seemed ludicrous for him to be a target, but we had to follow those leads first. It was only later that we started to think that Francine might have been the objective. She drove the car from the station to our house so it's entirely possible they thought they were attacking her, not Jonas. When you made a connection between the detonators, we realized there may be a link to the Zyklon Killer and we contacted you immediately about our interactions with Lawson."

"Yes, of course. I apologize if that came across as accusatory."

"Apology accepted. So, where do we go from here?"

"Do you believe that Mr. Lawson was responsible for the latest car bomb?"

Will let me answer.

"If the device was highly professional, most likely military, Lawson would therefore be a candidate. It doesn't make sense considering he just, for lack of a better word, retained me to help him. But the guy is highly unstable and he could have reconsidered minutes after talking to me."

"That could well be, Ms. Vega. I'd like to go over the materials that Mr. Lawson gave you with a fresh set of eyes. Perhaps something may jump out at me. By the way, Special Agent Allen, has the FBI made any headway in apprehending Mr. Lawson?"

"Let's just say that there are certain advantages Lawson has that keep him a step ahead of us."

We discussed a few more non-important issues and then Will and I left to go to our respective jobs.

14

I had to be in Madison, Wisconsin in two days for another Reverend Rally, as he liked to call them. I was to attend five of these rallies in five different states around the country over the next two weeks. I would be on the road that entire time. There are reporters who thrive on this. I was beginning to sense that Katrina was one such reporter. For me, at this point in my life, I was looking only at the difficulties. I know, I know; I want it both ways. I love being out in the field but here I am, whining about being out in the field. But if nothing else, this would be the longest I would be away from Rosa since the day she was born. That alone was going to kill me.

At the Madison event, The Reverend was to announce some major economic policy initiatives. To date, his rallies had consisted of diatribes: against immigrants, Muslims, Mexicans, the press, the current president, me. While this approach had served him well through the primaries and hurtled him toward the nomination, one of his aides obviously told him that he needed to inject some substance into his speeches if he was going to have any success in battling Governor Kent.

The rally was to be on Thursday evening. I had been burned too many times with flight delays and cancellations so I booked a flight for Wednesday night to be sure I was out there in plenty of time. I figured I could spend Thursday morning and afternoon chatting with some of the campaign staff to get some inside tidbits to flesh out my report.

In the meantime, I had a day and a half in New York and I quickly made arrangements to fill the time. I was able to secure an interview with The Reverend's first supporter, Georgia Congressman Pete Connors. He had recently assumed the role as Chairman of the Put God Back in the White House PAC. The interview was to be the following morning, in Staten Island of all places. But first in the evening, I was to have dinner with my old friend, Alexander Kent. While I was officially reporting on the McKenzie campaign, it wouldn't hurt to do some opposition research.

I didn't think it would be all that difficult to get up to speed with the Kent campaign, which was pretty much on autopilot. The man was a shoo-in for the nomination and, if the polls were accurate, for the Presidency. He had a squeaky-clean reputation. His opponents would occasionally try and pin something on him, but he'd laugh it off and nothing stuck. He was always careful in his responses and was so non-controversial as to be considered bland.

In many cases, this blandness would be a turnoff to the voters but he projected an everyman confidence that was appealing. He had every reason to exude confidence. His record of achievement was second to none. He'd performed miracle after miracle in New York, reviving a moribund economy with record-breaking job growth five years in a row. He was especially adept at attracting new high-tech businesses with high-paying jobs back to the Empire State.

Every quantitative and qualitative measure one could cite—economic, quality of life, environmental, crime, infrastructure development, you name it—had improved under his watch. And he did it with a legislature stocked with the opposition party, many of whom publicly supported his candidacy.

Topping off the package, he was tall and strikingly handsome, with gray only beginning to compliment his temples. He was a self-made man, the son of German immigrants who came to this country just after the war with next to nothing. He was not only his party's favorite for the nomination but he was the definitive pick for the Presidency. If Reverend McKenzie was to be his opponent, most prognosticators anticipated a trouncing of record proportions.

I knew Governor Kent's basic story but I needed to do some more intense background research to become better acquainted with the man. Who better to provide this information that his own son and campaign manager?

Alexander was already seated at the restaurant, a small French bistro, The Napoleon, in midtown, when I arrived. At first glance, he was a younger version of his father, which wasn't bad. He exuded the same confidence and ability. All too often, men of consequence had disappointing offspring but that could not be said of the Kents. I could have done much worse if I had stayed with him; yes, much worse.

He had already ordered himself a vodka martini and asked if I wanted one. I readily agreed.

"And she said we must get together, but I knew it'd never be arranged."

One of Alexander's idiosyncrasies was that he loved to quote lines from songs and movies. It was your job to either identify the source or, better yet, provide the follow-up line. I was ready for him.

"And she handed me twenty dollars for a two fifty fare, she said 'Harry, keep the change.' "

"Touché, Ms. Vega. So, how's that young daughter of yours?"

"Beautiful, and growing so fast. She's smart, too. Every day I'm astonished at something new she learned."

"And all this coming from an unbiased source."

I laughed. "Well, maybe not, but that doesn't make it any less true, does it?"

"And how's the most recent love of your life, The Reverend, these days?"

"I'm still trying to figure all this out. He's touched into something in the American psyche, something disturbing, but something nonetheless."

"The American people are better than what he's selling."

"Don't sell him short. I know you want your father to stand tall above the fray, but he's got to be careful that, while he's standing so tall and looking out at the horizon like a good captain should, he doesn't see the little people, the people who vote in droves, flocking by him to get to McKenzie."

"That's a great image. I have to tell Dad that one."

He pulled out a small notebook and scribbled down a few words. It reminded me of the first time I met with McKenzie—back when he was a small-town preacher and not a presidential candidate—and he pulled out a notebook to jot down his catchphrase "No Cheeks Left" while we chatted. I didn't think Alexander would appreciate the comparison.

"Great image or not, he shouldn't be discounted or ignored.

Remember what happened when Apollo Creed didn't give Rocky Balboa any credit and didn't train properly for the fight."

"Ah, using a movie reference before me. I must be slipping. Although we can't be complacent, we still have another three weeks of primaries before we even get into the one-on-one campaigning. We're going to have three debates and a vice-presidential debate. The lack of experience and training in our opponent's resume is only going to become more glaring as time goes on. You'll see."

"I hope so, but I keep hearing about voters in the swing states who want change, who want a non-politician who isn't beholden to special interests to come in and seriously shake things up. Add The Reverend's charisma, his plea that we need to bring God back into government and his ability to give people convenient scapegoats as the reasons for all their troubles make him formidable. On top of that, he's a master at delegitimizing those who disagree with him. I've personally been the recipient of this mastery. Don't sell him short."

"I think you're the one guilty of selling the American people short."

"I wish I had as much confidence in them as you do. Remember, I've witnessed up close how strong a distrust of Muslims we have in this country. Your father has to at least recognize this."

"Oh, he does, but he thinks that in the end, our goodness as a people will shine through."

I thought he was being extremely naive, but refreshingly naive nonetheless.

We talked some more politics but it was soon time to head home since I had to be out on Staten Island by 7:30 the next morning to interview the Congressman. I could count on one hand the number of times I'd been on Staten Island and most of those times were simply passing through to get to somewhere else. If Queens was a suburb to me, Staten Island was out in the sticks. Connors was there for some sort of prayer breakfast at 9:00 after which he had to hop a plane to get back to DC for a vote. So 7:30 it was.

I was excited about working with Jonas again. This was to be his first day back at work so he'd understandably be tired and probably wouldn't be all there, but I didn't care. He was back with me; that's all that mattered.

We arrived ten minutes early at the venue where the Congressman was attending the conservative conclave. We got to taping the interview right away.

"This is Francine Vega. I'm here with Congressman Pete Connors. Congressman, thank you for making time to talk with me today."

"It's my pleasure, Francine."

"Congressman, you were one of Reverend McKenzie's earliest supporters. In fact, you were present at Reverend George Warriner's rally a few years back where Reverend McKenzie gave his speech that catapulted him to national prominence."

"Yes, I remember that evening well. Even then, I could see something special in this fine man. It's no secret that I've got my own presidential aspirations and toyed with a run but once I met The Reverend and heard him speak, I knew I had to put my plans on hold for a bit. I'm a young guy after all."

I think he wanted me to either laugh or confirm his appraisal of himself. When I did not respond, he continued.

"We need an outsider to finally shake things up in Washington."

"Even if he has no experience at all in government?"

"That is not an impediment. On the contrary, his appeal is that he has no government experience. Experience in Washington only results in corruption, not in an enhanced ability to solve the country's ills."

"Congressman, you're now in your fourth term in the House. How has your experience affected you?"

"Ha, Ms. Vega. Nice shot, but let's keep our focus on the presidential candidate?"

"Fair enough, Congressman. To date, Reverend McKenzie has not yet provided much in the way of detail or positions on policy or issues affecting this country, yet people are supporting him in large numbers. Do you have any explanation?"

"Yes, I believe I do. The people are lost in the wilderness, wandering from oasis to oasis, but never reaching the Promised Land. They are looking for a leader who will inspire them, who will raise them up, to achieve greatness. The Reverend is just that person. He's a gifted man, a quick learner and someone who has already shown an innate ability to raise people up, to get them to work together, to bring us forward together as a country."

"Don't you think he'll need to quickly get up to speed on the various issues of the day?"

"Oh, he will. And he'll surround himself with the best people, highly respected people, who will get the job done."

"Well, I've heard people complain that he never answers a substantive question directly, that he resorts to platitudes and generalizations. How would you respond to the people who say this?"

"I would tell them to sit down with him for five minutes. I guarantee they'll walk away with a much different impression of the man. They would agree with me wholeheartedly that The Reverend is not only highly qualified to be President of the United States, but he is the leader that we need right now."

"There are also many who say that he's fanning flames of hatred and fear in this country, getting people to blame others for their lot in life. Moreover, they claim he is using religion as the tool to foment this hatred and fear. Don't you have concerns as a member of Congress about the historic separation of church and state in this country and that he would blur the lines by introducing religion into our government?"

"We need to get back to the strong core values that our country was founded on, the values that are embodied in the religion of our fathers and forefathers. The Founding Fathers never wanted for this to be a godless country; they wanted to keep established churches from ruling us. There is no fear of that happening with The Reverend. He will keep the ruling elites, whether they are from the worlds of religion, government or private entities, at arms length at all times. You can go to the bank on that."

"What about his feelings about Muslims and how they should be treated? He's been pretty vocal about his dislike for that religion. Again, getting specifics on how he would direct the government to deal with members of that faith has been difficult, but popular wisdom is that the measures he'd put in place would be quite draconian. How do you feel about this?"

"Well, Francine, I tend to agree with The Reverend on many things. People of all faiths need to come together and become Americans."

"Muslims haven't done this?"

"Not from what I've seen over the years. I'm always open to a frank discussion on the subject, however."

"Well, that about does it. Thank you for joining me, Congressman."

"Thank you for having me."

"This is Francine Vega, reporting from New York. I've been speaking with Congressman Pete Connors from Georgia. Now back to your local stations."

15

True to my fear and expectations, my flight to Madison, Wisconsin was canceled and I was re-booked for a flight the following afternoon. I arrived at the arena in Madison the following evening, only about an hour and a half before the rally.

Contrary to the underwhelming experience in New Jersey, this hall was packed with supporters. We reporters were herded into our pen, but instead of us being all alone surrounded by empty seats, we were in amongst the masses. Malevolent looks were cast at us from every direction. A few of us took the opportunity to go out and interview some in the crowd. I vacillated between joining them in hopes of getting a colorful quote or two for my report and hunkering down and waiting for The Reverend.

I made my mind up and was about to venture out when my phone pinged, indicating a message had just come in. It was a message from Alan that read: *I have information on Zyklon. Let's meet where it all began for us. You'll be back in NYC on July 22nd. Let's meet at 9:00 AM on the 23rd. Okay?* The man knew my schedule better than I did. He probably hacked into my calendar. I texted him back: *Okay.*

Rather than going out among the unwashed hordes, I sat back down in my seat. I had too much on my mind to conduct a proper interview.

Did Alan have a clue that could help to unmask the real Zyklon Killer? Why would he want to help me with Zyklon? Jacob Lawson was once his hero and mentor; now he was his mortal enemy. Proving someone other than Aaron Kaplow, Lawson's cousin, to be the killer would only be of benefit to Lawson, wouldn't it? While I would hardly think that Alan had anything against Kaplow, neither would he seemingly have reason to want to clear that man's name. What was Alan's motive in all this?

The only thing I could come up with was that in the past, Alan Westbrook had proven to be a surprisingly empathetic person. He was brilliant but deeply troubled by a host of demons, many of them inflicted on him by Jacob Lawson. His departing line to me the last time we met in Jonas's hospital room that, if Lawson were to kill him, it would only be finishing the job started on 9/11 when Lawson killed Alan's identical twin, Freddy. But through all that, he could show a remarkable level of concern for others. Well, maybe he didn't show concern for others, but for me anyway.

I did have a journalistic interest in uncovering the fact that the State of Texas had executed an innocent man. Alexander was correct. I am fervently against the death penalty in all but the most egregious cases. If I could come up with conclusive evidence that this man had been framed and the state had killed the wrong person, it would be quite a feather in my proverbial career cap.

However, all that was outweighed by my hatred for Lawson. I did not have anything against Aaron Kaplow but if the killing of someone close to Lawson made that reprehensible human being suffer, then it was worth the sacrifice. I could wash my hands of the whole thing with a clear conscience, but there were three ever-present reasons for me to keep moving forward on this: Wendy, Lena and Miriam.

Wendy deserved actual justice. Her murderer—if indeed Aaron Kaplow was innocent—must be found and punished. She was owed that much. The State had limited incentive to question the outcome.

When I contacted Lena after Kaplow had been apprehended, she was relieved that no other people would be subjected to the gruesome death her granddaughter had endured. However, she wasn't one of those who would say his execution would give her "closure". Only bringing Wendy back to her would result in closure. There was no closing the hole that was left in her heart.

The fact that the wrong man may have been killed and that the true Zyklon Killer was still out there is what would torment this good woman more than anything. I toyed with calling her immediately after the execution but I thought that unseemly. Now that I believed that Kaplow might not have been the killer, I thought it best to let her maintain her illusion that the Zyklon Killer was off the street.

I owed it to Miriam Berger, too. Long before she took her own life,

Nazi monsters had taken her life. Then, when she showed courage to relive her nightmare and try to make one of those monsters accountable for his horrific crimes, the door was slammed in her face. I couldn't insult her legacy once again as justice is denied, that a murderer allied with the Nazis would be allowed to walk free.

I must have jumped a foot when a trumpet blared over the loudspeakers. The spectacular was about to begin. The other reporters hurried back to their respective spots in the journalistic ghetto.

Everyone expected The Reverend to strut out onto the stage but that wouldn't happen for another forty-five minutes. Ethan Wethersby, a firebrand Fundamentalist Baptist preacher, kicked off the evening with an overly long and rambling invocation. He was followed in turn by two local political figures and a director of a community action center, whatever that was.

At last, the main event was about to begin. The lights went down as a local high school band that was sitting off to the side, unnoticed to most, launched into a spirited if slightly off-key rendition of Onward Christian Soldiers. The Reverend came onto the stage from the right, waving to the crowd.

He had used this song for his triumphal entry some years earlier at the mega-church where he first made his name. It was fine then when he was an itinerant preacher but now that he was running for President of people of all religions, I found the choice especially offensive.

He settled in behind the microphone as he accepted the adulation, which went on for an eternity. He was in no rush to quiet them down but then he raised his hand and the arena went silent.

"My friends—and my enemies, too—I have a special message for you today: at last, you have a candidate who will put you first. It may come as a shock to you but most politicians think the American public is lazy and easily duped. They think more about themselves than they do about you. They care more about special interests and lobbyists who lavish them with gifts and donations than they do about making your lives better.

"What makes me so different? That's probably the question you're asking yourself. I would too, if I were you. What makes me different is I've spent my whole life in the service of others. And this tiger is not going to changes its stripes.

"I wouldn't know a special interest if I tripped over one. That makes me scary to them. But I bet none of you are scared of little ol' me. You are the people who need help, and I'm the one you know in your hearts can do it.

"I hope you've come to know me over the past year and a half. I haven't BS'd you. I haven't tried to sell you a bill of goods. What I have tried to impress on you is the opportunity that is America. In this country, it's supposed to be that hard work, not who your parents are, determines your lot in life. My father was a laborer in a factory but here I am, running for President of the United States. I'm living a dream, and I'd like to take you along in that dream.

"But all too often the deck gets stacked against the good people of this country. Immigrants come in and steal our jobs away. There are those who do not share our values, our Christian values, and would seek to alter our way of life. I can go on and on but each one of you sitting here hearing my words knows what I'm talking about. It all must change, and I'm the only one who can change it."

I was starting to zone out. Despite the promise that he would be making a new announcement on initiatives to jumpstart the economy, I knew I wasn't going to hear anything of substance. It was the same old mantra about how America was being stolen away by "others". His economic policy would be that there were others who kept good, honest, homegrown Americans from getting their fair share of the pie and fully achieving the American Dream. Take care of those others, and there would be more than enough for everybody. He never has fully articulated what he meant by taking care of "those people" but it didn't matter to his faithful followers whose numbers were increasing by the minute.

People felt they were being ignored and The Reverend was the only one who was listening to them. Whether The Reverend could actually deliver and improve their lives was immaterial. He was in their corner; that's all that mattered.

After what seemed an interminable amount of time, the band once again struck up "Onward Christian Soldiers" as The Reverend and his entourage made their triumphal withdrawal off the stage.

I hooked up with Jonas immediately after the rally. He waited in the car until he got my message. He could have attended the rally, but he had no interest in hearing what The Reverend had to say. Furthermore, a black man in a sea of white faces would have been extremely conspicuous. He would have been subjected to one "what is he doing here" look after another. Even worse, he could have been used as a symbol that the message imparted here was resonating not just with working and middle-class whites. Jonas did not want to be any part of that.

I walked out into the parking lot where he was waiting for me with his camera and other equipment. The timing was perfect. I would go live on the national 11 o'clock news. We had about five minutes to get ourselves set up, but we wouldn't need even that long. It was so comfortable working with Jonas again.

"You all ready to go, J?"

"Let 'er rip, Frannie."

We ran through a couple sound checks and adjusted the lighting. Then we waited for our signal that we were live. Five minutes later, the call came.

"Good evening. This is Francine Vega reporting outside the Calumet Arena in Madison, Wisconsin where Reverend Malcolm McKenzie, a leading contender to be his party's nominee for the November presidential election, just finished speaking.

"Despite a full week of announcements that this speech was going to reveal some new policies regarding his economic plans for the country, Reverend McKenzie gave his usual stump speech.

"The packed arena did not seem to mind, however, as they cheered his every word, occasionally coming up with a chant of a slogan. McKenzie seemed to revel when they did this.

"One main difference was that this may have been the first time that McKenzie publicly attacked his presumptive rival, Governor Peter Kent, by name. As far as I know, prior to this, the attacks have been general broadsides on the opposition party and its collective candidates. Now that the field is narrowing down to the two candidates, the attacks are narrowing down, too.

"McKenzie continued with his theme that others—namely immigrants, Muslims and Mexicans—are responsible for the desperate economic plight of many of his followers. He will be the only one who can help put these people in their place to bring the country back to its former glory. The crowd responded enthusiastically to this assertion."

I concluded my report and I heard news anchor Kenneth Haynes over my earpiece.

"Francine, McKenzie has also been fond of stoking the crowd with attacks on the news media. Were there any such attacks this evening?"

"No, Kenneth, he was curiously quiet on that front this evening. We received a few nasty glances from the crowd but that was about it."

"Where is the campaign heading next?"

"Tonight was the kickoff of a Midwest six event tour over the next week, with stops in Gary, Indiana; Springfield, Illinois; Akron, Ohio; Ames, Iowa; and Independence, Missouri."

"Thank you for that report, Francine. That was Francine Vega reporting from Madison, Wisconsin. We'll take a break now for some messages from our sponsors and when we come back we'll review a startling new study on the safety of American-made automobiles."

We wrapped things up and headed back to our hotel.

The next two stops on the trip went pretty much the same. In fact, the three rallies were identical: the same message, the same theatrics, the same words, the same white faces. I was having trouble finding anything new to say in my reports. Luckily, at each event I was able to secure interviews with colorful local politicians who were in attendance.

Two hours prior to the rally at the Akron, Ohio as I was just stepping out of the shower my phone pinged indicating that a newsworthy message had been received. I went into the living room area and turned up the volume on the all-news station that was playing.

"Here's the latest on the situation at the Budget Travel & Gas Truck Stop just outside the Bryce Canyon National Park in Utah. At 4:40 local time, a middle-aged man armed with a semi-automatic weapon stepped out from between two parked vehicles and opened fire on a group of people, mostly retirees from Cleveland, Ohio, as they got off a bus after touring the park. Five people are reported dead and another thirteen were wounded. After emptying his magazine and then reloading to fire again, the weapon jammed at which point the assailant fled the scene in an old white Ford pickup truck with California plates. Because of the remote location, law enforcement and medical personnel arrived at the scene only around ten minutes ago to assist the wounded and to gather statements and evidence. A number of the more seriously wounded were transported by helicopter to the closest hospital with a trauma center in Las Vegas, Nevada. We will have more on this breaking story as it develops. We now return you to your regularly scheduled broadcast."

This lack of information and detail would not stop the various television stations from taking part in conjecture, idle speculation and conspiracy theories. There was a 24/7 news beast that had to be fed, and when something as juicy a meal as a mass shooting took place, it could not be sated. I knew this well for I was not only a feeder of the beast but an intrinsic part of its existence. You only hoped that along the way, you didn't get yourself out on a limb with your speculation only to have the branch sawed off behind you.

I arrived at the arena about a half hour early and got to my seat. Like the others, the hall was filling in quickly and would most likely be packed for the final event. Since the reporters had gotten used to the routine, only about half the press seats were occupied. Most would eventually be filled. Many reporters knew there was not going to be any earthshattering revelations so some would arrive late or not show up at all.

I was all set for another boring evening of sameness when The Reverend stormed out onto the stage without any of the usual fanfare or opening acts. As soon as he got to the microphone the room got quiet.

"My friends, I'm mad as hell and I'm not going to take it anymore."

A huge banner with those three words—the words I've come to hate with a passion—"No Cheeks Left!" unfurled behind him.

"I was once advised that, as a preacher, when I was wronged I was supposed to show my adversaries my other cheek. It was the Christian thing to do, I was told. Well, after today's news in which a terrorist gunned down nearly twenty of your fellow Ohioans in cold blood and in broad daylight, I can honestly say I have no cheeks left to offer. And neither should you. We have all been assaulted in a country where we should be able to walk tall, free and safe.

"I have just gotten off the phone with families of the victims, offering them condolences in their time of need. They all wanted me to give you the message emblazoned behind me. They wanted America to finally stand up for what is right and not be pushed around by a bunch of towel-headed camel jockeys."

This was a new one for him. His rhetoric had always contained plenty of anti-Muslim venom but never was it so blatantly vitriolic. He would be coy about his denunciations. Plus, something did not ring true here. The incident happened no more than two hours ago and law enforcement officials only recently arrived at the scene. I thought it far too early to release victim names and addresses, even to a presidential candidate. Also, the gunman had escaped. I'd seen nothing about him being a Muslim. I pulled out my phone to use my own inside source, my husband, to check it out.

"Aren't you still working?" Will asked.

"Yeah, I'm at the rally. You'll have to speak up; it's pretty loud here. There's something McKenzie said about the attack at Bryce Canyon that I wanted to run by you."

"Shoot. Ooh, bad use of that word. What is it?"

"He just stated that he spoke with families of the victims. Is any of that public knowledge?"

"I don't believe so. Our agents only recently arrived at the scene. They had to come out of Las Vegas. As a matter of fact, I was just reading an interim report giving a preliminary assessment of the situation that was attached to the BOLO about the suspect. Standard protocol is to seal off and secure the scene, which also includes the release of any information to the public."

"And the identity and background of the gunman? McKenzie just stated that he was a Muslim terrorist."

"That's way too premature. Not a whole lot to go on here. His description was middle-aged, average height and stocky with dark but not black skin and a mustache. There was such mayhem that nobody could say anything definitive about the guy. There's more description of his beat-up white Ford pickup truck than there is of the gunman."

"There's no way he could have spoken to the victims' families, is there?"

"It's highly unlikely at this point."

"Just as I suspected. McKenzie is making things up to fit his agenda. That gets me so mad. Can I use any of this in my report tonight?"

"There's nothing here that's confidential or if released would hinder our investigation, but let me make a few calls to make sure my info is up to date. I'll get right back."

Ten minutes later, Will called me back.

"Situation is exactly as we discussed. There is no way that The Reverend or his campaign would know anything about the suspect or the victims. Any inquiries about the case, especially from a presidential candidate, would have been routed through the Vegas public affairs office and they haven't heard from him. Just as a side note, they did get an inquiry on the status of the investigation and the condition of the victims from the Kent camp."

"Figures. Thanks Will. Looks like our friend is getting going now so I better listen. Talk to you later. Hug the kids for me. Love you."

"Love you back. Fava, don't do anything stupid."

"I won't, but I won't back down either. "

"I wouldn't expect you to."

I returned to listening to his speech. He was hitting his stride now with an anti-Muslim diatribe that the crowd was eating up. They fed off each other. I'd always found him to be a gifted orator, but those were always written out speeches that he delivered. This one, because of the circumstances, had to be more off-the-cuff and he was brilliant at it. I think he was even surprising himself at how easily the words flowed from his mouth.

I, on the other hand, preferred a tighter script that was thought out in advance and one was already forming in my mind. My adlibbing skills were non-existent, or maybe like The Reverend before this evening, they were as yet undiscovered and unrealized. In any case, the script of my report for this evening was forming in my mind. I jotted down a few of the key points I wanted to make to ensure I didn't forget them.

When the rally concluded, I rushed down to Jonas who had set up in front of the arena. Since there hadn't been anything new to report, I hadn't bothered doing on-air reports after the last two rallies. Tonight, however, was different. I called in and requested a slot, advising the producer of the general gist of what I was going to say. He thought it was newsworthy and approved a live report.

The Reverend had finished his rally a full half-hour earlier this evening than previous evenings. I guess he just blew himself out. As a result, we had some time to kill before my live report.

"How have you been feeling, J.? Any after effects of the explosion?"

"I get an occasional headache, but the doctors said that was to be expected. Other than that, I'm fine. It would take an awful lot to really hurt an ox like me. One good outcome of me getting blown up is Eunice and I are back together."

"That's great!" I thought about the love-hate, on again/off again relationship Jonas and Eunice have had over the years. "It is great, isn't it?"

"Oh yeah. The ole gal got a taste of what it might be to lose me and she came to her senses about how wonderful I am. She's not as much of a tight ass now. All is good."

"I'm happy for you, J. You deserve someone special in your life."

Just then I received word in my earpiece that we were going to go live in five minutes. We did last minute sound and lighting checks and were ready to go. I heard Kenneth Haynes introducing me and turning it over.

"Thank you, Kenneth. It's nice to be with you again.

"I'm reporting from outside the Akron Civic Center where presidential candidate Malcolm McKenzie just concluded his latest rally. As with his previous rallies on this road trip, the arena was packed with supporters. However, the address delivered at this rally was a departure from the usual speech for The Reverend.

"As many of you are now aware, a gunman opened fire on a tour bus in Utah, killing at least five people and wounding twenty more. In his speech, Reverend McKenzie made statements that implied that he had full knowledge of the details of the tragedy, despite the fact that little to no information about either the gunman or the victims has been released at this point in time."

I knew I was walking a fine line here as I was essentially calling the presidential candidate a liar.

"After speaking with an FBI source, I've been advised that the names of the victims have not yet been released. There is therefore little chance that The Reverend could have spoken to their families as he claimed this evening. Furthermore, there is very little information on the identity or even background of the shooter. As my source said, there is more information on the beat-up Ford pickup truck than there is on the shooter.

"Tonight, however, The Reverent prematurely used this shooting to incite the crowd, to foment anger in them, against Muslims. At this point, the gunman is on the loose and authorities have indicated they only have a sketchy description of him. Despite this, Reverend McKenzie has seized on this as an opportunity to advance his anti-Muslim agenda. He even used derogatory stereotypic terms to describe Muslims. At one point, the crowd broke into a chant using these same terms.

"While Reverend McKenzie appeared to be deeply troubled by the shooting, a number of observers in the auditorium questioned the timing of his tirade and whether he was capitalizing on an unfortunate tragedy for his political benefit. It may come out that the shooter was indeed an Islamic terrorist but until the facts come out, some people are recommending that it may be more prudent to not speculate at this time. The end result of his impetuous outburst could be an uptick in violence.

"This is Francine Vega, reporting from the McKenzie campaign in Akron, Ohio."

I could hear Haynes thanking me and taking over as we shut down the filming. Jonas was putting his camera away when he remembered he had my phone in his pocket. He took it out to hand to me when it buzzed. He automatically looked at it.

"Frannie, take a look at this."

I took the phone from him and looked at the display. The news alert message read: 'Cleveland Ohio mosque firebombed. 2 killed and 14 injured.'

"That didn't take long, did it Frannie?"

"No, it didn't."

McKenzie was so unpredictable that he could proudly take full responsibility or, just as likely, he could claim that his comments were completely unrelated to the firebombing. He'd want the world to think that he has such power, that the citizens were listening to him like he was already president. Of course, he'd make all the disclaimers about the lawless loss of life, but you could tell by his demeanor that he was proud of himself. We'd have to wait and see what his official comments and position would be.

Jonas and I made our way back to our hotel. Even though it was after midnight, I still wanted to watch the news for an hour or so and take a hot bath before going to bed. My plane to Ames, Iowa was not until around noon the next day so I could sleep in a bit. It seemed like a perfect plan.

I turned on cable news to find a breaking news report. After a car chase that crossed state lines three times and a pitched gun battle, authorities had captured the alleged gunman. He was gravely wounded. While his identity was not released, initial reports were that the man was an American of Italian decent. There was no indication he was a Muslim.

My phone rang. It was Frank. It was well after one in the morning, his time.

"Hey, Frank, it sure is a surprise to hear from you at this hour."

"Hi Francine. I have some good news and bad news for you."

"I'll take the bad news first."

"You're off the McKenzie campaign. Your report tonight got back to him and he was livid. He accused you of being biased and engaging in shoddy shock journalism. Your credentials are being revoked immediately."

"He can do that?"

"He can request anything he wants and we don't have to obey, but Janet Kahn already agreed to take you off."

"She what? Without a fight? We can't let him get away with this! We owe it to our industry to go to war with this megalomaniac!"

"Calm down. I didn't say Janet wasn't backing you or willing to fight McKenzie, but she wanted to do it in a different manner. First, Katrina is due back next week and I must admit that Janet is a woman of her word. It would have been easy to kick Katrina to the curb, but she didn't. As a result, you'd be out soon anyway."

"You did say you had good news as well, didn't you?"

"Indeed I did. Janet may be taking you off of this story but she's not kicking you to the curb either. She's been very impressed with your reporting, especially tonight's report. She said something about you having balls."

"Great big ones, but don't let Will know, okay?"

"Anyway, the good news is that you've officially become a talking head. Janet has an opening for a guest commentator on this Sunday's *Issues & Answers*. She wants you to fill that slot. She spoke with Richard Leitz, and he agreed wholeheartedly."

"Really? Me?"

Issues & Answers was the network's top-rated news program. Known for outspoken guests and sharp, candid and intelligent discussion on politics and issues affecting the nation, this show was every newsperson's dream of making it. Its host, Richard Leitz, was its rock star and was the reason anybody who was anybody clamored to be on the show.

"Yes, you. This all fell into place in the last hour or so. Janet wanted you to be on the show for this Sunday. You were to call in remotely. But then when McKenzie called her in an irate tirade demanding you be removed from the campaign, it all seemed to come together. She told me to make it happen and get you back to New York for a meeting tomorrow afternoon at 2:00 to get ready for Sunday's show. You in?"

"You bet I am! I'll catch a plane tomorrow morning. Thanks Frank."

"It's nothing, Francine. Get a good night's sleep."

15

I arrived for the meeting the next day, eager but also nervous. The host of *Issues & Answers*, Richard Leitz, was off-the-charts smart. He was educated at Dartmouth, Harvard and Cambridge with a PhD in sociology, a law degree and a Masters in journalism. I considered myself bright and well-read, but I knew I was going to be way out of my league. I hoped I could keep up with him and his guests. My only wish was that I not make a fool out of myself.

I arrived ten minutes early but six people were already seated around the table, waiting for the meeting to begin. This in itself was new to me. I was used to meeting attendees arriving for meetings at best right on time but most likely they'd drift in five to ten minutes late. I loved and respected Frank, but he has never run the tightest ship. I personally would have preferred a little more office discipline, but that was a matter of style.

Richard Leitz himself was at the table, chatting with Abbie Feldstein, a columnist for the Washington Herald and a regular contributor to the show, mostly on political matters. Richard got up when I entered the room and came over to greet me.

"Francine, welcome to our little gathering. I'm looking forward to you joining us and contributing to the show."

"I hope I can keep up, Richard."

"Oh, I've seen your work and read up on you. Raised by a single mother in Spanish Harlem, you went to NYU where you thrived. You've been with Action 6 News for eight years where you've built up quite a following. You were nominated for a Pulitzer in your mid-twenties after breaking what I consider to be the story of the decade. It's too bad that your boss, Frank McDermott, couldn't think of a single nice thing to say about you but I personally think he's jealous."

I laughed. Jealousy is definitely not one of Frank's attributes and it's sometimes embarrassing the way he gushes to others about me. It's almost like I was his daughter.

"Yeah, that's Frank, all over."

"Come, let me introduce you around."

Two of the attendees of the meeting would be on-air. The aforementioned Abbie Feldstein was one. I recognized her from the show. The other was Paul Parker, a network reporter who was working on the Kent campaign.

The other three people sitting there were the show's producers and whose names flew out of my head the second they were introduced. Each of them, after they were introduced, sat back down and resumed pecking at computers. A few minutes later, two other producer-types walked in with their computers and took their places at the table.

At precisely 2:00, Richard started the meeting.

"Thank you all for coming. Jeanette," he said to one of the producers, "Can you see if you can get Ed and Heidi on the monitors so we can begin?"

Jeanette typed furiously and it was not long until the two giant monitors on the wall came to life. On one monitor the face of Ed Coffey, a long-time network journalist who was a regular on the show, appeared. On the other monitor a full bookcase appeared. I tried looking at the titles of the books but they were all scholarly studies on a variety of international relations. It was my impression that the books were there as much for impression value as they were for information purposes.

We all sat quietly. After ten minutes, Heidi Jeldres, an expert on U.S.-Arab relations who worked at the prestigious Center on World Affairs, a conservative-to-moderate think tank, sat down in front of the computer's camera.

"Sorry if I'm late," said Heidi to all of us. "I just got back from a meeting with my daughter's teacher."

It was obvious from Ms. Jeldres' demeanor that the meeting had not gone well but you had to admire how she was able to compartmentalize her life and focus on our meeting.

"Not a problem, Heidi. We only just started."

Richard was obviously a stickler for punctuality but he didn't let on that he was annoyed that the meeting was starting late. If nothing else, I sensed he was genuinely a decent person and issues regarding the welfare of a daughter would rightly be a valid excuse for tardiness. Also, Heidi Jeldres was world-renowned in her field and he couldn't afford to antagonize her.

"First, let me introduce Francine Vega, who will be joining us for Sunday's show and I hope will be a regular contributor in the long-term."

"Thank you, Richard. I so look forward to being a part of *Issues & Answers.*"

"The big news is that I received word just before I walked in that Peter Kent has agreed to be our guest on Sunday's show. I spoke with his son, Alexander, to lay out the ground rules. To my surprise, there really weren't many. The candidate is willing to be on the show the entire hour, if we want. I'm tempted. Mr. Kent did ask to review a list of questions we'd like to ask in advance. He did ask that we be respectful and not be solely out for a gotcha moment. That's normal, but it's amazing that there wasn't anything else. Hell, we're discussing with The Reverend's camp such minutiae on questions, format, time, you name it that I doubt he'll ever agree to come on the show.

"Oh, and by the way, Alexander was thrilled that you're going to be on the show, Francine. Looks like you have a big fan."

"I interviewed him a few years ago and we've been friends ever since."

"Let's get to work and come up with a set of questions and how we can orchestrate this."

The session then fell into a freewheeling, spirited back and forth between all the participants. It was the producers' job to capture all of the ideas and then fashion them into a series of questions that could be asked of the presidential candidate. The topics were far-ranging going from immigration to trade to environmental protection to energy policy to the Middle East.

For the most part, as the newcomer I sat back and listened, taking notes but not really providing my own input. I was beginning to worry that Richard might wonder why I was there, wasting precious space on the dais. I was confident in my ideas and my ability to express them, but this was not a forum I was used to. I needed to assert myself more but I was having problems inserting myself or even getting a word in edgewise.

It wasn't until Heidi Jeldres made a statement that my feelings expressed themselves all over my face.

"It's become abundantly clear that Reverend McKenzie has no interest in the good of the United States or its citizens. He is only interested in promoting himself. He's on the ride of his life and it will keep his interest only as long as it's about him."

Richard obviously read the disagreement that was shown on my face as he held up his hand for everyone to stop talking, which they instantly did.

"Francine, I sense you disagree with that assessment of Reverend McKenzie."

I felt on the spot as everyone turned their eyes to me. It was now or never whether I was going to be an actual part of this program. I took a breath and launched into my take on The Reverend.

"No, I don't agree. McKenzie definitely has an overinflated ego and a thin skin, but I believe he is going at this campaign because of a sense that he is serving the country. He truly believes that God and morality have long departed from this country and that he's the one to bring them back. Serving himself is the last thing on his mind."

"Are you saying you believe he'd be a good President?" Ed Coffey asked.

"Not in the least. The man has no clue. His message is one of hate and fear. He keeps saying he's going to announce detailed plans of what he's going to do to address certain problems or certain issues but they never seem to materialize. Now, I know this is not a straight news program and opinion plays a great role but I don't think it's my place to express my opinion who would make the best president. Rather, I need to put the facts out there to help our viewers make an informed decision."

"It sounds to me that your time on the McKenzie campaign may have skewed your viewpoint, Ms. Vega," Heidi Jeldres intoned.

"Oh really? If I'm so cozy with him, why did The Reverend demand I be removed from his press corps?"

"He did?"

"Yes, he did. In addition, McKenzie and I have a history that goes back a number of years so there is no love lost here. But that doesn't mean that I don't want us as journalists to state things that aren't true to back a viewpoint. I continue to have some semblance of confidence that the American public will make the correct choice if they are presented with the full set of facts."

I looked over to see Richard smiling at the exchange. I think I passed the test.

16

Sunday morning came and I couldn't believe I was so nervous and excited. I did some breathing exercises to calm myself down, but it didn't work. I would just have to let adrenaline carry me through. Will arranged for Emma to come and watch the kids so he could drive me into Manhattan. He also wanted to see me in action in person and I got him permission to attend off to the side.

We arrived at the studio a half-hour ahead of the appointed time. I've been on-air for so many years, I knew how to do my own hair and makeup, but it's always best to let the hair and makeup experts touch you up some before airtime so I kissed Will goodbye to head over to them.

When I got there, Peter Kent was sitting in the chair.

"You're Francine Vega, aren't you?" he called out.

"Governor Kent, it's a pleasure to meet you."

"The pleasure's mine. Alexander has told me so much about you and I've seen your work myself. All quite impressive, I must say."

"I'm the one who's impressed. You'll make a fine President."

I thought to myself that he'd be a fine looking President, as well.

"I still have to make it through a campaign and election, don't I?"

He said that so as not to jinx himself but it was obvious that he was brimming with confidence. All the polls had him ahead by double digits, some by as much as twenty percent. Some pundits were talking a sweep of epic proportions. More than one pundit maintained that McKenzie would need to call on the "special relationship with God" (air quotes included) he'd developed as The Reverend to fashion a miracle to pull off even a close race.

"So are there any special questions you plan on asking me today?"

"I have a whole array of questions on numerous issues."

"Such as?"

I was unsure how much I should reveal. As a politician, Kent was practiced at handling any question with ease, brushing aside those questions he wanted to avoid but still making an appearance that he was being responsive. Giving the exact questions up front would give him an opportunity to think through his answers (and non-answers). As a result, the show would lose the spontaneity it was noted for.

On the other hand, I couldn't blow him off completely. He was pressing for something, and I didn't want to offend him. I had to give him something.

"One thing I've always been impressed about you is your record in regards to prison reform and sentencing guidelines. I'll probably ask if you would bring the same reforms to the federal level."

"Please do ask that. It's one of my favorite topics. We have the highest incarceration rate of any modern western nation. I find it hard to believe that Americans are that much more evil than other peoples. We are losing entire generations of young black men, wasting precious resources pursuing things like recreational use of marijuana.

"Alexander tells me you believe that Texas may have executed an innocent man and the Zyklon Killer is still out there?"

Even though this question was in the same general area of the justice system, the shift to this specific subject threw me off guard. I think that may have been his intent. This may be a standard interview technique of his and he was using me to warm up his skill before the show began.

"Yes, I've been given some information that is worth pursuing. Interesting that you should ask."

"Oh, it was somewhat related to what we were talking about. Also, I was personally involved in attempting to extradite Aaron Kaplow back to New York to stand trial for his crimes here. Have you made any headway in your investigation?"

"Not really. I've been pretty busy with my new work assignments. I..."

I almost blurted out about the NYPD discovering the connection between the detonator used in the bomb to blow up Jonas's car and that used on the day Wendy Smith was murdered but I caught myself.

"You were going to say something else?"

"No, nothing important."

"One thing I can do is warn you about going up against the State of Texas. Governor Lemaster is an ornery, vindictive son-of-a-bitch who will stop at nothing to keep you from proving his state executed an innocent man. Once he learns of your efforts, be prepared to be dragged through mud like you've never imagined. He'll make up things about you. I even believe that physical intimidation is not out of the question."

"You really got to know this guy, didn't you?"

"As I mentioned, I was personally involved in the extradition attempt. I made it clear that Kaplow was all his, once we were done, but I wanted justice for the victims in my state."

"I appreciate the warning."

"It's not just a warning; it's a prediction."

A chill ran down my spine. He was giving me a heads-up as to what a fellow governor might do to me but the tone of his warning made it sound like he himself was threatening me.

"I'll be sure to watch my back. It doesn't hurt having an FBI Special Agent as my husband."

"No, I suppose it doesn't," he laughed.

An intern stuck his head in.

"Governor Kent, Richard would like to go over a few things before the broadcast. Would you please come with me? Miss Vega, we'll be doing a run through in fifteen minutes."

"I'll be ready. Thank you."

The Governor got out of his chair and started to leave but before he did he turned to me and gently grabbed both my hands.

"It's been a pleasure getting to know you a little bit, Ms. Vega. I can see why Alexander goes on and on about you. Please, though, take my warning seriously. Be careful before you go down this road. I don't want you getting hurt."

Before I could respond, he turned and accompanied the intern out of the room.

The show went off without a hitch. I did get to ask Governor Kent about prison and sentencing reform as well as questions on a number of other topics. Regardless of what we threw at him, his responses were informed and well-thought out. He was able to not only draw on his experiences as Governor but also to express a vision of the direction in which he thought the country could be heading.

Each of us panelists brought up Reverend McKenzie at one or more point. While he didn't back down from contrasting their respective policies and ideas, he would not let himself be drawn into anything that could remotely be considered name-calling or a lack of respect for his prospective opponent. He just would not go there. He even admonished Heidi Jeldres at one point when he thought her questioning crossed a partisan line. With his poll numbers, he obviously could go out of his way to be magnanimous.

I do have to say that I was sorry when the show ended. It was not only one of the most exhilarating experiences of my life but also one of the most professionally affirming events I'd ever taken part in.

After the show, Richard came up to me and told he'd like to have me back as a regular contributor. He'd have his people draw up the necessary paperwork to make that happen. I felt authenticated. I was able to stand up toe-to-toe with the big boys on a national stage.

17

The next day I left for my scheduled rendezvous with Alan. I hoped I had understood his cryptic message to meet "where it all began" correctly as I got into the cab to head down to 367 East Third Street, between Avenues C and D. This was where I'd first met Alan nearly three years ago. However, Alan so often thought and spoke in a code of his own that it was sometimes impossible to accurately discern his true meaning.

When I told Will where I was going, he insisted that he was going to accompany me. He sensed a trap of some sort by Lawson. I told him I thought he was being overly paranoid. For one thing, Lawson would have no idea where Alan and I would be meeting.

I also thought Alan might be inhibited if Will were along. Even though Will had a history with Alan and could be counted as one of his friends as much as anyone could be, Alan's moods could have such swings that he might not show if he spied that Will was with me. I thought it better if I went to meet Alan alone. Will reluctantly agreed not to come along, although I knew full well that either he or one of his agents was going to keep me under surveillance.

The way I envisioned it playing out was that Alan and I would meet and he would give me some information or documents. That would be it. Alan was not much of a talker so there would be little in the way of conversation. Then, as I headed back to the subway, Will would pull up and offer me a ride, his camera and telescopic lens beside him. I'd be both angry with him for babying me and thankful that I have someone who cares enough to watch over and worry about me the way he does.

I arrived at the building at 367 East Third Street, between Avenues C and D, ten minutes before the time we were scheduled to meet. The five-story walk-up was a dump back when we met three years ago. Now it was an abandoned dump with boarded-up windows on the first two floors. From what I observed, the building should have been condemned years ago. The City finally realized it as well.

The neighborhood itself did feel somewhat safer than it did back then. At that point in time I made sure to have Jonas accompany me not only because he was my cameraman but also because of the intimidation factor his size offered. Today, I was going solo and I was thankful that in the intervening three years there had been some gentrification, so I didn't feel unsafe.

Of course, that didn't mean there weren't the homeless, rummaging through trashcans, looking for a bottle or aluminum can that can be redeemed for some spare change. After I'd been standing there about ten minutes one such denizen of the streets stumbled by me. I believe he was wearing on his body every stitch of clothing he owned, making one of the more fragrant men I'd ever encountered. Despite the temperature being a pleasant 75 degrees, he even had a woolen hat pulled down nearly over his eyes.

At one point he fell over, obviously drunk or high though it was only two o'clock in the afternoon. He regained his balance, but he still tottered a bit. It appeared that he was trying to determine where he was or even who he was. The thought of Jonas wandering the streets after the explosion popped into my mind. He appeared to be a drunken homeless man, just like this one. If it weren't for an observant Good Samaritan, he probably would have been left on the streets and may have died.

I contemplated assisting this gentleman but in the end I employed the practiced New York habit of pretending these people don't exist, but his stench made it extremely difficult. I wanted to help but I couldn't afford to leave this spot. Alan was always an extremely punctual person and he was due any minute. He was also a skittish person who was being tracked by a madman and if I weren't there, he would disappear. Heaven knows when he would return.

Two o'clock came and went and still no Alan. My vagrant friend had settled into a comatose state, leaning on a nearby lamppost. Thankfully he had relocated to a spot downwind of me. Once I was done with Alan I was going to call 911 to get some assistance for this gentleman. But where was Alan?

As I mentioned, Alan was always punctual. It was one of his many neuroses, but one I appreciated as I was always at least five minutes early to every meeting.

It got to be quarter after and I was about to give up and leave when a late model black Mercedes sedan pulled up to the curb beside me. The sedan had blackened windows so I could not see inside. I tensed up immediately. The last time I was this near a similar automobile I was forced inside at gunpoint to talk with Lawson.

The homeless guy groaned and shifted his position slightly. I was happy to see he was still alive but he was the least of my concerns now as the passenger side door opened and out stepped a sixtyish slender man with slicked back graying hair and wearing an obviously expensive tailored charcoal pinstriped suit.

"Ms. Vega?" he called out as he approached. At the same time, he reached his right hand into his inside vest pocket. I didn't know what to do. Should I run? Should I dive one way or the other to make me a moving target, more difficult to hit? Instead, of these options, I froze. The person who didn't freeze was the homeless guy who immediately sprung to action.

As soon as he had gotten to his feet, he whipped out a Glock, assumed a firing position and aimed the gun at the gray-haired man.

"Freeze," he shouted out, "FBI."

"Will? That's you?" I asked.

Will didn't answer me but kept his focus on the man, who was standing there petrified. All the color had drained from his face and I would not be surprised if at this moment his pants smelled as badly as Will did.

"Pull your hand out, slowly."

The man obliged. In his hand was an envelope, not a gun.

"I'm Special Agent Will Allen. Who are you and what business do you have with Francine Vega?"

"My name is Robert Howes. I'm an attorney at the law firm of Esposito and Liebowitz. My client, Alan Westbrook, requested that I deliver this envelope to Ms. Vega. That's all."

Will put his gun back in his holster.

"I apologize for scaring you Mr. Howes, but there have been several recent threats on Ms. Vega's life and we wanted to make sure this is not another. You can go now."

Howes turned and headed back to his car.

"Mr. Howes?" I called out.

He turned back toward me.

"Why are you here but not Alan?"

"I don't know. He sent me a text about an hour ago with instructions to come to this location and deliver the envelope."

He turned to walk away again.

"Mr. Howes? The envelope?"

"Oh yes. I'm a bit flustered, I'm afraid."

He walked over and handed it to me. He got into the car and sped away.

Will and I looked at each other in disbelief. My heartbeat had returned to nearly normal. I wanted to go and give Will a hug but his stench so repulsed me I was afraid I would gag if I did.

"I understand your need to keep an eye on me but did you really need to make yourself smell so foul?"

"Pretty good undercover disguise, huh?"

He was obviously so proud of himself that I didn't have the heart to point out how much of an idiot I thought he was being, so I just agreed.

"So, what does Alan have to say and why the cloak and dagger message sender?"

I tore open the envelope and found a brief note. I read it aloud.

My Dearest Francine,

If you are reading this note, most likely I am dead. Please go to the Federated Amalgamated Bank on the corner of 72nd and 3rd and ask for Mr. Ellsworth for further instruction.

Love,

Alan

"Dead?"

I couldn't believe what I was reading. I ran into Will's arms.

"Do you believe it?" I asked him.

"We'll do everything we can do to get the truth."

"Poor Alan. Such a lost soul. It has to be Lawson, doesn't it?"

"He'd be a prime suspect. Let's go to that bank and find out what's there. I'll meet you there in an hour. I think I have to go back and clean up some, ya think?"

"Nah."

We both laughed. As we were about to go our separate ways I happened to glance up to the apartment where Alan had once lived.

"Will," I called out to my husband, "look up at that fourth-floor window. Are those bullet holes?"

Will walked back to me and we gazed up at the window.

"Sure looks like it. Probably a drug deal gone bad. I'll put in a call to NYPD to look into it."

"Will, that was Alan's apartment back when I first met him. I have a bad feeling."

Will reached into his pocket and pulled out his gun once again.

"Wait here," he ordered.

"Like hell I will," I shot back, "if something is going on, I'd be more of a target out here on the street than with you. I'm coming up."

Will conceded defeat.

"You stay behind me then."

We walked over to the front entryway, which was boarded up but had since been pried open. We had to bend and contort a bit but we squeezed through and into the vestibule. We pulled out our phones and activated our flashlight applications as we started our ascent up the stairs. We heard some rustling and stopped in our tracks but we didn't hear it again.

"Rats," Will concluded as we resumed our climb.

We arrived at the fourth floor and headed over to Alan's former apartment. All of the doors had been kicked or jimmied open. Abandoned furniture, clothing and other household items were strewn about, making the footing somewhat precarious.

"Scavengers. I'll bet you won't find a speck of copper in this entire building."

The door to Alan's old apartment was shut more than the others. It was almost as if it had been carefully closed after someone departed. We walked in and it was impossible not to see him immediately. Alan's body was in a seated, slumped-over position on the floor under the window where we saw the bullet holes.

The front of his shirt was bloodstained with two observable bullet holes in his chest. Will knelt down to him and took his wrist.

"No pulse. His body is still warm. He was killed within the past hour, I'd say. The coroner will give us a more exact time. I'd better give Detective Kelly a call. It's NYPD's case, not ours."

Will obviously realized how cold and clinical he must have sounded as he stood up to stand beside me.

"I'm sorry, Fava. I know how much Alan meant to you, and to me."

"I know."

We both stood there, silent and in our own thoughts, for a minute or so. I knelt down next to Alan. If nothing else I wanted to close his eyes.

"No, Fava, don't touch him. There may be evidence. I'll call Kelly and hang around to make sure the crime scene doesn't get disturbed. You need me to call someone to escort you back to the office? Lawson may be out there, waiting for you."

"No, I'll be okay. I don't think he'll try anything."

I headed toward the door. As I passed the bathroom, something caught me out of the corner of my eye. I stopped dead in my tracks.

"Fava, please. I'll feel better if you wait until I can get somebody down here."

"You don't have to worry about Lawson hurting me."

"You don't know that."

"Yes, I do."

I pointed into the bathroom. There on the toilet, tied up and gagged was the lifeless mutilated body of Jacob Lawson. Will looked in.

"Whoever did this wanted Lawson to suffer. This was personal, very personal."

"Well, that reduces the number of people who wanted to do this to several thousand."

"Including our poor friend out there."

Will pulled out his phone and called Detective Kelly. Twenty minutes later she arrived at the scene with her team.

"My life has certainly taken a turn since meeting you two," she said in greeting as she walked into the apartment. "All I have to do is follow you around and I'll never be bored."

"Nice to see you, too, Detective," was Will's deadpan response.

"I assume you didn't disturb anything, correct?"

"I opened the door and then I felt for Alan's pulse, that's it."

"Remind me again who these people are."

I responded.

"The man laying by the window is Alan Starbuck Westbrook. He was our friend."

"He was the lottery winner, right?"

I resented Alan be reduced in such a manner, but I let it pass.

"Yes, he was."

"And the other man?"

"That was Jacob Lawson."

"The former Colonel who was on your most wanted list, right?"

"Yes."

Additional people—crime scene investigators and the coroner—filed in. We moved off to a corner.

"Any theories on what went on here?"

The question was obviously aimed at Will, the detective's law enforcement colleague, but I answered instead.

"This was Alan's old apartment when I first met him. Living in this hole is what he had been reduced to after Lawson murdered Freddy Westbrook, Alan's twin brother, and Alan went off the deep end. Alan had always believed that Freddy was killed in the terrorist attack on the Pentagon but he later learned that Lawson killed him on that day. I think Alan lured Lawson here to exact his revenge. Looking at Lawson's body, he may have been successful. Unfortunately, a third party showed up before Alan left and killed him."

"Interesting. You'd make a good cop."

I looked at Will.

"Yes, I've been told that before."

"Any theories on who killed your friend?"

"Not one. Other than Lawson, I wasn't aware of Alan having any enemies or even adversaries. The man was the ultimate loner, the classic computer nerd. As far as I could ever tell, we were his only friends, and we weren't close. Before contacting me recently, I hadn't heard from him in nearly two years."

"Why are the two of you down here anyway?"

"I got a text from Alan asking me to meet him in front of this building. It was where we first met. He had some information on the Zyklon Killer to share with me. We were instead met by a lawyer who handed me this."

I handed her the note, which she read silently. She then looked Will up and down, observing his ludicrous homeless outfit for the first time.

"Just out of curiosity, are you heading to a costume party or are you undercover for some reason?"

"Just trying to keep my sometimes pigheaded wife alive."

"I'm not even going to ask. So how'd you end up here?"

"I happened to look up and noticed the bullet holes. I thought the worst. The front door was pried open so we came up and found this."

"Okay. Well, I'm going to ask you to get out of here so my people can do their work."

Before leaving I went over to Alan one last time to say goodbye. I looked down at him, not knowing what I believed but hoping that he and Freddy were reunited at last. It was then I noticed something on his left pant leg.

"Detective, Will, come over here."

They complied and looked down at Alan's body.

"What is it, Fava?" Will asked.

"His pants. Look at his left thigh."

There was so much blood everywhere and the blood on his khakis did not look like anything special or out of the ordinary until one looked closer.

"Does that look like the letter Z that he wrote on his pants with his own blood?"

"Now that you mention it, it does. Does it say Z = A?" Detective Kelly asked.

"I think it does. It looks like he attempted another letter but he didn't make it."

"What does Z = A mean?"

"I don't have any idea."

"Maybe it's a formula of some sort," speculated Detective Kelly. "You say he was an eccentric genius. Maybe his mind just went haywire as he was dying. Or maybe these are simply the scratches of a man in agony as his life was ebbing away. I've seen some pretty strange things that dying people do as they try to hold onto life before they exhale their last breath."

She was making sense. The markings on his pant leg could be anything, or nothing at all, in which case I was reading way too much into this. But I didn't think so.

"Alan was trying to send me a message. He wrote on his pants with his blood for me to see. I first met and interviewed Alan on the street, like I told you. When I came back a few days later for a follow-up, I came up to this apartment and it was abandoned. Cleaned out totally. He was long-gone but he left a letter in an envelope with my name on it. He could tell from our one short meeting that I would be coming back. I think this is the same situation. He knew I'd be back. This was his parting message to me."

"But you have no idea what that message is."

"No, I don't. Since his original message indicated he had some information on the Zyklon Killer that he wanted to give me, I'm going to take a guess that the Z is Zyklon. But beyond that, I have no idea. It looks to me like he started to write another letter but he died before he could finish."

"I'm not totally seeing it," admitted the Detective.

Kelly called in the tech that was photographing the crime scene to take a close-up of the supposed writing.

"I have a woman in our forensics lab who is a master at this type of thing. If anyone can discern that he was actually writing something here and not just wiping his hands, it would be Kate. Oh, when are you planning to go to the bank and meet with this Mr. Ellsworth?"

"The bank'll be closed by now so tomorrow morning."

"I'd like to join you, if that's okay.

"That would be fine. Nine o'clock. Federated Amalgamated Bank on the corner of 72nd and 3rd."

"Got it. See you then."

18

We met Detective Kelly promptly at nine in front of the bank.

We walked into the bank and headed over to a balding overweight man with wireframe glasses who was just finishing up with a client.

"Excuse me, we're here to see Mr. Ellsworth."

"I'm Fred Ellsworth. How can I help you?"

"My name's Francine Vega, this is my husband, Will Allen and our friend, Jane Kelly. We got a message from Alan Westbrook that we needed to see you regarding some business we have with him."

I wasn't sure why we needed to see this man so I didn't want to let on that Alan was dead, that Will is an FBI agent or that Jane an NYPD detective.

"I thought I recognized you from TV when you walked in. Yes, Mr. Westbrook is one of our best clients. A month ago, he told me that you may call one day and he told me to give you this in that eventuality."

He reached into a drawer and pulled out an envelope. He emptied the contents of the envelope, a key and a computer thumb drive, onto his desk.

"The key," Ellsworth advised, "is to a safe deposit box that he had me set up for you to access. He just had the thumb drive delivered to me yesterday. I don't know what's on it. If you would like, I will lead you back to the vault where we keep our deposit boxes."

Will, Jane and I all rose to go back.

"I'm afraid only Francine Vega is allowed to accompany me to the vault. I'm sorry."

"Is that because of state or federal law or just company policy?"

"I really don't know. I assume it's company policy."

"In which case I'm accompanying my wife and Detective Kelly is coming with us as well."

Will pulled out his badge and held it out for Ellsworth to examine.

Kelly did the same.

"We're investigating possible criminal activity and the content of that box may hold some clues," Will stated. "If you like, I can make a few calls and get a warrant."

"No, that won't be necessary. Since your wife has been given full access to the box, it's up to her who would accompany her."

"Thank you."

Ellsworth led us into the vault and over to box number 265. I inserted the key and withdrew the box. At that point, Ellsworth left us alone.

"You kind of came down on that guy a little hard, don't you think?"

"Bank guys always annoy me. They're only one step above lawyers."

I put the box down on a table and we sat down to examine the contents. I opened it to find a letter and a cashier's check.

"Will, Jane, look at this."

I was in total disbelief as I handed the check over to Will.

"Am I seeing this correctly?"

"Yes, you are. This is a check for $200 million, to you."

"I guess I'm going to have to treat you two with newfound respect," Kelly joked.

"What's the letter say?" Will asked.

I read the letter aloud.

My dearest Francine,

I realize you must be shocked to see the accompanying check. If I somehow managed to survive, you can give the money back to me when we next meet. Otherwise, it is yours to do with as you please.

If it were not for you and Will, I would not have had a life these past three years. The fact that I may be dead by the time you read this does not diminish what you have given me. After 9/11 when I lost Freddy up to the minute I met you I was the walking dead. For the past three years, I felt purpose, all because of you. I don't fear death and if it happens, so be it. But at least for now, I kind of like living.

I trust you to put this money to good use. You're the type person who wouldn't know any other way. Please know that I retained the remaining $30 million that is still in an account here. My will stipulates that you will *get that upon proof of my death.*

In any case, don't give up journalism. It's what you were born to do. You're a natural at digging out the truth where others can't.

Keep your guard up when it comes to Jake. He's resourceful and vengeful. He needs you at the moment, so you are useful to him but once he doesn't think you to be of value, he'll eliminate you without remorse.

Have a good life. Enjoy your family. And keep searching for the truth.

ASW

"What should we do with the money?" I asked.

Will responded, "We should put it in an account but not touch it until we figure out what the hell is going on here. I have a feeling that, by giving it to you, he was also trying to protect it from Lawson but we don't know if there's anybody else hungry for it. We still have that $20 million that was put into our accounts in an effort to frame us that we tried to return to Alan but he wouldn't take it. Neither you nor I have ever touched that money; we'll just do the same with this pot."

Everything he said made perfect sense, but I must say I found the idea of sailing away on a yacht for a carefree life devoid of responsibility alluring. I resisted temptation and we deposited the check.

When I got back to my office I stuck Alan's thumb drive into my computer. My IT guys would be aghast that I did so, fearing that I would infect the entire system with a virus. I had no worries; if anybody could be trusted, it would be Alan.

I tried accessing the file but it had been written in an unfamiliar program. I searched to see if there was an application I could download to access it, but none came up. That was the furthest reach of my technological competence. I needed help. I called Stuart, the one IT guy who would lecture me the least on inserting an unknown device into my computer. Ten minutes later, he arrived at my desk.

He sat down and started typing furiously to crack the code. I left him to it. Fifteen minutes later he came to me, totally dejected and defeated. I called Will to see if one of the FBI anti-hacking gurus could take a look at it. I had the thumb drive messengered down to Will's office.

Three hours later my phone buzzed.

"Hi Will. Anything?"

"It took my guys a couple hours but they finally figured it out. They were complimentary of Alan's skill."

"And?"

"There were three files on the drive. Each file was encrypted differently so it took some doing to open them, but my guys finally opened them. Each file consisted of one sentence. The first, *Zyklon knew Jake circa 1994-96.* The second, *Zyklon will kill again, soon.* The third, *München Sieben.*"

"That's it?"

"Yup. I expected a whole dossier revealing Zyklon's identity. But then again, this is classic Alan."

"How so?"

"I bet he knew who Zyklon is and did have an entire dossier on him. But like our previous dealings, he'd only leak dribs and drabs to us for fear we wouldn't need him anymore."

"But he did tell us a couple important things."

"And they are?"

"That if in fact Aaron Kaplow was not the Zyklon Killer, neither was he a random selection to be the fall guy. He was specifically chosen not only to lead investigators astray but also to punish Jacob Lawson. Alan narrowed down the field immeasurably."

"Yes, he narrowed it down to people that Colonel Lawson pissed off over a five-year period, a time when he was accumulating his power. That puts the number in the thousands instead of millions."

"It's something anyway. We're heading in the right direction."

"Fava, Zyklon is dangerous. We also know he's not done killing. The closer you get to him, the more dangerous he's going to get. That cornered wounded animal thing, you know?"

"Will, are you saying the Bureau will take the case over now?"

"I don't know. It's all still highly speculative that the Zyklon is even out there. There's no real evidence. We only have the words of a disgraced army officer and a mentally unstable man, both of whom are now deceased. Not much to go on. As far as my superiors are concerned, this is a closed case and I suspect they aren't too eager to reopen a case when we have so many other cases to investigate."

"But I'm supposed to let it drop?"

Will said nothing in reply.

"I appreciate your wanting to protect me but you know I can't turn it over. Wendy would never forgive me."

"From the way you describe her, I don't think she would want you endangering yourself for her."

"Then I would never forgive me."

"Okay, but we work together. No more resistance so I have to dress in foul-smelling clothes to keep an eye on you."

"Okay. What do you make of *München Sieben*?"

"I have no idea. If I'm not mistaken, that means *Munich Seven*."

"Sounds like a German baroque string ensemble. I'd be somewhat surprised if that's what Alan was referring to."

"With Alan, you'd never know. I'd like to bring in Detective Kelly. She's good. I think she can help us a lot. Plus, Alan was murdered and his last known whereabouts was in the city. This would most likely fall under NYPD, not FBI, jurisdiction."

"I trust your judgment."

"That's what I like to hear."

19

A short while after I hung up with Will my phone buzzed again. It was Richard Leitz.

"Francine, can you come on the show Sunday after next?"

"Sure, any special guests?"

"None other than The Reverend himself. We, along with every other network, have been trying to get McKenzie on our shows for months but he successfully dodged us. Then ten minutes ago he called me and asked if he could appear. The only condition he had was that you be in attendance. That's why he's coming to us rather than the other shows.

"After Kent came on our show last week, the gap in the polls widened and McKenzie is starting to get nervous that he's going to get to a point where he'll never be able to make up the difference."

"I would think that I'd be the last person he'd want on the show."

"He's been taking a beating ever since it became known he kicked you out of his camp. The late-night comics have been having a field day with him saying that if he can't take the heat of criticism by you, how's he going to be able to stand up to world leaders who say derogatory things about him?"

"So I'm on a level with a third world despot now, right?"

"That about sums it up. In any case, he or his handlers think he has to get out into the public eye more and that extending an olive branch your way would not hurt. So the drill would be the same as last time. Thursday get together at two. If you can be here personally, great, otherwise we'll patch you in. We'll try and reach out to McKenzie on Friday or Saturday but if we can't, hopefully he can come in an hour or two before airtime. So we'll see you next Thursday?"

"I'll be there."

"Great. Have a good week.

Despite numerous communications between the network and the McKenzie camp, The Reverend did not arrive at the station until ten minutes before airtime. He offered no explanation or apology.

He was rushed in to makeup for a quick touch-up but there was no time for a sit down to go over the process or to clarify what questions would be asked. Richard was nearly ready to can the entire interview and instead go with a Plan B. Richard explained that, when it came to live interviews, there always had to be a contingency in case the guest did not show up. Even after McKenzie arrived, Richard was still tempted to punt the interview but at the last minute he relented and indicated it was a go. As he explained it, this was a presidential candidate who has not granted an interview to any network and it was quite a coup for us to be the first. Richard acknowledged he'd be a complete fool to brush off a presidential candidate in a huff.

The show began.

"Good morning and welcome to today's edition of *Issues & Answers*. I'm your host, Richard Leitz and with me today are Michelle Francis, Senior Fellow at the Brooklyn Institute for Politics & Economics, Andrew Robinson, National Political Correspondent for the Washington Sentinel and Francine Vega, News Anchor for Action 6 News in New York and who had most recently covered the national presidential campaign for this network.

"Today we are privileged to have as our guest Reverend Malcolm McKenzie, who is the presumptive presidential candidate for the Republican Party. Welcome Reverend McKenzie."

"Thank you, Richard, for having me on your show this morning."

"Glad to have you. I'd like to start off with asking you why you, a man of the cloth, want to be President of the United States."

"I received my calling to minister to the needs of my flock when I was only sixteen. I have followed that calling ever since but a few years ago I received a second calling, one to administer to the needs of the nation. This call was just as strong and it's been one that not only I've heard but the great people of this nation as well."

"Are you saying that your run for the Presidency is ordained by God?"

"Let's just say that there's been a deficit of godliness in this country and that it is my mission to bring this country back to its basic goodness, to its being worthy of God's mercy."

"Is that really the role of the President?"

"I can see no greater role. Who better than a President, who has all the earthly power any person could hope for, to make it happen? In fact, I see this as the primary leadership function of the President."

"Are you saying we ignore the constitutional requirement separating church and state?"

"The constitution states, 'Congress shall make no law respecting an establishment of religion, or prohibiting the free exercise thereof.' This was designed to keep the government from interfering in the affairs of religion and churches, not the other way around. There is no prohibition of bringing more of God and his morality into government. In fact, the foundation of this country is built on the Judeo-Christian ethics."

I couldn't resist interjecting.

"What about all the people who don't belong to the Judeo-Christian culture? How would they fit in to the country you're looking to create?"

The Reverend turned to me to address me directly.

"Ms. Vega, what a pleasure it is to be with you again. I do hope I'll see you at my next rally in Dubuque."

What a hypocrite! He knows I won't be there because he specifically barred me from being there. I was tempted to call his bluff and thank him for his invitation to tell him I would be in attendance but I thought better of it.

"Katrina Turow has reovered. I was only a fill-in while she was recuperating but she'll be back in time for your next rally."

"Thank the Lord she's healthy again."

"Yes indeed. Now back to my question. Is there going to be room and acceptance for those who, let's just call them non-believers."

"Of course there will be, but they have to realize and accept the pillars upon this great country was built."

"Reverend, I have a Jewish friend who's old enough to remember when the school day would begin with a recitation of the Lord's Prayer. She distinctly remembers being stigmatized after a schoolmate loudly told the teacher that she's not praying. Is that the America you want us to head back to where certain Americans are made to feel self-conscious about their beliefs? To be made to feel like they weren't full Americans?"

"I'm sure it wasn't quite as traumatic as you paint it, but in any case, we need to return to a set of common values."

I was about to respond when Richard spoke up. I don't think he liked the direction the discussion was heading at this early stage in the program and wanted to steer it on a different heading.

"Reverend, I'd like to address one of the criticisms leveled at your campaign. Namely, there seems to be a distinct lack of specifics or even plans for what you'd like to do as president. How do you respond to those critics?"

"Lincoln told us that our government is one of the people, by the people and for the people. However, if you talk with any person on the street as I've been doing for the past year, you'll find out that this is no longer true. They don't feel part of this government; they feel alienated from it. We've had eight years of plans and specifics on a variety of topics, but no inclusion. Like David who went to retrieve the lost lamb who wandered from the flock, my goal is to bring these wonderful folks back into the fold."

Michelle Francis spoke up.

"Mr. McKenzie"

"Reverend McKenzie," he corrected.

"Reverend McKenzie, you have stated that it is your primary goal to stop the bleeding of U.S. jobs to overseas. However, your statements to date don't seem to point in the direction of strong government action to make this happen. How exactly do you plan to create meaningful jobs?"

"By getting out of the way. By letting the free market do its thing, unfettered by burdensome regulation and high taxes. Once we do that, the jobs will come. I will ensure that government moves aside and allows for growth. I'm sure that Governor Kent is well meaning and I'll grant that his policies have shown some moderate success in New York, but they are not suited to the national stage. What he will do is to impose his will so that the states will be stifled in doing the things that they can do best. We have become a weak nation because we have become a dependent nation. We need to get our government back to the people, but if the people have been so weakened they can't take the reins then it's up to us in leadership positions to help them stand on their own.

"As I've ministered to my flock over the years, I've encountered many who were so dependent on their addictions that they could barely keep themselves alive, never mind function properly in society. They had to relearn how to live, how to stand on their own two feet, how to be productive human beings once again. I helped these people, as I can help those people of the United States who are too dependent on the federal government to stand on their own two feet. They need to be weaned off of assistance programs that promote dependency and stifle their initiative."

Every subject matter we threw out at him—immigration, national defense, foreign affairs, health care, tax policy—he parried in exactly the same way. He had ready answers regardless of the topic but the more he talked, the more it became obvious that he had few actual plans for what he wanted to do. He was, I have to admit, a persuasive speaker. He handled us with skill. But it was superficial.

Time was coming to a close and Richard took the opportunity ask one wrap-up question.

"Reverend, your appeal to the average voter is that you would be coming to DC as the ultimate outsider with no connections or strings attached to you. They say this would give you freedom to act exclusively on the public's behalf, not for the special interests. This has another side, however. You would also be coming in inexperienced, a neophyte. How would you overcome this inexperience and get things done?"

"I already have a list of experienced people I would surround myself with but, more importantly, I believe my policies are so common sense that they will practically implement themselves. I can't tell you the number of Congressmen and Senators who have told me that they wished they had the guts to put forward the ideas I've promoted. I have no worry on this score.

"Can you honestly tell me that the country and the world is getting along swimmingly with the experienced politicians in charge? We have been way too diplomatic in some parts of the globe. We have displayed weakness, not strength. I will restore our strength."

There was one last question I had to ask.

"But Reverend, you recently had me kicked off your campaign because of some critical reporting I did about you and your campaign. Is that the type of strength you're referring to, which could be interpreted to be thin skin, not strength? Do you believe you have the temperament to be the President of the United States? How would you handle the inevitable criticism you would receive on a daily basis as President?"

"I was wrong to react to your comments the way I did, Ms. Vega. We all make our mistakes. The measure of a person is how they learn and grow from them. I'm sorry."

That show of humility was unexpected and threw me so off guard that I missed my chance for any follow-up questions I wanted to ask.

The show ended and as was getting ready to leave, The Reverend walked up to me.

"It really is a pleasure seeing you again, Ms. Vega."

"Reverend, likewise."

"You really are the one who started me on this journey. I should be more appreciative than I have been to you."

I simply nodded in return as we went our separate ways.

20

When I got back to my desk, my phone rang. It was Detective Kelly.

"Detective, how are you today?"

"Fine, I tried to reach Will but I couldn't reach him. I figured you two acted as a team so I thought I would call you."

Again, the use of his first name rankled me. I had no reason to doubt Will's love and devotion but jealousy is not always logical, is it?

"Did you find anything?"

"Well, my lab tech Judy confirmed that Mr. Westbrook did indeed write Z = A."

"How?"

"She was able to lift his own fingerprint off the blood on his pants. I told you she was good. Any further thoughts on what he was trying to tell you?"

"No, Z has to be Zyklon. There's no other logical possibility. A? I have no idea, especially since he was unable to write any other letters. Do you know yet whether Alan was the one who tortured and killed Lawson?"

"If he did, he was careful about it. We would have expected there to be blood spatter or some other trace of Lawson on whoever did this. Mr. Westbrook is clean, except for his own blood, of course."

"I guess it doesn't really matter but it's hard imagining Alan torturing anyone, even his mortal enemy. I'd like to keep Alan's gentle soul image intact in my mind. You know what I mean?"

"Yes, I do, Francine. In both of our lines of work we meet so many shits that when we run across a good person we want to hold him or her in our hearts as long as we can."

"That's quite poetic, detective."

"Yeah, it happens every once in awhile. You do understand that I'll have to kill you if you tell anybody."

"Secret's safe with me."

While Detective Kelly expressed interest, there was little she could do to help me find the true Zyklon Killer, even after Alan's murder. The case was officially closed and I only had circumstantial hearsay from a wanted criminal who was looking to clear his cousin's name and from an eccentric loner who was enamored with me. Will was in the same boat. The FBI considered the case closed and had no credible reason to reopen it. They both had their plates full with their official duties and could not devote either resources or time to help me out.

It wasn't as if I had a lot of spare time on my hands to investigate Zyklon. Keeping current so that I could be a valuable member of the *Issues & Answers* team was taking a lot of my time. But I had to make time. I had to investigate Alan's cryptic messages on the thumb drive. *Zyklon knew Jake circa 1994-96.* Perhaps there was some connection between this and 'Z = A'.

I scrolled down my contacts list on my phone until I got to the name I was looking for, Captain Audra Fairchild. I hoped she was still at the Pentagon. I called the number I had and an official male voice answered.

"Office of Logistical Operations, Specialist First Class Weldon speaking."

"Captain Audra Fairchild, please."

"You mean Major Fairchild."

"She's gotten a promotion since I last spoke to her a few years ago."

"Can I tell her who's calling?"

"Francine Vega, I'm a reporter from Action 6 News in New York."

"If this is a press inquiry, you should go through the Army's Office of Press Relations. I can transfer you."

"No, it's not a press call. The call is more of a personal nature."

"Let me check if she's available."

A minute later, Major Fairchild came on the line.

"Francine? How are you?"

"I'm doing well, Major. I wasn't sure you'd remember me. Congratulations on your promotion, by the way."

"Thank you. And of course I remember you. In a way, you're responsible for my promotion."

"I am?"

"When Lawson was still around, I was tentative and indecisive, always looking over my shoulder. Once he was removed as a result of your work, I felt free and was able to do my job better. My superiors noticed and a promotion ensued. I meant to call you, not only for that but also for the work you did in getting Freddy justice. It meant a lot. What can I do for you?"

"First, I wanted to let you know that Lawson is dead. He was murdered."

"Forgive me for not appearing too upset."

"The bad news I have to tell you is that Alan was murdered, too."

"Alan? Oh no. Such a good man. It's a shame. Do they know who did it?"

"No, not yet, but that might be where you can help."

"Anything, what do you need?"

"I need to get any information you can get your hands on related to Colonel Lawson between 1994 and 1996. His schedules, meetings, highlights, I need everything. Do you think there are records that go that far back?"

"Please, we're the army. We record everything and then we keep all that information in warehouses for centuries. Can I ask what in particular you're looking for?"

"I believe the person who killed Alan, and probably Lawson as well, may have known Lawson during that period."

"I'll see what we have. I have a friend in records management who should be able to do a search and get me what you need."

"Can you get it soon? This person may kill again if we don't find out quickly who it is."

"I'll get him working on it today, as soon as we hang up."

The next order of business was to try and figure out what Alan meant by *München Sieben*. Munich 7. Will didn't have a clue. I then went on the Internet and plugged *München Sieben* into the search engine. What came up was a German police drama series that ran from 2004-2007. Alan could be extremely obtuse, but inserting a clue from a foreign TV show was a bit much.

My knowledge of Munich could fit into a thimble with room to spare.

It's a city in Germany, but I couldn't tell you what part. My only other knowledge of the city was that there was a terrorist attack there during the 1972 Olympics and a number of Israeli athletes were taken hostage and then were killed in a botched rescue attempt. Other than that, zilch.

It then occurred to me that Miriam Berger was from Munich. Perhaps the reference had to do with the war, which would only make sense given the modus operandi of the killer. I tried refining my Internet search by plugging in 'Munich 7 World War II' but again nothing of relevance came up. I thought I was on the right track, though.

I dug out my notes from when I was covering the Wendy Smith case. I hurried through the pages related to her and scanned the information on her great-grandfather, SS *Obersturmführer* Michael Strauss. He was from the Munich area. On a hunch, I looked up Hans Steiner, the SS Officer referred to in the folder that Lawson had given me. He was from Munich, too. Likewise, when I looked up the SS officers whose descendants had been killed by the Zyklon Killer, each was from the Munich area.

I had to bounce this off someone to help me reason through it. Will was on a stake out and I couldn't call him so I dialed Detective Kelly.

"Detective, when you were investigating the Zyklon Killer, I know you must have looked for connection between the victims but did you ever look for connections between the victim's fathers and grandfathers, in other words, between the Nazi officers?"

"You know that this case is considered closed, correct? It's quite a coincidence that you called since just ten minutes ago a directive was circulated telling NYPD personnel not to invest any more time, effort or resources on anything related to the Zyklon Killer. It's closed. Period."

"That seems like a strange directive, doesn't it? Do you get many directives like that?"

"Honestly, I can't say I ever remember getting a similar one, but we get indecipherable orders every day that we must obey. There's been some talk of a huge economic deal between New York and Texas that reopening a case like this could scuttle. I'm absolutely sure the directive is totally unrelated to the deal and that my superiors would never, ever let politics interfere with police work."

I let her sarcasm hang in the air for a moment.

"Are you saying you can't answer my question?"

"I'm saying I've gotten a direct order on this particular case. But if we were to talk hypotheticals, we can talk all day."

"So, on a hypothetical serial killer case, you would look for connections and commonalities between the victims, right?"

"Yes, of course we would. Now, let's say it was a case on which I was not the lead detective but one where I assisted because it was such a high-profile case. In many of these cases, there wouldn't be any connections we could find. As far as the lead investigator could tell, they were complete strangers to each other with no social, familial, financial, professional or any other linkage between them whatsoever."

"What about between the fathers or grandfathers of each of the victims?"

"On occasion, such a hypothetical serial killer would leave behind notes indicating that the ancestors were involved in a similar line of work but most likely there would not be an investigation of any connections between these ancestors."

"Nothing about any connections between them?"

"Not unless we found a reason to dig any deeper."

I couldn't stand playing this charade any further. I needed to get to the point.

"The FBI was finally able to crack Alan's code on the thumb drive and found out what were in the three files. Will was going to give you a call to fill you in but he's been up to his eyeballs on a case so I might as well brief you."

I could feel the iciness over the phone. It was obvious that the Detective was not pleased with not being briefed immediately on anything related to a case of hers, even if it was one she was ordered not to work on anymore.

"Go on."

"Each of the files contained a single line. The first was *Zyklon knew Jake circa 1994-96.* Jake is, or rather was, Lawson. The second was *Zyklon will kill again, soon* and the third was, *München Sieben.*"

"What's that mean?"

"It means *Munich 7.* I think Alan was giving us a clue as to the identity of the Zyklon Killer. The only thing I could come up with during an Internet search was an old German police drama by that name. Unless there's some information embedded in an episode of Munich 7—which isn't entirely out of the question with Alan—my theory is that there was some connection between the SS officer relatives of the victims. They all seem to be from Munich. I was calling to see if you could help me look into it."

There was a pause before Kelly spoke. I could sense that she was no longer pissed about not being kept apprised of news but was now uncomfortable about going against her directive.

"Detective? Are you still there?"

"Yes. We've moved beyond the hypothetical and are now looking at further investigation of the Zyklon Killer. I'm sorry, but I can't help you on it."

"What?"

"Yes, the orders were specific."

"But why? If nothing else, this could provide you with leads in helping to solve two of the NYPD's higher profile cases: blowing up Jonas and killing Alan. Whatever happened to the old line 'We'll follow this investigation wherever it leads?', which in this case leads to the Zyklon Killer?"

"I'm sorry, Francine, but this is coming from the very highest levels. The official position of the State of New York is that the Zyklon Killer has been apprehended and brought to justice. That's the end of it as far as the NYPD is concerned."

"And as far as you're concerned, Jane?"

I was sorely disappointed in her and this was the first time I'd referred to her by name and not be her title. After another pause, I continued.

"Hasn't Alan given you a probable scenario that confirms Aaron Kaplow' contention that he was framed all along? He could have been selected because he was Lawson's cousin and because he was an easy mark with his limited mental capacity. Isn't this alone enough to warrant additional investigation that they may have gotten the wrong guy?"

"This directive comes from the highest levels. I did push back but to no avail."

"And what about his message that Zyklon is going to kill again, and soon?"

"My superiors are already dismissing your guy as a wacko whose word is hardly worth reopening a closed case."

It was obvious she was spouting the company line but her heart wasn't in it. Her words were telling me one thing but her voice was telling me another. She wanted to help but she was running into a wall. Her next statement confirmed this.

"Francine, the joint effort New York and Texas are working that would benefit both states greatly. The Governor does not want anything that would antagonize Texas and jeopardize this effort at this point in time. Revealing that Texas may have executed an innocent man is something that would definitely sour relations."

"So someone else has to die because some money is to be made. Do you really want to be a part of that, Jane?"

Another silent pause.

"I'm sorry. I'll do my utmost to find out who killed your friend but there's nothing more I can do for you regarding the Zyklon Killer."

We both hung up, dissatisfied with the results of the phone call.

I could think of no contacts, German or otherwise, who could give me insight on what the *Munich 7* could be or why Alan thought it to be important. Jane had made comments about Alan's mental state and whether anything he said could be credible. Alan may not have been the most stable person on earth but I never had any doubt as to the veracity or importance of anything he ever said or wrote. If he left a message for me, it contained truth. Period. I had to follow this through.

My mind kept going back to Wendy, Lena and Miriam and their connection to Munich. It was then I decided to reach out to a contact that might be able to help me. I checked my watch and decided that it would still be working hours in Tel Aviv, Israel. I went into my contact list and located the name of the woman that I hadn't spoken to in over three years. The line buzzed with that distinctive tone of a foreign country. Finally, a man's voice came on.

"Shalom."

"Shalom. Is Rachel Stern there?"

"Yes, she is. Can I tell her who is calling?"

"Francine Vega, from New York."

She came on the line.

"Francine! To what do I owe the honor of this call? You're not trying to shame me into doing my job again, are you?"

I laughed. Although she was referencing a rather painful moment in our previous lives when I had to coerce her to be a true journalist, I could tell the comment was made in jest.

"No, not at all. I have a question for you."

"Shoot."

"Do you know what *Munich 7* is?"

"My initial guess is that it is a German version of *Maroon 5*. Do you have anything more?"

"I think it's something that goes back to World War II. Are you familiar with the Zyklon Killer?"

"Yes, as you can imagine, anything that involves the use of Zyklon B is going to get Israel's attention. The Zyklon Killer was just executed, wasn't he?"

"I have reason to believe that they may have killed the wrong man, that the Zyklon Killer is still alive and may attack again. One clue that may help identify the actual killer is *Munich 7*. I did an Internet search and the only result I got was an old German police drama. I somehow don't think that's it. I believe it may have something to do with the war since all of the SS Officers connected to Zyklon's victims were from Munich."

"I don't know anything about it but I know a man who may be able to help you."

"Can you give me his number?"

"I can do even better. I'll give you his address. He works for the Israeli mission to the U.N. at 800 Second Avenue in New York. His name is Ari Klarsfeld."

"Klarsfeld? As in Serge Klarsfeld, the Nazi hunter?"

"Yes, Serge is his uncle. His mother survived the war and settled in Israel, where Ari was born. Ever since an early age, Ari has been interested in his aunt and uncle's work."

"Do you know if he's in the States now and will be willing to talk to me?"

"We became friends when I interviewed him after one of the Hamas uprisings in Gaza, so I know him pretty well. If he's around, I can guarantee he will want to speak with you. I can see him salivating right now at the chance to be part of such a story. I'll give him a call right now and call or text you back."

"Thanks, Rachel. I really need to arrange a trip to Israel so we can catch up."

"Or better yet, I need to come to New York. I haven't been there since your wedding. Maybe this story will grow like your previous one and I'll get the station to pay my trip. Say hi to that wonderful husband of yours. Bye."

I thought to myself that like Jonas, Rachel was another friend that I've moved on from and only contacted her when I needed something. I hadn't sent so much as a postcard in three years. Luckily, because of the distance between us, she didn't hold it against me but I knew that even if she worked in the next room, I probably wouldn't have kept up with her. I had to change this in myself. I had to make time for the people I cared about.

An hour later, I got a text from Rachel telling me that Ari Klarsfeld could see me but I had to get down to his office in the next half hour. After that, he was heading to the airport to head back to Tel Aviv. I threw everything down and ran to the street where I was able to flag down a cab in short order.

Because of traffic, the cab ride took a full twenty minutes to get downtown. Then I had to go through screening and security to get into the building. He had called the front desk and given them my name but since it was around lunchtime, there was nobody to come down to escort me upstairs. I waited in the lobby a half hour, which extended into forty-five minutes and then an hour. I had the front desk check again, but they got no answer.

I despaired that I would not be able to talk with Mr. Klarsfeld especially after I got a text from the office advising me that I was back to covering The Reverend, at least temporarily. He had scheduled an impromptu press conference for that evening up in his upstate hometown of Wayland, New York, and he called Janet to specifically request that I attend. I felt like a yo-yo. I called Jonas and asked him if he were up for a road trip. 'Hell yeah, Frannie.' was his enthusiastic reply. I asked him to grab my overnight bag that I keep under my desk in case situations like this arise. Early in my career I missed out on a story because I wasn't prepared. I vowed that it would never happen again.

I then checked with Emma to see if she could spend the night with the kids since Will was still on his stakeout and might not get home until the following morning. Luckily, she had nothing planned and was able to stay with them.

The press conference—for which we were provided no details and, as a result, rumors were flying over the Internet, including that he was calling it quits and abandoning the race—was scheduled for eight. The time to get to Wayland from the City was about three and a half hours. However, we would be leaving just as the evening rush hour was beginning so we had to allow an extra hour. That meant the latest I could get the car, pick up Jonas (he still was not cleared to drive) and be on the road was around three thirty.

It was now after one and still there was no sign of Klarsfeld. For all I knew, he could be on his plane back to Israel right now, leaving me in the lurch. I was about ready to tell the guard that I'd have to come back a different day when a somewhat tall man in his mid-fifties with a thick shock of silver-gray hair framing a handsome, weathered face pushed his way briskly through the revolving door and entered the lobby. He was carrying a plastic bag of what appeared to be food and drink.

"You must be Francine Vega," he called out to me. I nodded.

He walked over, put the bag on the floor and reached his hand out for me to shake, which I did.

"I'm so sorry to keep you waiting. I trust it hasn't been too long. I hope you don't mind but I got an incurable craving for deli and had to rush down to Katz's on Houston Street for some sandwiches. Am I being stereotypical or what, huh?"

I wasn't sure what to respond, so I remained silent.

"You know, it took me a full year after being posted here to pronounce Houston correctly. I always wanted to pronounce it like the city in Texas but I've finally got the 'ow' sound down."

He seemed proud of himself and his transformation into a New Yorker.

"Let's go up to my office and eat these. I hope you haven't eaten. I have a pastrami on rye and a corned beef on rye, both with lots of mustard. If you wanted tongue, you're on your own. I can't even stand the sight of it. We can split or you can have one or the other. I love both. I got a couple knishes and some Dr. Brown's cream soda. A veritable feast."

We started towards the elevators.

"I thought you had a flight to catch to go back to Israel."

"I only tell people that to see how serious they are about seeing me. You'd be surprised how many people say that it's urgent they see me but when I tell them they have to get to me within a half hour, they can't make it. I find this little ruse an easy way to separate the wheat from the chaff. You're obviously wheat."

We exited the elevator and strode to his office. He unlocked the door and we went in. I was surprised at how modest the office was. It consisted of a single room with a desk and there was no staff. On the walls were pictures of various Israeli Air Force planes.

"Those are planes I've flown during my service. I'm actually still in the Air Force. If there were an emergency, I could be called up, although I'm getting a bit long in the tooth for that although being a small country you never know."

"Thank you for seeing me on such short notice."

"Well, your reputation precedes you. I was a low-level diplomat when Prime Minister Rosen was indicted and sent to prison, largely because of you."

"Since you're willing to see me, I guess you weren't much of a fan."

"The man was a corrupt boor. Israel is lucky to be rid of him. It hasn't hurt my career either being under a new regime. So when Rachel called, telling me you wanted to chat, I had to jump at the chance."

"But I had to be put through the wringer first to make sure I was serious."

"But of course," he replied with a twinkle in his eye.

"So what do you want to talk about? Rachel was rather sketchy but she did say something about the Zyklon Killer."

Keeping an eye on the clock, I gave Ari a greatly summarized version of all I knew about the Zyklon Killer.

"So, I have reason to believe the Zyklon Killer is still alive and may kill again. The main reason I'm here to see you is one clue my friend Alan left for me before he was killed. He wrote *München Sieben*, which I believe means *Munich 7*.

Ari Klarsfeld said nothing for a few seconds, sitting there with an astounded look on his face.

"*München Sieben*, I haven't heard that term in years. You're sure that's what your friend wrote?"

"Absolutely. What does it mean?"

"In the Nazi-hunting world it had special meaning, but over the years many of us began to believe it was nothing but a myth. Maybe it's real after all."

"What is it?" I was getting impatient.

"*München Sieben* actually has two references. The first, as you've already surmised, refers to the seven SS officers who escaped in the waning days of the war. Most if not all were believed to have made it safely to South America. None were ever captured. All would be long dead by now."

"Now it makes sense. They my be dead but they had children and grandchildren. That's who the Zyklon Killer is going after. Six descendants have been murdered thus far. There is one left. We have the names of the six. Who is the seventh?"

"Over the years, many people believed the *München Sieben* to be a myth. Remember, Munich is largely believed to be the birthplace of Nazism. It was where Hitler first made his name after the First World War. It was the site of the Beer Hall Putsch, Hitler's coup attempt. It failed and he was sent to prison but it burnished his credentials and gave him time to write *Mein Kampf*. He was released to adulation of the masses after serving only a portion of his sentence. What I am saying is that Munich was a hotbed of Nazism and scores of officers, soldiers and party members came from that city. The seventh SS officer could be one of hundreds."

"What's the second reference of *Munich 7*?"

"Seven tons."

"Seven tons? Of what?"

"Seven tons of gold. These SS officers supposedly put aside every speck of gold they could lift off the Jews—wedding rings, jewelry, dental fillings, you name it—and hid it away. Legend has it that they hoped to bring the gold with them when they fled to South America but the Allies arrived before they could transport it. Legend is that it's hidden away somewhere, waiting to be discovered."

I pulled out my phone and went online, punching in 'worth of ton of gold'.

"An ounce of gold is worth about $2000. That would make the current value of a ton of gold about $64 million and then seven tons would be $448 million. It's never been found?"

"Not according to popular legend."

He handed me his card.

"I have an appointment I have to get to. Please, feel free to contact me if you need anything more or have any additional information you can share with me. The number is my international number. The phone will ring anywhere in the world. Good luck with your quest. And be careful."

"I will, Mr. Klarsfeld."

21

It was like old times riding with Jonas as we headed up the Thruway. As a matter of fact, three years earlier, we had taken this exact trip together. The difference this time is that I was driving, which meant the trip would take at least a half hour to forty-five minutes longer than the last time.

I had no idea what The Reverend was going to talk about today or why he had reconsidered my banishment. I thought that Katrina should have been making the trip but the company wasn't taking any chances of her rushing back without a final doctor's approval.

Without his rallies to bolster him, The Reverend had been eerily silent over the past week. Then, almost on a whim, he announces a press conference only hours before it was to be held in a remote corner of New York. If he were hoping that this would result in minimal coverage, he was going to be sorely disappointed.

When we arrived, news vans and cars choked the streets of this small town. Every conceivable network, newspaper and other legitimate and illegitimate news outlets were represented. How they would all fit into this small Methodist Church was anybody's guess.

We had enough time for me to do a short intro prior to the press conference. Jonas set up his camera in front of the church and we had a few takes. We reviewed the takes quickly and then Jonas sent the best one in to the station.

Jonas opted to stay in the car, surfing the web on his phone. There probably wouldn't have been room for him anyway and the event would be covered with one camera that would provide a shared feed to all the news outlets.

I walked up to the front door of the church and was greeted by a burly man with a bushy black beard, more a bouncer at a bar than a greeter at a church. He looked me up and down and then asked me for my name, which I gave. He nodded and called over an earnest skinny woman with a long blond ponytail. He whispered something in her ear and then told me to go with her.

We walked together silently back out of the church. I was getting anxious, not because I feared for my safety or anything like that but I feared I was being escorted back to my car. The Reverend had made it clear that I was persona non-grata on his campaign but then he relented. Now, he could be relenting on his relenting. I didn't have much choice but to follow this young woman wherever she was leading me. She offered no explanation or even an offer to chat.

We left the church by the front door and, when we got to the sidewalk, we turned right and at the next house, turned into the walkway. The young woman knocked on the door, which then opened pretty much immediately.

"Thank you, Alice," The Reverend intoned. "You can head back to the church. I'll be along shortly."

She nodded and departed, leaving me standing there on the porch. He then turned to me.

"Won't you please come in, Ms. Vega? I promise I won't bite."

I walked in and he invited me to sit on the flowered couch in the living room.

"You're probably wondering why I wanted to see you alone."

"A couple questions to that effect had crossed my mind."

"Well, first I want to ensure that everything we say here will be off-the-record."

"If that's the way you want it, yes, it is."

"Good. I called you here to apologize to you for my ham-handed attempts to bar you from my campaign. I'm rather new to this and am not as thick-skinned as I should be. You're the one who's as responsible as anyone for starting me down this road."

"Don't remind me."

He laughed.

"Touché. But because you're the unwitting impetus for me being a candidate, I take your criticism to heart, especially because it contains so much truth. I've developed many friends as well as enemies in the press but, to paraphrase Ugarte in Casablanca, because you despise me, you're the only person in the press I can trust."

"I don't despise you, Reverend."

"Of course you do, and I'd have no respect for you if you didn't despise me."

"You wouldn't?"

"No, I wouldn't. I've tapped into something here and I've ridden the wave, but it's a malicious and malignant wave. I've tapped into the meanest and cruelest aspects of the American psyche. I've preached love and goodness my entire life, but now all I ever talk about is hate and fear. And the audiences eat it up. When I get in front of the crowds and they react to my new message, I feed on their enthusiasm and keep giving them more. You've recognized this in me from day one and that's why you despise me, with good reason. I attack the media but they are an essential component of American democracy.

"You are doing your job in calling me out. And you fear for the future of this country if someone like me becomes President. To tell you the truth, so do I. I am so far in over my head that it's scary. It's almost like I'm Chance the Gardener from *Being There*. I say these things that I know are a total crock of shit, pardon my French, but people take each word as a pearl of wisdom.

"Then I saw the full impact of my words. After my most recent diatribe in which I spread false information, a mosque was firebombed. A mother and her baby were badly hurt. A baby. She's only three months. She's still in the hospital. It's still fifty-fifty whether she'll pull through. A baby. God help me that I was responsible for that."

"Why don't you quit?"

"I've traveled this too far down this road to turn back. I've locked up the nomination and the convention is in two weeks. It would be a total disservice to the people who have worked for me and supported me to say to them, 'Sorry, just kidding.' I owe them my fullest effort to the bitter end, and I plan on giving it to them. Who knows, maybe they see something in me that even I don't know I have. My greatest fear is that it's not what they've seen in me but what I see in them, and it isn't pretty.

"I know there are rumors that I stopped holding my rallies because we're strapped for cash. That isn't true. I simply needed a break from my supporters. We'll be back on the road again tomorrow. I'm going to give a speech in Utah tomorrow and a rally in Nevada the day after that and then it's on to Los Angeles for the convention. I do hope you'll be along for the ride."

"Katrina will be back in the next couple of days, so she'll be taking back over."

"Good. She's evidence of another of my failings. I'm glad she's well enough to resume.

"My only salvation is that Governor Kent is going to annihilate me. He's going to kick my ass but good. Regardless of what I say about him publicly, he's a good man who has been a fantastic governor for this state. He'll make a terrific president, but you didn't hear that from me. The country will be in good hands. Anyway, enough of this baring of my soul."

"I hope it was cathartic for you, Reverend."

"Yes, it was. I thank you for your time and for your indulgence, Ms. Vega. There are not many people I could have such a chat with. Now, I'm sure your colleagues are getting restless. Shall we get on with the press conference?"

We thought it better that I go out the back entrance first and then work my way over to the church separately from him. I entered the church and was escorted to my spot. Five minutes later The Reverend entered the church through a back entrance and walked somberly to the altar.

"Thank you all for making the trip and joining me here this evening. Many of you came a long way. I know it's normal for a candidate to make a statement and then open it up for questions but let's get to the main event and I'll take questions right off."

It was obvious that the genuine feelings he expressed during our private talk affected him. He was tentative and defensive in answering his first couple of questions, which was so unlike him. When he was our guest on *Issues & Answers*, he was so confident and easy in his answers even when he was giving non-answers or saying nothing at all.

I don't believe he was trying to use me when we had our chat or that he was trying to get me to change the things I was saying about him. He really did need someone to confide in, and I was that lucky person. While it may not have been his intention to change my feelings towards him, our talk did have that effect and now I found myself feeling sorry for him. It was bothering me to see him this way so when it came time for the third set of questions, I raised my hand. The Reverend noticed me immediately and called on me.

"Reverend, can you describe your service as an army chaplain in Iraq during Desert Storm and how that would impact you in any decision you make to send us to war?"

The other journalists looked at me in amazement and annoyance that I was giving him such an easy question, especially when many of them sensed they had him on the ropes. The Reverend gave me the slightest of nods, acknowledging and appreciating that I was giving him a softball to help him get back on his game. It worked. I could literally see his faith in himself return in full as he answered my question.

I'm certain that this was not the proudest moment in my journalism career. A part of me felt like I had sold out, like I had been subjectively coopted. However, I felt pretty good at that moment about myself as a human being.

22

The planets must have been aligned because we had an evening where the entire family could have dinner together. Will had no stakes-outs. I had no rallies to attend or Zyklon clues to run down. The kids had no basketball practices or band performances.

I decided I would use the occasion to cook for my family. My cooking skills are still a work in progress but one dish has long been my pride and joy: arroz con pollo. It was my mother's specialty and I used to love to help her make it. She taught me all the little steps that enhanced its flavor. For example, where the recipe called for regular long-grain rice, she would use the Arborio rice used in risotto. She also used a touch more saffron than was called for.

I called Jonas and asked him to join us. It would be his first trip back to my house since the blast.

"But you just said you wanted a quiet family evening."

"Which is exactly why you need to be here."

He still wasn't driving so I told him Will would pick him up after work and they'd ride out to Queens together. I invited him to stay the night or, if he'd wish to get back home, we'd drive him to Brooklyn, no problem.

He hemmed and hawed a little more, saying he didn't want to be an imposition. I wasn't going to take no for an answer but I didn't want to order him (as if I had that authority) or shame him (not that Jonas could be shamed) into coming so I decided to play dirty. I handed the phone to Stella, my seven year-old daughter.

"Uncle Jonas," she pleaded, "won't you come to dinner? We miss you."

She handed the phone back to me.

"What time is Will going to pick me up?" he said with a sigh.

"That's more like it, J. He'll get you around five-thirty."

"Ya know, you don't fight fair, Frannie."

"And proud of it."

Jonas and Will got to our house around six thirty. Dinner was set for seven. Jonas tried playing with the kids the same way he had a few months ago but I could tell he was still limited so I had to tell them to go easy on him. They seemed to understand. Rosa was delighted at seeing Uncle Jonas again, and at under two, she was more his speed at this moment.

We had just sat down for dinner when Stella turned to me to ask a question.

"Fava, what's Zyklon?"

The question out of a seven year-old's mouth caught me totally off guard. I looked at Will for guidance but he simply smiled back, curious as to how awkwardly I was going to handle the situation. I decided to see if I could punt on this one but in any case I was going to tell her the truth.

"Zyklon is a German word. It means cyclone, which is another word for tornado. You remember when we watched *The Wizard of Oz* together last month?"

"I was scared of those talking trees."

"Me too, and the flying monkeys, but you remember when Dorothy was in the house and the wind was blowing hard. She looked out the window and says to Toto, "We must be up inside the cyclone!" Well, that's what a Zyklon is, except it's in German."

"Oh, is a Zyklon bad?"

"Like many words, it can have good or bad meanings."

"I guess a Zyklon Killer is bad. I heard you and Daddy talk about the Zyklon Killer and you were very upset."

"Well, Zyklon, in this case, is very, very bad. We were upset about the people who died because of a person who calls himself the Zyklon Killer."

"Why did they die?"

"He killed them. He is a sick person who killed some very nice people."

"But why?"

"He has his reasons, but none of them make sense to any of us."

"Is he going to kill you or Daddy or Uncle Jonas?"

I reached over and pulled her to me, giving her a big hug.

"Of course he's not going to hurt any of us. There's no reason for you to worry. What put these crazy thoughts in your mind?"

"Ricky said that the Zyklon Killer blew up Uncle Jonas's car."

"Who's Ricky?"

"Ricky Jones. He's in my class. His Dad is a policeman."

Will and I looked at each other.

"Stella, honey. I don't want you to worry about this anymore. Your Daddy and I and Uncle Jonas will be fine. Your Daddy's the best Special Agent in the world, isn't he?"

She nodded.

"I can't hear you." I started tickling her, causing her to smile and then laugh out loud.

"Who's the world's best Special Agent?" I repeated.

"Daddy! Daddy's the world's best Special Agent."

I went back to hugging her closely.

"That's more like it. And because your Daddy's the best, he's going to protect all of us. Right?"

I pretended like I was going to tickle her again.

"Right, Fava. Daddy's the best!"

After dinner, we let the kids go up to their rooms for bed and Will, Jonas and I went into the office. We called Detective Kelly. She and her team would be the only other people who would have any knowledge about the Zyklon Killer's possible relation to blowing up Jonas's car. We had to find out about who this "Policeman Jones" was.

Kelly picked up.

"Hi, Jane. I'm here with Francine and Jonas. There's something we need to talk to you about pertaining to Zyklon."

"Okay, but as I told Francine, this is a closed case and I can't do any work on it."

"I know all that. I just have one question. Have you spoken to anybody about the possibility of the Zyklon Killer still being alive?"

"Only my captain. Why?"

"During dinner this evening my seven year-old daughter told me a boy in her class, Ricky Jones, said that the Zyklon Killer blew up Jonas's car. Stella said that Ricky's dad was a policeman. She was scared for us because she's heard us talk about the Zyklon Killer—we'll have to be more careful about that in the future. Since you're the only one besides us we could think of who knows anything about Zyklon, we wanted to talk with you."

"I certainly didn't say anything to anybody especially since I received a direct order not to do anything more regarding the Zyklon Killer."

"Do you know this policeman, Jones?"

"Doesn't ring a bell. We have 34,000 officers in the department and Jones is such a common name that without some additional information it's the proverbial needle in a haystack. I really have to go now."

"Okay. Bye."

"That was certainly unhelpful," I offered after she hung up. "I wouldn't think it would be that difficult to track down a police officer who has a child at Stella's school. She's a detective, for God's sake."

"Yes, that was odd. I think the order to lay off Zyklon was presented to her a lot stronger than she originally told us. We'll just have to go the rest of the way without her."

"Just like old times, eh?"

I'd almost forgotten Jonas was with us mainly because he had fallen asleep halfway through our conversation with Detective Kelly. Ever since the explosion, the poor guy only had half the energy he used to have. He'd gotten stronger as time progressed but I doubted he'd ever be back to what he used to be. It seemed a shame to wake him so I put a blanket over him, gave him a kiss on the forehead and we went up to bed ourselves.

23

The next morning I was at my desk getting prepared for the following Sunday's *Issues & Answers* when my phone rang. It was Major Fairchild.

"I'm afraid I don't have much in the way of information on Jacob Lawson's schedule or activities for 1994-1996."

I thought it interesting how she studiously avoided calling him Colonel. In her eyes, the man was a traitor and did not deserve any sort of respect.

"I thought you said the Army had records on everything and that you keep them forever."

"We do. And I'm sure there are copious records on Lawson during that period but it's all classified; in fact, highly classified. The man served in Special Ops at that time. He got his promotion and came to the Pentagon in late 1996. That's when Freddy and Alan got close to him.

"The stuff he did in the mid-1990s must have been highly sensitive. Just the little poking around that I did raised some red flags. I'm curious exactly what it was he did, but not enough to risk my career over."

"I'm sorry if I created problems for you."

"No problems. I was able to fend off the inquiries easy enough. I hope this little bit of intel helps you."

"I think it does, or will anyway. Thank you, Major."

After I hung up, I pulled out a pad of paper to summarize what I knew to date.

- *Lawson was in Special Ops between 1994 and 1996 during which time he knew the person who would later become the Zyklon Killer.*
- *The explosives used in both Jonas's explosion and the blast that may have been used to divert police away from Wendy Smith's murder had the same "fingerprint" and seemed to be military grade.*
- *Therefore, a reasonable supposition is that the Zyklon Killer may*

also have been Special Ops.

- *Whoever Zyklon is has a special hatred for Lawson to the extent that he (or she but most likely he) would frame a cousin Lawson loves for the murders.*
- *The motive behind the murders may not be as clear-cut as the notes left with the victims. Based on how Munich 7 is interpreted, there could be a more basic motive: money.*
- *Zyklon will kill again, soon.*
- *Z = A?*

There were still too many unanswered questions and no time to answer them before he struck again. I had to stay focused and concentrate on what I could learn, not what I didn't know. I had to find out who NYPD Officer Jones was and how he knew about Zyklon.

Will volunteered to do some inquiries but I had a better idea. If there were anything nefarious about this Jones fellow, it would probably be better if innocuous little ol' me made some inquiries rather than the FBI. I called the school. A friendly middle-aged woman's voice answered.

"You've reached P.S. No. 32. This is Debra Holliston. How can I help you?"

"Hello Ms. Holliston. This is Francine Vega. I'm Stella Allen's mother. Stella's in second grade there."

"I know Stella. A delightful little girl."

"Yes, she is, thank you."

It's interesting how I would often introduce myself as Stella's mom but I would never do that with her older brother, Albert. Albert was old enough to remember his mother before cancer took her away and it's been a slow process getting him to accept me as a part of the family. He's getting there, but it's still a process, for both of us. Stella, on the other hand, was much younger when her mother died and as a result welcomed me as a mother. I continued.

"I was hoping you could help me out. Stella has a classmate, Ricky Jones, with whom she wanted to set up a play date and I was wondering if you could give me his parents' number so we can set it up. I don't want you to do anything that will get you in trouble."

"I don't see anything wrong with this. In my day, when we wanted to play, we played. We didn't have to schedule our fun times. But you can't be too careful these days."

"No, we can't," I agreed.

I could hear clicking on her keyboard over the line.

"Here they are. James and Holly Jones, their number is 347-555-7842."

"James Jones is a policeman, right?"

"I know he works for the NYPD, but I'm not sure in what capacity. Mrs. Jones is a court stenographer."

"You've been very helpful, Ms. Holliston."

"Let me know how the play date works out."

"I will."

I waited until evening to call, increasing the chances that James Jones was there. If he answered, I decided I was going to be perfectly blunt and ask him straight out. Often you can learn as much from a non-answer or a denial as you can from a response.

"Hello."

It was a man's voice.

"Hello, is this James Jones?"

"It is. Who's this?"

"My name's Francine Vega. My daughter, Stella Allen, goes to school with your son, Ricky. Yesterday, Stella told us your son told her that the Zyklon Killer was responsible for blowing up the car of my friend, Jonas Clarke. Do you have any idea why he would have said such a thing?"

Click. The line went dead. I hit a nerve.

The next morning, I called the general NYPD number to see if I could narrow down where exactly James Jones worked, what he did and how he got to know about the Zyklon Killer. I got an automated system that led me through a series of commands. Every third or fourth step in the inquiry, the prompt would remind me that, for an emergency situation, I should dial 911. I eventually landed on a directory where I could type in the name of the person I wanted. I was advised after typing in James Jones the there were twelve of them scattered across various precincts throughout the city.

I wrote down the information on each Jones. Not one was stationed in our precinct. That would have been too easy. I would have to call each one and hopefully I would recognize the voice of the James Jones with whom I'd spoken. For the other James Joneses that I encountered, I'd have to come up with a plausible excuse why I was calling. I was going to work my way down the list when one of the entries caught my attention. This James Jones was stationed not at one of the precincts but at headquarters at One Police Plaza in lower Manhattan. I'd start there.

"NYPD, Information Technology Bureau," an earnest female intoned.

IT! That would explain him knowing about Zyklon. I would have thought Detective Kelly too professional to blab out something as sensitive as this. It had to be someone who could tap into her system. I still had to verify this was the correct Jones.

"My name is Francine Allen," I replied using my married name, "I'm calling regarding his son, Ricky, who's a student at P.S. 166 in Queens."

I knew that invoking his son's name would get him to the phone. Plus, since it did involve his son, nobody could accuse me of lying to a police officer.

"Hello."

It was my turn to hang up. It was definitely the right Jones. Now I had to figure out why he had knowledge of Zyklon. Was he the Zyklon Killer? I didn't think so. If he were the serial killer, I doubt that he would be talking about Zyklon so openly that his seven-year old son could pick up on it. But did he have some sort of connection to the killer or did he just innocently stumble on this information? I agreed with Will that Kelly was too much of a professional to casually talk about this subject so that Jones could pick up on it.

One credible possibility was that Jones wormed his way into Kelly's emails or other electronic data management system. If the detective were anything like me, she'd keep copious notes on anything and everything. I bet that after each of our conversations, she would sit at her computer and memorialize what we had just talked about. It would be a breeze for an IT person to ferret those notes out and read them. But why? Why Kelly? Did he have some sort of grudge against Kelly and was looking for dirt on her? Or was he instructed to look into her by someone else? Or was the guy just killing time, doing what geeks do in their spare moments? If so, he could have innocently stumbled on her notes about Zyklon while surfing and then excitedly mentioned this to his wife. These were the questions I needed to investigate.

Given how Kelly reacted to our inquiries, I wasn't counting on the NYPD to provide me much in the way of background on Mr. Jones. Desperate times called for desperate measures and I had to bring in the heavy guns. I had to go to the interns. I walked down the hall to see Frank.

"Hey Frank."

"Francine, I hardly see you anymore. I'm all confused as to whether you still work for me or not."

"Me too. All I know is money keeps showing up in my bank account every other week so I must be working for somebody."

"What's up?"

"Zyklon. You have any industrious interns with Internet savvy willing to do something more substantial than delivering tapes or fetching coffee?"

"Yeah, I have one. Her name's Heather Abernathy. Sharp and a go-getter. She is a rare intern who actually applied for the job, not someone who's here because she someone's daughter."

"Great. I need her to get me some background info on somebody. Nothing much. I just don't have the time."

"Sounds fine. I'll have her see you."

An hour later, Heather walked into my office. She was petite with short light brown hair and overly big glasses. I guess mousy would be an accurate adjective. I was trusting that her nerdy appearance was an indication of what she could do in finding information on James Jones.

I laid out what I needed. I thought she understood what I wanted but her voice was so soft that it was impossible to hear or understand her. She departed my office, leaving me wondering what if anything I was going to get.

The next day she came back. I was on the phone with my back to the door. When I hung up and turned around I nearly jumped out of my seat to see her sitting there. I had no idea how long she'd been in my office, patiently waiting.

"Hi Heather. You find anything?"

"This man is almost as boring as I am."

She caught me off guard with her self-deprecating comment and I couldn't help but burst out laughing. I was about to correct her but I couldn't help but to agree with her. Instead, I asked for details.

"How so?"

"He grew up in a small town in Indiana and is married to his childhood sweetheart. He has two kids, James, Jr. who's eight and Emily, who's five. He went to college at The Citadel in South Carolina where he majored in computer science. He served in the army for three years after which he went to work for the NYPD where he's been for the past twelve years. He's a lifelong Chicago Bears and Chicago Cubs fan, although he does go to the occasional Mets game.

"There's nothing unusual about his financials. No big deposits or withdrawals that would be red flags."

"You were able to access his financials?"

"Don't ask."

Another attempt at humor, but I wasn't going to react or probe any further.

"Anything more?"

"No, just boring. No criminal history, not even a parking ticket."

"Did you find any connection between Jones and Detective Kelly."

"Nothing that I could see. I checked his credit cards and did not see anything like hotel or restaurant charges that would give hints of an assignation."

"Assignation?"

"You know, an affair?"

"I know what the word means. I was just surprised to hear it used in casual conversation. You haven't done anything illegal, have you? Delving into financials and credit cards?"

Heather gave me a look.

"I know, don't ask. So I won't."

"I also looked at Jones's cell phone history. There was nothing out of the ordinary. He calls his wife a lot. But he did get one call from a blocked number that lasted thirteen minutes. I tried, but I couldn't get the number."

"When was the call?"

"Three days ago."

"That is interesting. Anything more?"

"Nope, that's about it."

"Thank you so much, Heather. You've been extremely helpful. I really appreciate it."

"Have I helped you?"

"Very much so."

"If there's anything more I can do for you, let me know. I do have to admit that I was nervous and apprehensive when Frank said you wanted to talk to me."

I was shocked.

"I'm that intimidating?"

"Not that I've talked to you but you're one of my heroes. I didn't know what to expect."

"Well, I'm glad I got to know you and would be happy to work with you again."

She left. I really did want to work with her again. There was something endearing about her, and that doesn't even touch on the quality of her work. Despite all the information she gave me, all I had about James Jones were questions. Most importantly, who was the owner of this blocked number with whom he talked for thirteen minutes?

I called Will and laid out everything Heather had told me. I wanted to see if the FBI could help in uncovering the blocked number.

"How did you get this information? No, wait. I don't want to know. As a sworn law enforcement officer, I'd be obliged to investigate and I'm sure you don't want me arresting whoever it was that illegally obtained all this info. Furthermore, in order to determine who the blocked person is, I would have to get a warrant. In order to get a warrant, I have to convince a judge that there is probable cause of a crime being committed based on legally-obtained evidence, which I do not have."

"Okay, okay. I get your point."

"I'm not trying to be difficult. I just need more to work with. Store away what you've learned. It may come in handy later. You'd be surprised how often that happens, usually when you least expect it. Something will happen that'll trigger you to remember and you'll make the link."

"Great, but in the meantime, the Zyklon Killer kills again."

"And if he does, it's his sin, not yours."

"Tell that to the next Wendy Smith."

"That's why I love you so much."

24

There was still the issue of the *Munich 7*. I had a list of six SS Officers who were purportedly part of this group. Who was the seventh? Was it Hans Georg Steiner, the man that Israelis thought they killed in the botched raid? If so, were any of his descendants the next potential victims of the killer?

I dug Ari Klarsfeld card out of my purse and dialed the number. After ringing a few times, he picked up.

"Hello, Francine. How are you today."

It gave me a shiver that he identified me from the number. The card I had given him had my office number, not the cell number from which I was now calling. I guess in his line of work, he had to know such things.

"I'm fine, Ari. And you?"

"I'm doing well. It's exceptionally hot in Tel Aviv this afternoon but, like you Americans, many Israelis have become slaves to their air conditioning units. How can I help you today?"

"Hans Georg Steiner. I meant to mention him when we met. Is he the seventh of the *Munich 7*?"

"Ah, *Herr Qualitätskontrolle*. He's not the ideal way to start off a conversation with an Israeli. His botched raid still gnaws at us. In answer to your question, yes, he is rumored to be part of the mysterious *Munich 7* group."

"Do you have any information on what ultimately happened to him?"

"Only rumors. After we got Eichmann, we were over-confident and felt we could catch any Nazi fugitive. That lasted until the Steiner fiasco. After that, we laid low, which gave him and other Nazis the opportunity to change identities yet again and relocate. One rumor is that he fled to America, but that is unsubstantiated. I am sorry I cannot give you anything more."

"Thanks, Ari. Be well."

This was another piece of information that might not appear useful now but should be stored away that may be useful at some later time. In the meantime, I had to return to my real day job.

The presidential campaign was becoming more heated and more pointed. The final primaries were held and both candidates, The Reverend and The Governor, had each secured enough delegates to lock up their respective nominations. They just needed the convention to formalize and validate the process.

Since the candidates had now been unofficially narrowed to these two men, the attacks began. It was curious how neither of the two men themselves resorted to the name calling and mud-slinging. That didn't stop their surrogates and campaign officials from resorting to such tactics. Each side, of course, claimed that its candidate wanted to take the high road but because the other candidate started with the negativity, he had to respond in kind.

The Governor's representatives called his opponent an incompetent and uninformed demagogue whose message was one of hate, fear and divisiveness. McKenzie's aim, Kent claimed, was to establish a theocratic state. McKenzie would toss out the Constitution and replace it with the Bible, Kent trumpeted.

For his part, the main theme for McKenzie's spokespeople—most notably Pete Connors—was that Kent had been bought and sold by the corporations. He was in the pocket of the special interests, not the people. With Kent, it would be the same old story in Washington, with no change in the status quo.

Issues & Answers this week was going to focus on the two candidates, their policies and plans. Two Congressmen—Bradley Anson of Utah for McKenzie and Sheldon Wayland of Connecticut for Kent—would act as surrogates for their respective candidates. Al Harrison of the Times would join Richard and me as the panelists grilling the two Congressmen.

I read up on both surrogates and watched taped interviews they gave over the past couple of years. Both men were the far extremes of their respective parties. In truth, neither represented the mainstream beliefs of either their respective parties or candidates.

Anson was a blustery blowhard who was not shy about giving his opinion on anything and everything. He was a creationist and climate change denier. He believed in following the intent of the founding fathers, which he interpreted to mean that any American should be able to carry any firearm he wanted whenever and wherever he wanted. He believed that government taxation and regulation were the evils that kept America from achieving greatness. He wanted the United States to end foreign entanglements and wars.

Wayland was soft-spoken but equally committed to his causes—universal healthcare, social justice and gender/racial/religious equality. He believed in sensible gun control measures and banning the sale of assault weapons to the average citizen. He supported an equitable tax system that required the rich and the corporations to pay their fair share. He believed in the role of government in regulating the excesses of industry. However, he could also be quite vague when it came to paying for all the things government was supposed to do.

Richard did not let either know that the other would be attending, hoping to get a more spontaneous interchange. What he did not count on was them showing up and then turning around and leaving as soon as they found out the other was also there.

Despite their profound political differences, Anson and Wayland were close friends. They played tennis together all the time. The previous week ago, however, they had a blow-up behind closed doors that spilled out into the public. They'd probably kiss and make up in the next couple of weeks but at the moment, they could not stand to be together in any room smaller than the House chambers.

Most people would be totally rattled by such a turn of events, but not Richard. He always had a Plan B. As soon as he realized that neither congressman would stay, he was on the phone calling other legislators, government officials and pundits to fill the void. There is no shortage of people who love to hear themselves talk and it didn't take long for replacements to be confirmed. There were two other Congressmen—my old friend Pete Connors from Georgia for McKenzie and an up and coming liberal representative from Massachusetts, William Pryor, for Kent—who could get themselves to our studio in DC with no problem.

We would patch them into our broadcast.

I was upset that all my research on Anson and Wayland had gone to waste. Connors was a known quantity to me but I knew nothing about Pryor. I was counting on Richard to do his usual job of polishing the rough edges that his co-panelists and I may exhibit.

The show went off without a hitch. Richard began with not-so-subtle digs at Anson and Wayland. In essence, he called them both thin-skinned, petty cowards, saying that the show was better off without them. He then introduced the two Congressmen who would be participating, heaping copious amounts of praise and accolades on each of them.

I'll have to say that there is probably not one issue on which I am in agreement with Pete Connors but I've come to have a grudging admiration for him as time has gone on. He's so far right that I find many of his ideas scary, but he's consistent. No one can ever accuse him of flip-flopping or shifting positions to buy votes. I also get the sense that he respects his opponents and their right to have opinions different from his own. Lastly, he's both intelligent and civil. That's a rare combination these days.

I could see why Pryor was a comer. He was young, good-looking, articulate, smart and had an easy-going way about him. He and Connors had intense debates on everything we threw at them but they never sniped at each other. They were obviously having a good time throwing their ideas out there and then defending them from the onslaught from the opposition. They both proved to be master fencers, thrusting and parrying over the course of a full hour.

When the show was done, we were all exhausted and exhilarated at the same time.

"Best show ever!" exulted Richard. "We should invite our guests at the last minute from now on. I thought the spontaneity today really added to the show."

"You think we convinced a few undecided voters to go for one candidate or the other?"

"Maybe, but what we did today is even more important. After today, no voter who watched our show can claim they went to the polls uninformed. We can't ask for anything more than that."

It was always rewarding and fun to be around someone as enthusiastic as Richard. He truly loved and believed in what he did for a living. He reminded me of my mother when she was doing her community organizing work. She'd come home in the evening so inspired about what she did during the day that I often couldn't get a word in edgewise about my day. But I didn't mind one bit. I fed off her enthusiasm. I was doing the same now.

I received a call from the network that Katrina had been cleared to return to full duty on the presidential campaign. I could tell from the tone of the phone call that the network executives would prefer that I stay on the McKenzie campaign and they would find another gig for Katrina.

I didn't think they had anything against her but they didn't want to change horses yet again midstream. Viewers like consistency. Going from Katrina to me and then back to Katrina was confusing. I thought the two of us were relatively interchangeable, but the execs didn't agree. I was polling pretty well these days from my appearances on *Issues & Answers* and they wanted to exploit whatever popularity I may have had.

I told the network that I had made it clear that I would do this job until such time that Katrina was able to return and I was going to stick to that commitment. This had been Katrina's chance of a lifetime that bad luck had sidetracked. I wasn't about to abet that bad luck and keep her from coming back. She wouldn't forgive me, and neither would I.

If Katrina felt she needed me to assist her for a period of time, I was more than willing to do that. But if she believed she was strong enough to go it alone, then so be it.

Frankly, I was leaning towards not wanting to continue. The Zyklon investigation was not getting as much of my time as it should. Plus, Richard had made it clear that he wanted me to be a permanent fixture on *Issues & Answers*. That in itself was a dream come true. I could just imagine my mother, if she were still alive, bragging about her daughter, the talking head!

I used to watch *Issues & Answers* and all the other comparable shows thinking that it seemed so easy. Now I realize that the reason the shows look so effortless is that a ton of work goes into each show. I've been lucky that I could skate through the shows I've done on the level of preparation I've put in thus far, but I knew that wasn't sustainable. For one thing, I consider myself a pretty intelligent person but the people we get on the show both as guests and as panelists are off-the-charts brilliant, experts in their various respective fields. In order to not be totally intimidated by these people, I need to be as prepared as I can be. Traveling around on an exhausting presidential campaign doesn't give you a lot of time for such preparation.

With all that was going on and with my newly emerging feelings of inadequacy, the one thing on which I was making a special effort to nurture was my relationship with my friends and family. I had to carve out time for Jonas. I disrespected him once; I wasn't going to do it again. Rosa and Stella appeared to be adjusting to my scheduled but Albert was reaching a tough age and needed me to be there for him.

With all this floating around in my head, I gave Katrina a call.

"Hi, Katrina. Welcome back!"

"Thanks, Francine. It sure feels wonderful to be healthy again."

"You ready to tag along with the Reverend again?"

"I don't know, Francine. I spoke with Cates, you know, the VP at the network, and he made it clear they would prefer to keep things the way they are. It's all right. I don't blame you in the least. The main regret I have is not going to the convention in Los Angeles."

"Those bastards. Katrina, you didn't give them an answer yet, did you?"

"No, I told them I'd like until morning."

"Good. Don't do anything. I'll be back to you within the hour. Just hang tight."

I hung up and dialed Richard.

"Hey, Richard. You weren't just blowing smoke when you told me how much I added to the show, were you?"

"Of course not! You've become an invaluable asset."

"Good. I quit."

"What?"

I proceeded to tell them what they were doing to Katrina and that I couldn't work for a network that acted in such an underhanded way.

"Don't do anything. Give me a few minutes."

It worked like a charm. I still wasn't high enough up the food chain to get things done at the executive level, but Richard Leitz was. Ten minutes later my phone rang, it was Katrina. She was as excited as a schoolgirl.

"What did you do? Cates called me back. It was all a big misunderstanding." I could practically see her doing air quotes as she said this. "They're sending a car for me in a couple hours to get on a plane to head out to Reno for a rally. Then it will be over to LA for the convention. I don't know how to thank you, Francine."

"For what? I just brought them to their senses about what a great reporter they have in Katrina Turow. Knock 'em dead out there."

Ten minutes later, my phone rang again.

"Hi, Richard."

"Now, about that conversation we had."

"You mean the one about the lineup for next week's show? You know, the one we're doing together."

25

Katrina was back on the trail with The Reverend again and she seemed more energized than ever. McKenzie made a special point of reaching out to her to welcome her back and he seemed much less antagonistic towards the media than he had been. He made sure to tell Katrina that he missed me and hoped I would be able to attend the convention.

I would like to have attended one or both of the conventions but, like I mentioned, my plate was pretty full. In addition, I went to one four years earlier. Frank had gotten me in and, quite frankly since there was no drama to conventions anymore, one was enough for me.

Both conventions had the expected results with no drama whatsoever. All the requisite speeches were made, party platforms were drawn up and approved and everyone left with a fervor that would lead them to victory in November. Party faithful expressed certainty that their side was the only way to restore America back to its predominance on the world stage. We analyzed and dissected these views on our weekly *Issues & Answers* program.

There were no surprises for vice presidential picks for either party. The Reverend went with Pete Connors. Governor Kent selected Senator Patricia Rinz from Wisconsin. She was a solid choice, a competent two-term Senator from a swing state.

America was working like it was supposed to work. The voters were being informed and would ultimately make their decision.

There were the traditional bumps in the polls for each party after its convention concluded, but then the polls settled down to a twenty to twenty-five point lead for Kent. This lead only increased after their first of three debates. Kent picked McKenzie apart on every single issue. The Reverend's rebuttals only dug the hole deeper. It was a sad and depressing thing to watch.

The day after the first debate a messenger arrived at the station with an envelope for me. In it were two tickets to a Peter Kent fundraiser at the Grand Hyatt sent to me by Alexander Kent. The younger Kent enclosed a note telling that it had been way too long since we had seen each other and he wanted me to attend with a guest of my choice, his compliments.

The campaign must have been flush with cash to give away high priced tickets like this. Either that or the campaign was hoping to get good coverage from me, but since I hadn't ever been that tough on Kent, that didn't seem the case. I settled for Alexander being a nice guy and being sincere that he'd like to see me again and this seemed like a golden opportunity to do so.

I checked with Emma. She'd stay with the kids until I got home. Now I had to figure out who would attend with me. Will was out in Seattle at an FBI Forensics Conference. I went up to Jonas to see if he'd like to go.

"I appreciate the offer, Frannie, but do I look like the type who has a tuxedo laying around? And this ain't a body that can go into a store and buy one off the rack. Anyway, Eunice and I are trying to make a go of it again. She's been real sweet since the accident. Since you were the one that broke us up before, I don't want to push my luck."

"Wait a second. I broke you up?"

"Not exactly, but Eunice is the real jealous type and she thought we had a thing when we used to spend so much time together."

"I hope you disabused her of that idea right away."

"Oh, I did. Many, many, many times but Eunice is rather headstrong and believes what she wants to believe. The explosion made her see the light and I don't want to set her off again."

"You and she are a couple pieces of work, J."

"Ain't that the truth. Give me a hug before you walk away, ya hear?"

I asked Frank but he and his wife had tickets to the opera. They were going to see a special performance of La Traviata at the Met after which they were going to have a romantic dinner at Tavern on the Green and maybe a carriage ride around the park. I conceded that it sounded a lot nicer than a rubber chicken fundraiser.

I was now down to my B Team dinner companions when I had an idea. I had promised Ari Klarsfeld a dinner for his help. Maybe I should see if he was in town. There would be no doubt that he'd have a tux at the ready, being that he traveled in diplomatic circles. This could even be amusing to him, given the line of work he was in. I called his number.

"Francine, delightful to hear from you again. You don't have any more ex-Nazis you need information on, do you?"

"No, not this time," I laughed. "I'm calling for something much more mundane. Are you by any chance in New York right now and if so, are you available this evening?"

"Yes, on both counts. Mundane or not, you have me intrigued."

"I have two tickets for a fundraiser for Peter Kent tonight at the Grand Hyatt. My husband is unavailable and anyone else I'd ask doesn't have a tux for the occasion. I hate to make it sound like you're so low a choice but would you like to attend with me?"

I was sure that sounded as awkward to him as it did to me and he'd tell me to get lost.

"I'd love to. An outsider getting an intimate peek at the internal workings of American politics and with such delightful company? Who could resist such an invitation?"

"It'll probably be a collection of boring speeches, but if it takes such an illusion to keep the seat next to me from being empty, I won't try to dispel that illusion."

"What time do the gala festivities begin?"

"Eight. It's black tie."

"I wouldn't have it any other way. I'm looking forward to seeing you in a gown. I'll meet you in front of the Hyatt at a quarter to eight."

"Great. See you then."

His comment about wanting to see me in a gown made me nervous. I hope it was simply banter and he wasn't expecting anything more than dinner and pleasant conversation. I made a point of telling him that Will was "unavailable" instead of out of town hoping that it would convey that I wasn't interested in more.

However, my mind did momentarily flashback to the short fling I had had with Farad Sahari before I met Will. Like Ari, Farad was a suave, handsome internationalist and both came from the same part of the world. Farad and I were only just beginning to get to know each other before Alan killed him in a jealous rage. I sometimes wonder if we had a chance if he had lived. We were from such different worlds. Just our religious and cultural differences alone seemed insurmountable, but I still think of him occasionally.

I knew nothing about Ari personally. He was about Will's age, was Jewish and descended from famous Nazi hunters. That was about it. He was engaging and intelligent and it was a pleasure to spend time with him. That much I knew.

Enough of this schoolgirl dreaming. I had some work to do and then I had to get myself out to Queens in time to shower, do up my hair and makeup, dress and get back to Manhattan before 7:45. I figured I'd take a subway home but arrange for a car service to the affair; make that to the fundraiser.

The car hit a bit of traffic so I didn't arrive at the Hyatt until about five minutes of eight. When the car pulled up in front on 42nd Street, Ari was standing there waiting. He did look dashing, I must say. He opened my door and helped me out.

"As I guessed, that gown was worth waiting for. You look wonderful."

My periwinkle blue, form-fitting, off-the-shoulder gown did compliment my skin and eyes perfectly. What I was most proud of was that the last time I wore this gown was prior to Rosa's birth and I was still able to fit into it. More precisely, I was able to once again fit into this gown after a lot of hard work to regain my figure after the birth of my daughter.

Ari gave me his arm and we walked into the ballroom together. Alexander was already there, speaking with a group of people. When he noticed me, he smiled, excused himself and headed over to greet me. He gave me a big hug.

"Francine, I'm so sorry for the last-minute notice but I'm so glad you were able to attend."

It was only then that he seemed to notice there was a man standing beside me. He had never met Will but he knew that my husband was older than I and probably assumed that Ari was Will. I was about to introduce Ari when an aide came by and advised Alexander that his father needed him to start the festivities. Alexander excused himself and headed up towards the dais. We went to our table.

At our table were Wesley Smith, a Black multimillionaire who had made his fortune in software development and his partner, Olive, who herself was a brilliant consultant to start-up businesses; Vincent Mazzei, an environmental attorney and, Becky, his wife; Alan Bookman, a venture capitalist and his date whose name I didn't catch.

We sat down and the two seats next to me were vacant until Diane Marrow and her partner, Susan, hurried in to occupy them. Diane was a well-known—and controversial—affordable housing advocate and organizer. I'd never met her or covered her but I'd seen plenty of stories on her over the years. My hunch was that she, like Ari and me, had been given complimentary tickets.

"Ms. Marrow, it's a pleasure to meet you. My name is."

"I know quite well who you are Ms. Vega."

I wasn't sure where she was going with this, whether she was going to be hostile and antagonistic or whether she had simply seen me on TV. Then a tear came to her eye.

"Your mother was my idol. I'd only met her a few times but I try to emulate her every day. She was such a champion of the downtrodden and underprivileged. It was such a loss for the world when she passed away."

"Thank you."

"I'm so glad you have chosen a field in which you can follow in her footsteps. Don't ever lose that."

"I sure hope not to. Let me introduce you to my friend, Ari Klarsfeld."

They shook hands.

"And what do you do, Mr. Klarsfeld?"

It occurred to me that Ari had never told me exactly what he did so I was curious to hear his response.

"I'm with the Israeli government, I work at the consulate in cultural affairs."

"That sounds fascinating," Diane responded. "I've often heard the term cultural affairs, but I never have been told what that means."

"I spread Israeli culture and I have affairs."

He let that hang in the air in an uncomfortable silence and then he burst out in a hearty laugh.

"I'm sorry for that attempt at humor but honestly, I've never figured out exactly what it means myself."

Just then Alexander approached the microphone. We all turned our attention to him.

"I'd like to welcome you all and thank you for coming. You may ask why we even need evenings like this. I'm sure that many of you have said to yourselves that Governor Kent has such a commanding lead that it would take an event of biblical proportions to change the expected outcome. Well, to borrow a story my father's worthy opponent continually trots out, I'm sure that Goliath went into his match with David with the same attitude. We cannot rest until the votes are counted in November and your contributions and attendance tonight will help us toward the goal of serving this great country of ours.

"So, I'll let you enjoy your meals but be assured that we are chaining the doors shut so that you have to endure me droning on once again before we get to the main event, my father, the Governor of this Great State of New York and the future President of the United States."

We had our dinners, the main course being a choice of beef tenderloin or salmon, with appropriate appetizers and desserts. The conversation settled into small talk on various topics. I spoke with everyone at our table but more naturally gravitated to Diane and Susan for sustained conversation. Ari seemed equally at ease interacting with the capitalists as he did with the housing organizers but nothing in any of his conversations that I overheard gave me any clue about the man. He was adroit in skillfully sidestepping any question he did not want to answer about himself. The man remained a mystery to the point I still wasn't sure whether he was expecting more from me later in the night.

We were sipping our coffee when Alexander came back to the podium.

"As promised, I'm here to bore you once again but I promise that I won't be long. I know you're anxious to get to the main event but he'd be angry with me if I didn't give him an appropriate setup. So here I go.

"I think everyone in this room will agree that this is a most unusual Presidential campaign. Never have the choices been more stark and obvious. On the one side we have competence, experience, a verified record of success, devotion to the Constitution and a love for America.

"The only part of this that our opponent shares is that he loves this country. I don't doubt that. But the man has absolutely no track record nor has he shown any level of competency in much of anything nor does he have any experience beyond running a small-town church. That is important; don't get me wrong. The number of people who get their spiritual guidance from these small churches I would guess run into the tens or even hundreds of millions, but it hardly prepares you to be President of the United States.

"But let me return to the love of America my father and Reverend McKenzie share. In many campaigns, one of the issues that starkly separate the candidates is their respective military service. This is not one of those campaigns. Each candidate's military service to his country was exemplary. Both served with distinction in Operation Desert Storm.

"We were bouncing around ideas of things to try on the campaign and someone threw out the idea of attacking The Reverend's military service since he was only a chaplain. The Governor cut him off before he could even finish the sentence. 'That man,' he said, 'was on the front lines with only a Bible to protect him. You try that sometime and let me know if you survive. That takes a special kind of character and bravery that not many people have. I'll let that suggestion slide this time because we're just throwing out ideas here. That happens to be a terrible one. But everyone here should be on notice that I will not tolerate such talk in the future and if I hear of it again, that person will be out on his or her ear.'

"My father knows of no greater service to our country than to serve in the military. He put his own life on hold to go to Iraq as an infantryman and then again served with distinction as an officer in Afghanistan after 9/11. My father always claimed it made a better man of him.

"It was his dedication that made me enter The Citadel for my undergraduate studies and then to dedicate three years in the Army. I was lucky enough to be selected for an elite Special Ops unit. I'd tell you what we did, but then I'd have to kill all of you."

Laughter erupted throughout the ballroom. I would have joined in the laughter but two things he just said—The Citadel and Special Ops—jumped out at me. I remembered Will's advice. You collect evidence and input along the way. Some of it is useless. Some of it is useful right away. The rest gets stored away and may be useful at a later time. I had just recently heard of someone else, James Jones, who had attended The Citadel. And Alan had written of Lawson actually having known the Zyklon Killer in the mid-1990s but it is impossible to track the killer down because Lawson was doing highly classified work with a Special Ops unit at the time. Perhaps Alexander could be a link in both cases. Perhaps he had run across Jones at school or had known whom Lawson associated with when he worked in Special Ops.

Both cases were long shots. The Citadel is a fairly big school with over 3,500 enrolled students. I didn't even know if the years they attended coincided. And I am sure there are multiple Special Ops units in the army so Alexander's and Lawson's paths most likely never crossed.

But in both cases it was my responsibility as a journalist to get the answers. And I had to do it quickly. Alexander was bound to head out on the road again and I may not have a chance to talk with him again until after the election. I reached into my bag as surreptitiously as I could and pulled out my phone. I was hoping I could discreetly send a text without it seeming too rude. If I was called on it I could claim that I was a concerned mother who had a year and a half old infant at home that I needed to check up on. That's a foolproof standby.

Keeping the phone under the table I composed a text to Heather.

Heather, Could you check on when Alexander Kent went to The Citadel and whether it was the same time James Jones did. Also, I'd like to know when Alexander served in the Army. Please get back to me ASAP. Thanks.

Fifteen minutes later, shortly after Governor Kent had started his speech, my phone vibrated with a return text from Heather.

Kent attended The Citadel from 1989 thru 1993, the same years as Jones. Kent went directly into the Army after college and served from 1993 to 1998.

I put my phone away. This could be a great break and perhaps Alexander could give some clues that could ultimately lead to the identity of the Zyklon Killer. Or it could be yet another in a long line of dead ends.

He may well never have met or even heard of either James Jones or Jacob Lawson. But I'd never know unless I asked.

I thought back to Detective Kelly telling me she had direct orders to back off on investigating the Zyklon Killer. It may be related to some high-level economic development deal in the works between New York and Texas that New York officials did not want scuttled due to the investigation of someone who had already executed. By all appearances, this directive came from the highest levels of the government, perhaps from the Governor himself. I had to be careful how I asked my questions. Otherwise, Alexander might shut down completely.

The Governor completed his remarks. It was basically his stump speech tailored for the New York audience; he added nothing new. At the end was a receiving line for everyone to wish the Governor well in the upcoming election. Ari and I made our way up to Alexander and the Governor.

"Thank you so much for inviting me, Alexander. It was a great affair. Best of luck to you, Governor. Let me introduce my companion for the evening. This is Ari Klarsfeld. He works at the Israeli Consulate."

"My pleasure," the Governor said as he extended his hand. "Klarsfeld? By any chance are you related to the famed Nazi-hunters?"

"Yes, they were my aunt and uncle. I share their passion in my blood, I'm afraid. As a matter of fact, I first met Ms. Vega here when she was doing some research on a group of ex-Nazi SS Officers who escaped after the war. They were known as the *Munich 7*. Ms. Vega is quite the researcher herself as she was able to discover that the victims of the Zyklon Killer were each descended from one of these officers. The only officer whose descendants have not been identified is Hans Georg Steiner."

I could tell that Ari was looking for some sort of reaction from the Governor and his son. There was nothing as far as I could tell. I was curious whether Ari saw something I didn't. I was also curious to see where the conversation would lead after that but we didn't get the chance as we were summarily dismissed.

"That does sound fascinating and it is certainly a pleasure to meet you Mr. Klarsfeld and to see you again, Ms. Vega, but I have many guests to say goodnight to," said the Governor as he hurried us along.

We gathered our coats from the check area and headed out to 42nd Street. Only then did Ari speak up.

"Let's walk for a little bit. It's a beautiful night and there are some things I want to discuss with you."

"Okay."

We walked down 42nd Street towards the East River and then turned left on Third Avenue. I felt a little conspicuous in my gown and high heels but I didn't mind. I was anxious to hear what he had to say.

"Interesting reaction by your Governor, no?" Ari asked.

"He couldn't get us from away from us quick enough, could he?"

"He spent plenty of time chatting with other guests, so I can only surmise that it was something I said that hurried us along."

"What in particular do you think he reacted to?"

Ari paused for a few seconds, weighing what he should say next.

"We have more information about Hans Georg Steiner than I have let on. We lost track of him in Argentina but we happen to know that he fled that country and came to the United States in 1951 under a false passport. We almost trapped him at Idlewild Airport, which you know as JFK, but he eluded us and came in through Boston. He changed identities again and we lost him totally at that point. We never did find him."

"Do you think he's still alive?"

"No. He was in his forties during the war so that would put him well into his hundreds. I hardly think that's probable. But what we do think is that he married and had children."

"Do you think the Zyklon Killer may be after one or more of those children?"

"It may sound callous but I really don't care. If descendants of SS Officers get killed off, it really is not any of my concern. I'm sorry. I know you felt a closeness to one of those descendants, Wendy Smith, but I can't as a Jew feel such a closeness."

"Then why do you care if Steiner is dead? I'm sure you don't believe in visiting the sins of the father down on the children."

"You are correct. I do not. But what I do care about is the gold. If the $400 million in gold is still out there, I am determined to find it and give it back to those from whom it was stolen. That gold was ripped out of Jewish mouths and from the wedding rings wrenched off their fingers. It was from their legacy. The money, if found, can do a lot to help Jews who are in need. It can't bring back the dead or make the grotesque violation they endured any more palatable, but maybe it can help eliminate some present suffering they are now feeling."

"So the Israeli government believes the gold is real, not just a myth?"

"We really don't know, but it is worth our effort to continue pursuing it until proven otherwise."

"You think Steiner's children know where the gold is?"

"I haven't a clue, but I'm not going to rest until I find out."

"What does all this have to do with Governor Kent?"

"We've had suspicions for some time about the Governor's background. His biography doesn't add up. He was born in 1961 to German parents who supposedly emigrated from Germany a dozen or so years earlier. We've searched for the father's name, Maximilian Kent and could find no record of him anywhere in Germany. Granted, many records were destroyed or in shambles after the war so it could all be true. Still, we had our doubts.

"When you called, I jumped at the opportunity to accompany you not only for your charming company but also to perhaps acquire some physical evidence that we could use for analysis."

"And did you find such evidence?"

"We'll see."

He pulled a handkerchief out of his coat pocket. He unfolded it to show me a cocktail glass.

"I lifted this after Alexander Kent put it down on a tray. We should be able to lift enough DNA off of it for comparison purposes."

"Comparison with what?"

"Believe it or not, we have tissue samples taken from Steiner. His appendix burst while he was commandant. The SS doctor was away so they forced a Jewish doctor to operate on him. The operation obviously was a success but a few days later they took the doctor out and shot him for violating the purity laws. But before he was killed, he preserved some skin and tissue in a sealed glass container and hid it away in a place only he and his bunkmate knew about. His scientific training told him that it could be useful someday.

"His bunkmate survived the war and carried the sample with him, ultimately to Israel. It was well enough preserved that a few years ago our scientists were able to characterize the DNA. We'll see if this matches."

"And if it does?"

"It could mean nothing but it is information that could be useful at some later time."

"I've gotten a lot of that recently."

"It could also mean that the Governor and his son may be in a lot of danger, if the Zyklon Killer is still alive as you suspect. I remember you saying that Wendy Smith had no clue that her great-grandfather was a Nazi. It could well be the same here. I'll let you know what we find out."

"Thanks, Ari."

The next day I went to the office and I called Heather in.

"Heather, I'd like you to do some research for me. Does Frank have you doing anything important right now?"

"Nothing that couldn't wait."

I made a mental note to double check with Frank. In her eagerness to work with me, Heather would tell me anything.

"I want you to find out everything you can on Governor Peter Kent's father. From what I understand, there are a lot of holes in his life story. Do your magic and fill in as many of those holes as you can. Got it?"

"Absolutely! I'll get right on it."

I went back and forth on whether to make the next phone call I wanted to make. Ultimately, I placed the call to Edward McKenzie, The Reverend's brother and campaign manager.

"Hello, Francine. This is a pleasant surprise."

"Hi, Edward. How's your brother's campaign going?"

"Quite well, actually."

The latest poll numbers had The Reverend down by twenty-three points and there wasn't a single battleground state where he held a statistically significant lead. Edward was obviously lying but it was his job to remain optimistic.

"I've lost track, are you still at the State Department or did you resign to run Malcolm's campaign?"

"I'm on a leave of absence at the moment."

"But I assume you could have access to State Department records if you want, right?"

"I have my ways. Why?"

"I'm doing background stuff on the campaign. I'd like to see what sort of official information there is on Peter Kent's father."

"Whoa! That's a can of worms I'm not sure I can or want to open. What do you need it for?"

"Background stuff. With your brother's autobiography— congratulations on the book being Number 1 on the New York Times Best Seller list for so long, by the way—the story of your parents is well known. Kent's parents, on the other hand, are a mystery. His father emigrated from Czechoslovakia in the early fifties, lived in upstate New York but when you ask people from the area about him, they know very little. He kept to himself, is the common reply."

"I just don't know what I can do for you. It would seem to smack of illegality or at least it would be unethical for me to use my position to make this type of inquiry for information related to the campaign."

"I understand," I responded in the most dejected voice I could muster without sounding too over the top. "I'm just trying to use my sources. I'll go through the general State Department press office to see what I can get."

"Good luck with that. You should get a response about three years into the Kent Administration," he responded ruefully. He paused and I didn't respond on purpose to let the silence hang there. Finally, he sighed and then spoke. I knew I had him.

"I know a guy that will keep things entirely confidential. I'll make the request and ask that he send you the information directly."

"Thanks, Edward."

"I'm glad you and my brother are playing nice these days."

"Me too. Good luck."

"Thanks, we need it."

After I hung up I sat there wondering why I was going through these motions and what I would do with this information once I got it. The answer to the first question was easy. It's news and it's what I do. Any investigative journalist worth his or her salt given this opening would dive in to see where such a story could lead.

The second question was more problematic. What if Peter Kent's father was a notorious SS officer? What good could come of reporting it other than feeding the public's insatiable need for sensationalistic tidbits? Could releasing such information have the potential to turn the campaign? Would I simply be besmirching a good man who would probably be a terrific President because he is descended from a devil? Does being descended from a devil negate all the good a man's done throughout his life? Can any of us be held accountable for what our parents may have done?

The reason I settled on was that the Zyklon Killer was still out there and his next victim could be Kent. If it were true that Steiner was Kent's father and he didn't know about it, I could be doing something to help save his life.

I took a deep breath and told myself not to rush into things. It was no use to fret over what may not happen. I would see what Ari and Heather came up with and take it from there.

26

It did not take Heather long to get back to me. The next morning, she walked into my office.

"The man was a ghost. The only things I could find on him were that he was married to June Wentworth on August 3, 1956, and he died on March 30, 1984. There wasn't even a mention of a funeral service. He just died. There are no public pictures of the man. I couldn't find any employment history. I couldn't find any church affiliation or social clubs. Nothing."

"Interesting, but at this point not unexpected. Thanks."

Heather started to walk away, obviously dejected that she could not give me more.

"Heather, hold on."

She turned around and eagerly came back.

"Close the door," I instructed.

I then proceeded to pull out a picture of Hans Georg Steiner taken probably in about 1939 or 1940. He was in his full SS uniform, complete with hat with the skull directly over the brim and the Nazi eagle above that. He stared into the camera with a smile that expressed the confidence that Germany was well on its way to conquering the world.

"How are your Photoshop skills?"

"Pretty good."

If they were anything like any other of her skills, I was sure she was massively underestimating her abilities.

"Do you think you can remove the hat and uniform from this picture and make him look like a regular guy in a nondescript shirt?"

Heather did a double take when she saw the picture of a Nazi SS officer.

"That shouldn't be difficult," she responded.

"I'm going to tell you something that cannot leave this room. You can't tell it to your family, your boyfriend or any of your friends."

"I don't really get along with my family or have a boyfriend or any close friends, for that matter."

It broke my heart not only that she said this but also that she believed it so matter-of-factly.

"I want you to promise."

"I promise, but you don't really need it. What kind of journalist would I make if I blabbed everything I heard?"

"Not a good one," I conceded. "I apologize for assuming otherwise. What I'm telling you that is confidential is that this Nazi, Hans Georg Steiner, may have been the father of Governor Peter Kent."

"I kind of figured that out. Why else would you have me researching Kent's father and then show me this picture?"

"You got me there. This is confidential because it may or may not be true and even if it is, we have to think through whether it's newsworthy enough to possibly influence a presidential election."

"Do you really think it could?"

"I don't know; I really don't. It could produce a big yawn on the part of the voters or it could be used to chip away at his credibility. The interesting thing is that many people have labeled much of the hateful things McKenzie spouts as being Nazi-like propaganda. It would be ironic if Kent is the one taken down because of a Nazi connection."

"My mind is spinning with that one."

"As you can see, that is why this information—or more precisely rumor—can't be discussed with anyone."

"I understand."

"Good. Now see what you can do with that picture. Don't do too good a job. It still has to look like a photo from the late 30s/early 40s when you're done."

Heather got up to leave but before she got to the door I called out to her.

"Oh, and I don't want to hear any more crap about you not having any close friends. You have at least one, remember that."

She smiled and left.

An hour later she came back.

"I hope this is what you're looking for. If not, I'm sure I can retouch it."

I took the picture from her.

"It's perfect, absolutely perfect. The hair looks like a style from the forties as does the shirt. You even kept the photographic technique and feel from that era intact."

"I had to go through a whole bunch of old pictures from back then to get it just so."

"All within an hour. You're amazing, Heather."

"Thank you."

"Are you up for a field trip tomorrow?"

"Am I? You bet I am?"

Her enthusiasm reminded me of myself when I was younger. I especially appreciated her response after I learned that she wasn't scheduled to work but would be cutting classes for the opportunity to work with me.

"Okay, then. Be back here tomorrow at around 7:30. I'll get us a car and we'll take a ride up to the Governor's hometown of Clearwood. It's about a four-hour drive. I hope to be back in the evening but bring a change of clothes in case it takes longer than expected and we'll share a room up there, if that's okay with you."

"You bet it is!"

After Heather left I went over to Jonas's station to see if he wanted to tag along. I didn't especially need him for this job. In fact, having him along with us might hurt us by making us less conspicuous in this tiny upstate New York town. Luckily, he had to be on assignment with another reporter so he couldn't make it but I could sense he appreciated being asked.

When I arrived at the office the next morning precisely at 7:30, Heather was waiting, as I expected she would be. We got into the Chrysler the office had allocated to me and we were on our way.

"So, what made you want to be a journalist, Heather?"

"I wasn't supposed to be. I was supposed to become a doctor. My parents are both doctors, my father a cardiac surgeon and my mother a pediatrician. I was expected to follow in their footsteps. When I didn't, they practically disowned me."

"You don't have to go into it if you don't want to."

"No, it's okay. It is what it is. Anyway, when I was young the son of the mayor of our town started convulsing. He was only four years old. They rushed him to the hospital where my mother was on call. My mother did what she could but, within a half hour, the boy passed away. The mayor and his wife blamed my mother and wanted her brought up on charges. The boy's body was whisked away and buried before any autopsy could be performed. The mayor was powerful and had everyone in his pocket. The cops, the courts, the ME, you name it.

"My mother was about to be charged when a TV reporter started looking at it and raised some questions. At that point the family decided they wanted to cremate the boy but the reporter was able to convince a State judge to issue an injunction and order an autopsy. It turned out that the wife was a heroin addict and the boy had swallowed some of her stash. My mother was exonerated and went on with her life and career.

"While my mother was appreciative of the reporter's efforts, she just thought he was doing his job and did not deserve any special credit or praise. I, on the other hand, was totally enthralled with what he did. He dug for truth and didn't stop until he got it. I was ten years old at the time, so I guess it was a bit early to be deciding on my profession, but I couldn't think of anything I'd rather do in my life. In any case, I knew I didn't want to go into medicine.

"When I reached high school, I made known my career choice, which precipitated a number of fights over how I was throwing my life away on such foolishness. When it came time for college, these fights only intensified. When I became a junior, my parents made it clear they would pay for the rest of my schooling only if I came to my senses and went to medical school. I would not so they cut me off without a penny. I paid for my remaining two years of college and am now paying for grad school myself."

"It's funny but I was also inspired by a newspaperman, Francisco Rosario, who helped my mother in battling a drug dealer in our building. In my case, my mother embraced my career choice decision. She thought I was pursuing a noble calling."

"And your father? What does he think?"

"I've never met my father. He abandoned my mother and me when I was a baby. He's probably somewhere in the Caribbean. Maybe he knows who I am and is proud of me. More likely, he'll figure out who I am and come looking for money some day."

"I'm sorry."

"Don't be. It is what it is."

"So what exactly are we doing today?"

"We're going to comb the town to see if anybody recognizes the picture."

We arrived at Clearwood at around noon. This town was so tiny it made The Reverend's Wayland look like a major metropolis. The town center consisted of a general store, a pizza joint and the town hall. We decided to start with the town hall.

It was an old wooden structure with a white clapboard exterior over which a huge cupola/bell tower presided. Inside was a hallway clad in oak paneling leading to various municipal offices. We went into the clerk's office. A fortyish severe looking woman sat behind the counter.

"Can I help you?"

"I hope so. My name is Francine Vega and this is Heather Abernathy. We're reporters working on a story. I was wondering if you might know this man. This photo was taken back in the war so if he's still alive he'd be in his nineties."

"He doesn't look familiar. Why are you looking for him?"

"It's a human interest story about a woman in Brooklyn who's also in her nineties looking for the love of her youth before she dies. All she has is this picture. Her mind is going so she can't remember his name but she knows he came from this town. My boss thought it worth a tank of gas to come up and check it out. You know how it is."

She laughed.

"Oh yes, I know how it is. Do or die, right? Anyway, he doesn't look familiar but I know someone who knows anybody and everybody who's lived in this town for the past fifty years. If this guy ever lived around here, Jimmy Williams would know him."

"Jimmy Williams?"

"Former police chief. He retired about ten years ago. Since then he's spent his time up at his cabin by the lake, fishing and generally keeping to himself. But he loves company. I'll give him a call and tell him you're coming up. Here's his address. It's about a three-mile drive."

She pulled out a pad and wrote down the address.

"It's sweet, what you're doing. Giving that woman this special gift before she dies is so nice. I can only hope someone does something so kind for me when my time comes."

Once we got to the car Heather asked the obvious.

"That was uncomfortable, wasn't it?"

"Yeah, you have to expect that when you lie. Sometimes it gets turned back on you like it just did. You just have to tell yourself that you're lying for a higher purpose and not let it bother you."

"Why didn't you want to go at it directly and talk to the clerk about Governor Kent and his father?"

"This little town has been inundated with reporters over the past year all wanting to get some new angle on the new President. The poor people here have talked and talked about the Kents and probably don't want to say one more word about them. If we came in directly, they'd either clam up or give the stock answers they've been giving for the past year. Either way, we'd never get any useful information. Let's go talk with Mr. Williams."

Heather was absorbing everything I was telling her. She really wanted to learn the business. I was only hoping I was a good enough teacher.

Ten minutes later, we arrived at Jimmy Williams' cabin. It was a small white building with moss green shutters. We walked around the building to the lakeside and found Mr. Williams sitting in a rocking chair on a screened-in porch.

"Ms. Vega, come on in, both you and your friend. Clara told me you'd be coming over."

We walked up a set of stairs to the porch. Jimmy Williams indicated for us to sit down.

"Can I offer you a beer or something else to drink? No? Okay, let's talk. And please don't give me a cock and bull story about some dying woman's wish. You're too far up the food chain to be working on the "human interest" story you described to Clara. Clara's a wonderful town clerk but she's not the sharpest arrow in the quiver. We may be a hick town but we do have satellite dishes and I've seen your work on the presidential campaign and on *Issues & Answers*. Tell Richard Leitz I love his show, by the way."

"You're right, there is no dying woman and this is related to the Presidential race."

"There now, don't you feel better?"

"As a matter of fact, I do. It's always much easier telling the truth. You don't have to remember as much. Please apologize to Clara for me."

"Nah, she'd be crestfallen if she thought she was helping you for a different purpose than what you told her. I'll let her keep her illusion that she assisted in a noble purpose. So, why exactly are you up here and what do you want from me?"

"There is so little on Governor Kent's father, not even any pictures. I'm sure reporter after reporter has been up here asking about Maximilian Kent. I'm afraid I'm just another one of those. I thought you folks would be so sick of reporters asking about Kent and his family that you wouldn't give us the time of day."

"You're correct on that, so you thought lying to us was the way to go?"

"When you put it that way it doesn't sound so great, does it? It seemed like a wonderful idea at the time."

He laughed.

"Yeah, I hear you. As police chief, I used to lie to people all the time to get what I wanted so I can hardly judge. The one thing I have to say about your little ruse is that it got you to see me. I've been kind of forgotten out here and that's how I like it. Folks like Clara have done a great job of shielding me from the likes of you, no offense."

"None taken."

"As a result, I've blessedly not talked to one reporter, and I'm the guy who knows everything about this part of the world. And that includes knowing Max Kent. So, I'd hate to see you waste all this time coming up here from the Big City. Ask what you want."

"Thank you, Chief Williams. How well did you know Max Kent?"

"Very well. In fact, I was probably the only one in town who knew him well. When he first moved into town, he searched me out. He concluded that, with his thick accent, the people here would be suspicious and would probably ask me to check him out. He was right on that count. He beat them to the punch and came over and introduced himself. We talked for a bit and then he asked me if I liked fishing. I did and we became regular fishing buddies.

"We'd talk about many things out on that boat. He told me about growing up in the Sudetenland section of Czechoslovakia and how tough it was living under Nazi rule, even though he was one of those Germans that the Nazis were quote/unquote liberating. As the war progressed, he was conscripted into the army but just before he was about to report, he ran away and joined the Czechoslovakian underground. He was almost captured a number of times but he admitted he lived a charmed life. After each escape, he'd have nightmares of being stood in front of a firing squad.

"Eventually he escaped Czechoslovakia and migrated to the one place you'd least expect: Germany. He got himself a cane and pretended a limp. He found a small town and claimed to be a wounded veteran from Munich but could not live in a large city anymore. He gained acceptance by volunteering to organize the home guard. Eventually, when the Americans approached he simply walked into army headquarters one day and gave them valuable information about troops remaining in the area. He was able to become friends with a captain whose brother worked in the State Department and was able to secure papers to emigrate.

"The man could tell a great story and I'd listen for hours out in that boat, captivated by his tales. I was too young to serve in World War II but later served my country in Korea so I could tell a couple war stories myself but I took a back seat to Max.

"Max was a private man. I'd invite him to get-togethers but he'd always decline, claiming he had business to attend to. I think he was self-conscious about his accent and how people would react to it. I respected that. People can be pretty judgmental about superficial things."

"Yes, they can. What business was he in?"

"Import and export."

"Of what?"

"He never said and I never asked. He seemed to make a nice living at whatever it was and that was good enough for me. He'd constantly be out of town for weeklong business trips. His wife, Martha, was the more social one. She'd do all the shopping and be out and about in the town. She was the one who would attend all of Peter's school functions."

"Is she still alive?"

"No, she passed a couple years before Max did. I tried visiting him during those two years but he wouldn't see anybody. I think he eventually died of a broken heart.

"One other thing he loved to talk about was Peter. He was so proud of that boy. Even though he never attended Peter's sporting or other events, he knew everything about that boy. I don't think he fully understood baseball but he could recite every one of Peter's statistics. He was so proud when Peter got accepted to Cornell, but at the same time he was so sad that his son was going away. He'd be so proud that his son got to be Governor and now has a good shot at being President."

"One thing I wanted to ask you is about a picture Heather found. Like I mentioned, there don't seem to be any photographs of Maximilian Kent anywhere but Heather is not to be deterred and found this picture but we can't be sure it's him. Would you know?"

I pulled a copy of the massaged photo out of my bag. I tried to mask my nervousness. Jimmy Williams was a sharp guy and, while Heather had done a magnificent job of photo-shopping the picture, it wouldn't be beyond Williams to notice that it had been doctored. To be caught in another lie would be the death knell for our investigation.

Williams took the picture and examined it.

"Wow, this is sure a relic, isn't it? I can't say for certain because it's so old—and so am I—but this sure looks like Max. I just can't swear to it. Wait a second."

I held my breath, certain I was about to be found out.

"See that?"

He pointed to the left side of Steiner's neck near the collar of his shirt.

"If I'm not mistaken, that looks like a birthmark. Same birthmark that Max had. I'm still not 100% sure but I'd have to say that is Max Kent."

We chatted a little longer but we left soon thereafter to get back to the city before nightfall.

"That was dicey for a little bit there," Heather noted in the car.

"I thought I blew it but we rallied. Plus, for all that he professed to like being alone, I think he welcomed the company. He liked being someone of importance again."

"Thank you, Francine, for including me today. I know it was something you could have done on your own. You sure didn't need me in there."

"There was a point where I wished I had sent you in blind on your own. I was the one who almost blew things. In any case, I appreciated having someone with me, someone I could trust."

"So, you have at least partial confirmation. What's next?"

"I have a call in to the State Department to see if they have any info they can share."

I was going to confide that my contact in the State Department was Kent's opponent's brother, figuring she'd get a kick out of it but then I reconsidered. It would be unprofessional to reveal my source.

"What are they looking for?"

"I want to see if there is any record of Maximilian Kent coming into the country, whether he ever got citizenship, whether he ever applied for a visa, things like that."

"What's your guess?"

"I'm guessing that they won't be able to find anything, that he illegally entered the country through a back door and then kept a low profile for the rest of his life. I also may be able to get DNA confirmation."

"What? DNA? How?"

I explained how a sample of Steiner's tissue was preserved and getting the glass Alexander drank out of. It was another in a long series of long shots.

"I still have to decide what to do when and if it's determined that Steiner was Kent's father. Is it news? What if it's enough to turn the presidential election on its head? Do I have the right to do that, especially if I believe his opponent to be a totally incompetent pretender? We have to consider that they may be future victims of the Zyklon Killer if indeed Peter and Alexander are in fact descendants of Steiner."

"That's all really deep, isn't it?"

I don't know if it was the seriousness with which she asked such a question or whether the question was so profound as to be ludicrous that we both burst out laughing. It was the type laughter that fed on itself that we laughed so hard I had to pull over to the side.

"You know how to put things in perspective, Heather. Thanks. I needed that."

Two days later my phone rang. It was a 202 area code out of DC. I answered.

"Ms. Vega? My name is Stuart Clinton. I work for the State Department. I believe we have a mutual acquaintance. You were looking for some information?"

"That's correct."

"Well, there is absolutely no information about the comings and goings of the person of interest. No record that he ever entered the U.S. or left it. I checked with other agencies and there is no record of him having an employment history or a visa of any type. As far as the United States of America is concerned, the man never existed, at least never within our borders. I'm sorry I couldn't give you more."

"Oh, you've helped immeasurably. What you told me doesn't surprise me in the least."

"Great. By the way, one more thing."

"We never had this conversation."

"Right, take care."

We still needed DNA confirmation but the pieces we'd put together so far all pointed in the direction of Hans Georg Steiner being Peter Kent's father. First, we started with Ari's intuition, which I surmised was never too far off. Then there was Peter's reaction to the mention of Hans

Georg Steiner. Jimmy Williams could not absolutely confirm that Steiner was Maximilian Kent but he thought it could be.

What rang true to me was how well Steiner, if that's who he was, was able to hide in plain sight. It would make sense that he would immediately search out and befriend the chief of police. That would cut off the majority of naysayers and curious. He could then tell the chief all about his past, or at least a plausible past, that made him neither a coward nor a hero. He could then be a recluse but one that was proud of his over-achieving son. That would further endear him to the chief.

He worked in some import and export business, but there is no record of him working anywhere. He could have spirited enough money away from Germany that he and his family lived on for decades without the need to earn any subsequent income. That would solve the problem of having to file tax returns.

Again, I asked myself why I was going through this exercise. No answer was forthcoming but then one thing dawned on me. Thus far I'd been so focused on my quest that I overlooked the most obvious reason, the Zyklon Killer. Thus far, the Zyklon Killer has murdered descendants of six of the *Munich 7*. Supposedly, the apprehension and execution of Aaron Kaplow took the Zyklon Killer out of circulation but I had subsequently learned that he most likely was not the killer but had been framed, set up. This meant that the killer was still out there.

Alan had written that the Zyklon Killer would kill again, and soon. His note, as was his habit, had been as cryptic as a clue in a complicated riddle but now the next victim became crystal clear. He had saved the best for last. It had to be either Peter or Alexander Kent, the direct descendants of the remaining *Munich 7* SS Officer.

Framing Kaplow would throw the authorities off the scent, opening the door to carry out a plan to assassinate one of the Kents. It would be a crowning achievement, especially since it would have to be done with scores of Secret Service officers surrounding Kent. The Zyklon Killer had proven extremely resourceful thus far. The lengths he went to in framing Kaplow is something you'd find in a spy thriller. But getting past the Secret Service?

Another thought crossed my mind. Since Kent was the ultimate target, the fulfillment of a career of killing, would the Zyklon Killer want to go down in glory? He had already proven that he had no objections to killing innocent people; perhaps he had no qualms about himself being killed in the process.

Regardless of what the DNA analysis showed, if I could investigate and deduce that Steiner was Kent's father, so could the killer. I had to warn them. I went into contacts and dialed Alexander Kent.

"Alexander, I think you and your father might be in great danger."

"My father's running for President. That comes with the territory."

"I'm not kidding. I truly believe you are the next targets of the Zyklon Killer."

"You're still on about that? One thing I admire about you is your tenacity. Once you grab onto something you're like a pit bull that won't let go."

"I'm serious."

"I believe you are. Please explain to me then why we may be the next targets."

"The killer has been going after descendants of a group of Nazi SS officers who escaped after the war who were known as the *Munich 7*. They've killed descendants of six of those officers. My research points to your grandfather being Hans Georg Steiner, the seventh."

"Now you're bordering on delusional, Francine. My grandfather fought against and fled from the people you describe. But, to be on the safe side, I'll raise this with the Secret Service and my father. We'll be on high alert. How about if we get together next week? I'm in Dallas now and then we're doing a five-state tour. We'll be back in the City a week from Friday."

Any further discussion was futile. If we proceeded further I was just going to continue to be patronized.

"Okay, give me a call when you're back in town."

I called Will next.

"Will, I think I figured it out. I know who the next victim of the Zyklon Killer is going to be. It's Governor Kent or Alexander. I spoke with Alexander but he blew me off. I'm really concerned."

I explained everything to him about learning Kent's father's identity and how it all now made sense. Something was in the works to kill the Presidential candidate.

"I'm sure the Secret Service detail covering Kent has the situation under control. Those guys are real professionals. I'll give the head of that detail a call to tip him off and make sure they're on their guard. Remember, though, that the last Zyklon murder took place over three years ago. Maybe Kaplow actually was the guy or maybe the killer just retired. I trust you, Fava, but I'll have a tough time making anyone else believe based on what appears to be a lot of circumstantial conjecture. We need hard evidence. If it's there, it'll come out. It always does. In the meantime, fretting only succeeds in giving yourself an ulcer, nothing more."

"You're right, hon. I'm sorry. I'm over-reacting. Once the idea popped into my head, it kind of took over. There's no reason to believe anything will happen, at least not immediately. Thanks for talking me down. You're always so level-headed."

"We're perfect together, a yin-yang. See you tonight. Love you."

"Love you, too."

I'd spent so much time on this that I'd neglected my prep work for the next *Issues & Answers*. A bunch of economic experts will be discussing their various opinions of what would happen to the national and global economies depending on which candidate gets elected. I can barely keep my own checkbook balanced, never mind understand the intricacies of world economics, trade, fiscal policy and whatever. I took some economic courses in college but I learned just enough to pass the tests and, once the tests were done, all that knowledge seeped out of my head. I would be totally out of my league with this subject matter and told Richard as much. He acknowledged my shortcomings but he wanted me to participate anyway. He'd thought I'd bring a fresh, novice perspective.

Frankly, I think I was being used like a canary in a mine. He had received extensive economic training at the finest schools and these experts would be talking a lingo he'd understand. However, he was worried about his viewing audience. If my eyes were glazing over or if I was getting lost, he'd know the viewers were as well. At that point, he could go back to the expert and make them explain what they had just said but in more understandable clear English. Hopefully, he'd see the light bulb go on above my head and then proceed to the next discussion. I had mixed emotions. On the one hand, it was nice to be needed but on the other hand it was somewhat insulting to be used as the class idiot who needed things dumbed down for them.

Ultimately, the show went off better than I expected. I sold Richard—and myself—short. I certainly did not keep up when the discussion was about esoteric economic theories but I gleaned enough from what they were saying to throw in some real-life examples that related directly to the average American's pocketbook. Afterwards, Richard told me that my contributions in this regard were invaluable and made the show a success. I went home feeling quite good about myself.

27

I wasn't sure whether I was pleased that once I got into prepping for *Issues & Answers* I had totally forgotten about Zyklon, at least for a little while. I thought it showed great focus to be able to immerse myself and focus on the job at hand while blocking out extraneous distractions. However, I began to worry that I was losing my ability to multitask and handle multiple things all at once.

I could always compartmentalize my different projects, but that didn't mean I'd totally erase the ones I wasn't working on completely from my consciousness. That's what I had done here and I was wondering if there wasn't some sort of psychological reasons behind it. Maybe I was looking for something—anything—that would push a topic like a serial killer using a genocidal gas out of my mind and out of my life.

After I finished the show I hurried back home to Queens to concentrate on another compartment of my life that had been sorely neglected of late: my family. I wanted a Sunday afternoon with no cellphones, no Zyklon, no presidential races or anything else outside of Will, Albert, Stella and Rosa. We packed up the car and took a drive across the Whitestone Bridge with our ultimate destination being the Bronx Zoo.

Ever since I first met Will, my relationship with his son, Albert, has always been a work in progress. Unlike Stella, who's three years younger than he and had limited thoughts of her mother, initially was resentful of me for taking the place of his mother. I tried to make it clear that this was not my intent, but this is not easy to explain to a pre-teen.

We were making some headway but then when Rosa was born, he saw himself as being pushed back a slot and new resentments emerged. With a whole lot of patience and special attention paid to him, we've worked ourselves back to a place where we can possibly be happy with each other. Some days are of course better than others but I can at least feel that we're heading in the right direction.

We had a great day at the zoo. It took a little doing but I was finally able to get Albert to go on a camel ride with me. I suppose it wouldn't have done too much for my cred if someone had recognized me and taken a video of me inelegantly bouncing around on the back of a camel, but I didn't care in the least. I don't think Albert and I had ever been closer.

We'd brought the stroller for Rosa but Will insisted on carrying her. I'm not even sure why we own a stroller. Both Will and I see them more as tools for lazy parents than for the kids. So, we carried her around all day. She, like everyone else, had the time of her life. The only tense moment was when a lion roared. While Albert and Stella were delighted, Rosa shrank back in fear and started to cry. Albert was the one who helped calm his little sister down.

After that she was fine, enjoying all the sights and making her own sounds that approximated their names. Eventually, she wore herself out and fell asleep in Will's arms.

We all did a little bit of everything that day. As soon as the kids hit the back seat, they were asleep. I wouldn't be far behind them. As Will was working his way through traffic back to Queens, I reached over and took his hand. It was a perfect day.

I was proud of myself for turning the ringer off on my phone for the entire afternoon and I did not check it even once. When we got home, I couldn't help myself and I checked my messages. There were seven of them. Most could wait but there was one from Ari asking me to call him. I had no idea if he was still in the States or back in Israel but I dialed anyway.

"Ari, how you doing?"

"I am fine. We got the DNA results back. Mixed results, I'm afraid. It's a fifty-seven percent match. While they were able to extract DNA samples from the Steiner tissue, there was a lot of degradation over the years. As you can imagine, the tissue wasn't stored in ideal conditions over time and may have been subjected to heat, cold, the air, you name it. Combine that with the fact that we are comparing the sample to that of a possible grandson, not a son, drops the probability even more. While not conclusive, our law enforcement officials here say that, combined with all the circumstantial and other evidence you've gathered, the odds are that the grandfather is indeed Hans Georg Steiner. It's just not something that would stand up in a court of law."

"Thanks, Ari."

My initial reaction was to call Alexander back and hit him again with my plea to take additional steps to protect himself and his father. This new news didn't provide conclusive evidence but it might be enough to tip the scales. Perhaps he would not simply dismiss me out of hand as he did before.

I pulled my phone out of my purse and went to my contacts. I was just about to hit Alexander's name but then Will stopped me.

"Fava, the situation is no different than before. Ari's information doesn't confirm or deny anything about Kent's father. You're getting too caught up in the story again. Take a deep breath and don't rush into things. It's better to wait until Alexander is in town and you can talk face to face."

"You're right," I sighed.

The next morning, I was at work when my phone rang. It was Katrina.

"Hi, Katrina. How are things out on the trail?"

"Weird. I had dinner with Malcolm McKenzie last night."

"Really? That is weird given your history."

"He called me out of the blue. He wanted to put that history behind us."

"And you believed him?"

"He invited me to dine with him and told me I could ask him anything I wanted. I was floored but skeptical. I felt like I was walking into a trap, but it was too good an opportunity to pass up.

"When we got together, he was open and charming. He apologized for all I went through. I kept waiting for something else to happen but it never did. He let me ask anything I wanted. He answered everything but some responses were more nuanced than others. It was most congenial and we left on such great terms.

"The one thing that I found most interesting was that he claimed to be sorry he ever got enmeshed in the "Destroy Mecca" controversy. He said he got caught up in it and believed it when he first said it. Then, when his more rabid fans pushed him on, he got rabid himself. His brother had gone through a bitter divorce with his Muslim wife and that pushed him into it even further. His brother has since had somewhat of a reconciliation with his wife and as a result has softened his stance on Islam, which he, in turn, passed on to The Reverend.

"McKenzie realized how wrong it was to preach genocide on the basis of a personal experience but he's too far down the road to turn back. He admitted to me that he was too weak a man to face the criticism if he turned back."

"Your chat, was it on the record?"

"Yes, as a matter of fact, he insisted that it be so at the beginning of our dinner. I could record the conversation if I wanted to."

"Did you?"

"Yes, I still had my reservations about our meeting and expected a trap, but there wasn't any trap."

"So, what are you going to do now?"

"I'm going to go ahead with it and report our dinner on tonight's news. I just wanted to bounce it off you to see if there's something I'm missing here."

I contemplated revealing that, in my opinion, McKenzie was terrified that he could actually somehow win this election. He was looking to use Katrina as a way to ensure that he would sabotage his chances. I personally thought it was overkill; his campaign was already down the tubes with no hope of recovery. The reason I didn't say anything was that he had stipulated that our conversation was off-the-record. To state my thoughts would have betrayed that trust.

"I see no downside to reporting. You have truth on your side, backed by a tape. Go for it."

"Thanks."

A few hours later I received a text from Alexander advising me he was back in town and wondered if we could get together the following evening. He was staying at l'Hôtel, one of the chic new boutique hotels on the Upper West Side and asked if we could meet there at 7:00. I agreed.

I took a cab up to 83rd Street and walked into the hotel. The lobby was ultra-modern with geometrically shaped amber-colored chairs and sofas. Various neon-lit designs adorned the wall. Off to the left was a stainless-steel bar and stools. Alexander was seated on one of these stools holding what looked to be a mojito. I did not see any guys with earpieces so it was obvious he wasn't taking my warnings seriously.

"Can I buy you a drink?"

"One of those would be great."

We sat and chatted, mostly about the campaign. He kept saying it was almost too easy but he was expecting an October surprise that would tighten things up somewhat. He didn't think there was any hope for McKenzie, however. He decried the state of the opposition party for letting it get itself to the point where someone like "The Reverend", which he said with great mockery, could be their standard-bearer.

"The far-out wackos have taken them hostage. My father has always been able to reach across the aisle but, over the past couple of years, he's had a tougher time dealing with them. They're always looking over their shoulder wondering who's listening in, looking for ammunition to use against them in the next primary.

"For the remainder of our conversation, which is a little more on the confidential side, perhaps we should go up to my room. I reassure you that I will remain a complete gentleman."

I laughed. "I think I've known you long enough to expect no different."

Alexander paid the bill and we headed to the elevator, which we took up to the 18th Floor. Just as we got to his door, my phone rang. It was Heather.

"Do you mind if I take this? It's my assistant."

"Go right ahead."

"Hi, Heather. What's up?"

"Francine, on a whim I did some checking and found out some interesting things."

"Such as?"

"Well, I was doing a timeline and decided to check on Peter Kent's schedule over the past ten years to fit into that timeline."

"I'm not even going to ask how you accessed such information."

"Well, he did spend a lot of time in Albany, which I found reassuring."

"Heather, I'm in the middle of a meeting so, unless you have something of note, I'm going to have to talk to you later."

"No, wait! He was in Paris for a trade conference on March 30, 2010."

I was starting to get a little annoyed.

"So? That hardly seems extraordinary given his position. Why do I care?"

"Because he was also in Austin, Texas for a National Governors Association meeting on April 7, 2007."

"Are you sure?"

"Yes, after I saw these items on his official schedule I checked online to confirm that those events happened on those dates. They did."

What Heather was driving at became clear. I made a mental note to teach her that, as a journalist, she needed to get to her point much quicker, that she needed to summarize of her main points in her lead sentence.

I had to be careful. Alexander was only about six to seven feet away, checking his emails. I didn't want to let on that Heather and I were talking about him or his father. I turned my back to him.

"Thanks, Heather. Let me know if you find anything more."

I kept the phone up to my ear. I was having trouble processing this information. It couldn't be true, could it? What she was telling me in itself was innocuous enough. However, put together with everything both Alan and Lawson told us made for a frightening conclusion.

Zyklon knew Jake circa 1994-96. Both men were Special Forces during the same period. Lawson pissed off people wherever he went. If Alexander knew Lawson at all during that period, it's not inconceivable they could become enemies in a short period of time. It's also not inconceivable that Alexander knew that the best way to get back at Lawson was not directly but through one of the few people he loved.

Alexander's Special Forces background could also explain the military-grade detonator used in the explosion of Jonas's car.

München Sieben or *Munich 7*. All six of the victims were descendants of a group of Nazi SS Officers that had escaped Europe (and being held accountable for their war crimes) known as the *Munich 7*. A large amount of evidence pointed to the Kents being directly descended from the seventh, Hans Georg Steiner. One aspect of the Aaron Kaplow trial that weighed heavily against Kaplow was that his mother was Jewish whose family had been murdered in the camps. This played into the prosecution's theory that the killings had been a deranged attempt at revenge.

However, an alternative theory could be that an heir to one of the *Munich 7* would be as deranged in an attempt to wipe out the past of their horrific kin by killing off the other six Nazis. Or maybe it could be a more primal motive. Perhaps the rumors of seven tons of gold are true and the heir to Hans Georg Steiner is hunting for clues about how to get his hands on the gold, killing as he goes along.

$Z = A$. Alan's dying message scrawled on the leg of his pants made sense now. Zyklon equals Alexander.

Zyklon will kill again, soon. This is the only one of Alan's observations that has not yet come to fruition or can yet be explained. A shiver ran down my spine.

Maybe I had totally misread everything. There could be a dozen alternative explanations that I should consider, but nothing was coming to mind. I only hoped that I hadn't given myself away by questioning him about Steiner the other day.

The phone was still planted to my ear even though Heather had hung up minutes ago. I decided I would try to surreptitiously call Will but then I noticed Alexander was watching me intently. He held out his left hand; he wanted the phone. When I hesitated, he pulled his right hand out of his pocket and in it was a gun. It was a Smith & Wesson E-Series pistol (Will's influence that I could recognize the make and model) with a silencer on it. I handed the phone over to him. He looked at the display and saw 'Heather' but that the call had ended.

"She's someone else from work," I offered meekly as he placed the phone on the end table beside him.

"I know. An intern."

"You know who my interns are?"

"As the old saying goes, 'Keep your friends close but keep your enemies closer.'"

"When did I get to be your enemy?"

"When you first covered the Zyklon Killer. I knew you weren't going to let go. I had to keep a close eye on you. So what were you and Ms. Abernathy talking about?"

"You and your father. She discovered that you were at conferences in both Paris and Austin on the dates of both killings."

"The world is full of coincidences, isn't it?"

"Yes, but combined with all the other coincidences, a good case could be made."

"The operative word in that sentence is could. So, you didn't know for sure before that?"

"Not conclusively, no."

"You're not as good as I thought."

"Sorry to disappoint."

"I'll get over it."

"Can I ask you one question: why Zyklon?"

"I thought I explained that in the notes I left at the scenes."

"Let's just say I'm a skeptic, especially after I heard the legend that *Munich 7* may also refer to seven tons of gold."

"Pure fantasy invented by my grandfather to throw the Nazi-hunters off his trail and that of his comrades. He knew that pure greed would be enough to send the hunters in a hundred different directions."

"Wait a second. Your grandfather died years before you were born."

"Yes, my father knew who his father was and the horrific things he did."

"Aren't you following in your grandfather's footsteps, killing innocent people whose only sin was who they were descended from?"

"It was unfortunate they had to be sacrificed, but it was for the greater good. There will always be potential SS and Gestapo types, just waiting for their opportunity to reemerge. My grandfather was a verified monster, but he loved his family. If he thought his son or grandson would be executed for his sins, I believe he would have thought twice about the course he was taking. Maybe he would have remained an innocuous anti-Semitic accountant."

"And how was your cause advanced by killing Aaron Kaplow and Alan Westbrook?"

"Aaron Kaplow was both pure revenge and a diversionary tactic. I hated Lawson. He was my CO when we were sent on a top-secret mission to Azerbaijan. The operation went south and we had to get out. My best friend, Kevin McCarthy, was seriously wounded and was slowing us down. After awhile, Kevin told us to leave him and get out of there. I'm sure you've seen this in the movies before. The wounded man says to leave him behind and save themselves but his buddies tell him to shut up. No one gets left behind. Instead, Lawson says okay. He stripped Kevin of anything that would identify him as an American, put a Russian GSh-18 pistol in his hand and then he ordered us to leave. We left him there to die. You don't do that and I vowed that I would avenge Kevin someday.

"When I learned that Lawrence Heinz, who was descended from Rudolf Becker, one of the *Munich 7*, lived in Austin and that Lawson's beloved cousin lived in Waco, just a stone's throw up Route 35, it was like manna falling from heaven. To top it off, I learned that George Kraml, another descendent of an SS officer but not a member of the *Munich 7*, lived in Waco and it gave me a perfect opportunity to set up framing Kaplow. Kraml thought that he was saved but he was never a target.

I knew that however careful I may have been, I could have unwittingly left a clue at one or more of the sites. I couldn't have the authorities coming down on me before I finished my mission. I needed a diversion and the unfortunate Aaron was a perfect two birds with one stone. So, like the explosion I set off to divert cops from Wendy Smith's apartment, I set the trap for Aaron. He even fell for the free trip to Paris to complete the frame-up.

"At the time, I didn't know you had a relationship with Lawson and that framing Aaron would draw you into it. Blowing up your friend's car was supposed to happen outside your home to throw you and your husband off your games. I also thought you'd figure that Lawson, being the psycho he was, had reconsidered his deal with you and was backing out. As a result, you would back out. Obviously, I sold you short.

"The guys I hired to follow you and rig the car to explode were complete morons. The timer got stuck and the car blew up on the FDR instead out front of your house. I'm glad your friend wasn't killed."

"And Alan's murder?"

"A tragic mistake. I'd drawn Lawson into a trap in order to torture and kill him; my hatred was that great. At the time, I thought it was a stroke of genius pretending I was Alan Westbrook and then luring Lawson to his old apartment. I'm no slouch with a computer but I'm a Neanderthal compared to Mr. Westbrook. I didn't realize that he'd hacked into both my computer as well as Lawson's and knew where we were. He simply showed up and I panicked, shooting him a number of times."

"He hated Lawson as much if not more than you. I doubt he would have attempted to stop you. He probably just wanted to ensure the job was done."

"I realize that now."

"In fact, I bet he was trying to kill multiple birds with one stone by arranging for me to meet with him at the exact same time you and Lawson would be there. He knew that Will or one of his agents would be accompanying me and they could catch both the Zyklon Killer and Jacob Lawson at the same time."

"That makes sense."

"Why did you lure Lawson to Alan's old building?"

"The security of an abandoned building mixed with the poetic justice of killing Lawson in the former home of an adversary."

"So, you've made your grand statement. What's next? How is killing me going to advance your cause?"

"Kill you? You greatly misconstrue the reason I asked you up here."

"You can pardon my confusion since I'm looking down the barrel of a gun, one with a silencer no less."

"My apologies. I needed you to listen to what I had to say."

"So, what exactly did I misconstrue?"

"Please take a look at the desk over there."

I looked over and saw two piles of paper with handwriting on them. One pile was just one page. The other appeared to be two or three pages.

"They are both the God's honest truth. One is more complete than the other, that's all. I am putting you in the unenviable position of using one or the either of these, or both of them, or neither, as you see fit. Tell my father that I love him but I can no longer live with this evil coursing through my veins, and neither should he. Tell him I'm sorry. Thank you, Francine."

With that, he turned the pistol so that it pointed at his right temple and then he pulled the trigger. The gun made a muffled report, after which it fell from Alexander's hand as his body dropped to the floor. It all happened so quickly that I didn't have a chance to tell him not to.

"Alexander, what have you done?"

I couldn't move for a few seconds. There was no reason to; it was obvious he was dead. Alan's words ran through my brain: *Zyklon will kill again, soon.* I was too late. The Zyklon Killer had indeed struck again but this time the victim was the Zyklon Killer.

I dialed home on my phone.

"Will, can you leave the kids at Emma's and come here immediately? You may want to have Detective Kelly join us. I'm at l'Hôtel on Broadway and 83rd Street in Room 1803. Please hurry."

He must have heard the distress in my voice because he just responded, "Okay, I'll be there soon." Then he hung up.

I went over to the desk to look at the papers there. I grabbed a tissue so as to not touch anything before the police arrived. Both pages started off with the same preamble.

I, Alexander Kent, leave this testament and confession of my own free will. My close friend Francine Vega is about to witness the extreme action—ending my own life—I am about to take. She is in no way a part of this or even knows that it is about to happen. I have chosen her to be a conscientious reporter who will give an honest accounting of all I write here. I have chosen her because of the hell she has endured due to the empathy she felt for one of my victims, Wendy Smith.

I, Alexander Kent, am the Zyklon Killer.

I framed Aaron Kaplow for two of the murders in order to wreak revenge on my mortal enemy, Jacob Lawson, who was Kaplow's cousin. It is unfortunate that Mr. Kaplow was implicated for my crimes and that the State of Texas executed an innocent man. My soul will bear the weight of this sin, as well as the murder of six other innocent people, for all of eternity.

On the computer on this desk, you will find a folder named Zyklon that chronicles the methods, times and other details of the murders I committed to prove that I, not Kaplow, am the killer.

I stand by the notes I left with each victim explaining why they were killed. Although the six people who were murdered by me were themselves entirely innocent, they were descended from such evil they were still culpable.

We live in constant danger that a new despot will emerge who will give tacit permission for the evil that exists in some people's heart to reemerge. The new SS Officers of our era may act differently and reconsider their actions if they have the knowledge that, even if they are able to evade justice during their lifetimes for their heinous crimes, punishment may be handed out to their progeny.

For this very reason, the punishment of the sons for the sins of the father, I am taking my own life as I am the grandson of the Nazi War Criminal, Hans Georg Steiner, whose crimes are well-documented and can be found chronicled in this computer file.

At the bottom of this statement was Alexander's signature.

I next reviewed the second statement. My bottom jaw must have nearly hit the floor. Then I re-read it because I could not believe what I was reading. No, I had read it correctly.

I made sure not to touch anything, using the tissue to handle anything. I knew these would be taken away as evidence and I didn't want my fingerprints or DNA anywhere near the statements or the computer. I also wasn't sure what would happen to the statements once they were taken away. They were so explosive that I envisioned them being destroyed so I took out my phone and took pictures of each page. I checked the pictures to make sure they were legible. I also made sure the signature on each one was visible.

I sat down and waited for Will to arrive.

28

Twenty minutes later there was a knock on the door. I opened it and, before Will could even walk in, I was in his arms. Up to this point, I'd kept my emotions in check but now, in his embrace, I couldn't hold back as I sobbed.

"Fava, what is it? What's wrong?"

It was then that he looked past me and saw Alexander's body on the floor.

"Oh my God. What happened?"

I still couldn't respond. Detective Kelly, whom I hadn't even noticed standing there with Will, gently moved us out of the doorway so she could enter. She walked over and knelt beside Alexander to feel if there was any pulse. There was none. She looked up at me.

"Francine, can you tell us what happened here?"

By this time, I had regained a modicum of composure.

"What you see here was the final act of the Zyklon Killer."

"I don't understand," she responded. "You saw the Zyklon Killer? Why didn't you call 911 instead of Will? It would have improved our chances of catching him? Can you give us a description?"

Will understood immediately what I was saying.

"No Detective, I don't think there's any need for that. There, lying on the floor, is the Zyklon Killer."

"Suicide was his act of atonement," I continued, "for not only his own sins but for that of his grandfather... and of his father.

"On the desk are two different versions of Alexander's life as the killer. He assured me that both are accurate representations; one is simply more complete than the other. Alexander gave me the choice to publicly release one or both or neither of these. Also, as you'll find out on the documents, on that computer is a folder providing detailed accounts of each murder he committed. He claims it contains information that only he and the police would know, thereby verifying that he, not Aaron Kaplow, was the Zyklon Killer.

"Before he killed himself, he gave me a full accounting of how and why he framed Kaplow and his motives for killing."

"Did you touch anything in the room?" the Detective asked.

"Not after he shot himself. When I came up here, it was only to talk. I had no reason to avoid touching anything so you may find my fingerprints, but I remained in that half of the room. After he turned the gun on himself, I went over to read the statements, but I used tissues to turn the pages."

"You came up to his room knowing he was the Zyklon Killer?"

"No, I didn't know until I was up here. I had a bunch of circumstances that pointed in that direction but I never conceived that it was he. I thought that he or his father might be the next intended target because of their lineage. Instead, I received a phone call while I was standing here that confirmed the fact that he was Zyklon. I was about to call Will when I looked up and he was pointing the gun at me. I thought he had lured me up to kill me because I knew too much. He then advised me that he brought me there to be his witness. After he told me all he had to, he turned the gun on himself and fired. It all happened so quickly. That's about it. Of course, I'll sit down with you and your people to give a complete statement."

Kelly headed over to the desk, pulled latex gloves out of her bag and put them on and then read the statements. I expected to see some sort of reaction when she read the more expansive one, but there was none. Instead, she pulled out her phone and took pictures of each page before putting the sheets back in their original places.

"I could fully envision this evidence disappearing. Am I safe in assuming that you thought the same thing and took pictures because you didn't trust me?"

I nodded.

Likewise, after she powered up the computer and accessed the Zyklon folder she pulled a thumb drive out of her bag. She inserted the drive and proceeded to copy the files over. Once done, she pulled the drive out and handed it to me.

"I know that if down the road this computer or folder goes missing, you'll send me a copy, right?"

"Yes, I will."

"Good. Now let me call my people to come and process this scene. Will, why don't you take your wife home. I'm sure she's exhausted. She's given me enough for a preliminary account. I'll have one of my detectives contact her tomorrow for a complete statement."

Will started to lead me out when Kelly added one more thing.

"Francine, do whatever you will with the information you gathered here. I'm certain you'll do the right thing. Whatever you do, be assured that I'll have your back."

Again, I simply nodded.

The next morning Will accompanied me to my office. I printed out four copies of Alexander's statements. Then we went over to Frank's office.

"Hi, Frank."

He looked up from his paperwork and was surprised to see Will was with me. He stood up to shake hands.

"Will, nice to see you. To what do I owe the pleasure?"

"Not pleasure, I'm afraid."

"Frank," I asked, "can you see if Richard can meet with us this morning? It's important."

"I ran into him on the way in. I'll call and see if can come over right away."

Fifteen minutes later, Richard Leitz walked into Frank's office.

"Hey Frank, hi Francine. What's up?"

"Richard, this is my husband, FBI Special Agent Will Allen."

"Well, the fact that you introduce him with his full title tells me something's up. I assure you, I thought those deductions were valid."

We all laughed, but it was short-lived as I walked over and closed Frank's door. I responded as I returned to my seat.

"I'm sure Will can go over those deductions with you later but right now we have something much more important to discuss. We need to decide whether we want to play a role in deciding who will be the next President of the United States."

"Now I'm intrigued. Let's talk."

"Last night, Alexander Kent committed suicide. I was there; I witnessed it. The official announcement should be going out sometime today after the family has been notified. His suicide in itself is news and will be reported but that's not what I wanted to talk with you about. This is what I want to talk to you about. These are two statements—two suicide notes—Alexander left. He told me they are both the absolute truth. One is simply more expansive and inclusive of more truths than the other and he gave me permission to use either or both or neither of these."

I handed out copies of Alexander's statements and gave Frank and Richard a few minutes to read through them.

"As you can see in the statements, he confessed to me that he, not Aaron Kaplow, was in fact the Zyklon Killer. I also have a computer folder with information backing this claim as well as the method and reasons for framing Kaplow for the murders.

"What I am proposing is that I read the longer statement on the air. It's just too important to keep under wraps, but it will have repercussions, even to the point of deciding who will be the next President of the United States. Do we as a network have the courage to take this step?"

"Has any of this been corroborated?" Frank asked.

"They are Alexander's words. He signed the statements. He told me himself that this is the truth. I've never seen as close a father and son as these two. He had no interest in lying or in scuttling his father's presidential bid. He had an interest in correcting the historical record so that he would no longer be living a lie.

"Alexander was fully aware of the firestorm this could generate. That's why he gave me a multiple of choices, including burning these pages. I'm choosing not to do that. I believe that what's on these pages is the truth, and we should never run away from the truth."

"I don't know, maybe we should run this by the lawyers," Frank offered.

"Well, that will bury these words for sure."

"I just don't know."

"Frank, we can't hide the truth. Don't do it for me; do it for Wendy Smith. She deserves the entire story behind her and the other victims' murders to be aired. Her grandmother deserves the truth."

"There are so many ways this could come crashing down on us. We need to proceed carefully and consider all the angles so we don't end up in jail. What do you think, Richard?"

Richard didn't say anything. He hadn't uttered a word since our bantering when he first arrived. He looked at me, then at Frank, then at Will and then back to me.

"Let's do it. On Sunday's show. Today's only Tuesday, so that will give a respectful amount of time to mourn the dead before we strike. I know I'm sounding like a heartless bastard here but we're talking about a serial killer who took the lives of a number of innocent people. My sympathies lie not with him or his father but with the truth and the victims.

"We'll lead off the show with you. You'll get as long as you need. I'm going to invite the Governor to attend or to send a rep, but I'm going to wait until the last minute. I don't want to give him and his lawyers time to pressure the network to get us to stop. You do realize there is going to be quite a shit-storm. I hope you're ready for it."

"I am."

"Good, I only hope I am. I'll talk with you later, Francine. Frank. Will, it's a pleasure meeting you."

Richard got up and left.

"Francine," Frank said, "I'm sorry. I should have been gung-ho for you. I froze and didn't back you. Thank God for Richard Leitz."

"I know that in the end, you'll always be there for me, Frank. You were just being practical, asking questions that needed to be asked."

"No, I was being scared. Like a little kid."

Over the next few days, I wrote and rewrote and rewrote again what I was going to say. Alexander was a vicious serial killer of innocent people—including a person I had grown close to—and yet here I was feeling some level of sympathy for him. In his own twisted mind, he was doing a noble thing, preventing future SS officers from coming forward. He even saw his own death as contributing to that cause. Still, I had to keep telling myself that the bottom line is he was a ruthless killer. I can't appear to be glorifying him or even complimentary of him.

We were about ready to go to bed when my phone buzzed. It was a 212 area code, but I didn't recognize the number. I was going to ignore the call but then I remembered when I first received a call from a 672 area code, which happens to be Antarctica, and it turned out to be Alan who somehow was able to route his calls through that continent for security purposes. I answered.

"Hello?"

"Francine, it's Jane Kelly. Is Will there? If so, put me on speaker."

I did.

"Hi Jane, what's the latest?"

"Lots. First, the ME has officially ruled the death a suicide. You're off the hook, Francine."

"I didn't realize I was on the hook, Jane."

"Don't take it personally. Formalities, you know the process: everyone's a suspect until they've been eliminated. Anyway, I've only been able to file a preliminary report on the suicide itself. I didn't want to include any mention of you two or of the statements or computer until I've had a chance to talk to my captain, which won't happen until tomorrow. We let the governor know that his son has been killed and that we suspect suicide but we didn't get into details, especially no details about the Zyklon Killer.

"I gave the computer and papers to my friend, Sergeant Billy Bentley, who oversees the evidence vault even though they weren't yet officially logged in as evidence. He put the computer and papers in a secure locker but, as feared, they've disappeared. There is no record of them being signed out or removed, but they're gone.

"I absolutely trust Billy. He wouldn't have done anything. I did call my captain, who's out of town now, to fill him in on the situation. He was the one who suggested I wait in filing the report or telling anyone about the details until he returned.

"The fact that the evidence was lifted leaves only a couple of possibilities. One is my captain. He could have sent out an alert and set the wheels in motion, but I don't think so. I've known Oliver for fifteen years and I would be shocked if he would resort to something like this. The only other people who knew the details are my team and the ME's office. Again, I don't see it. I don't see any of them being involved or politically inclined. The only other possibility is that my phone may have been compromised."

"You were bugged?"

"I'm having one of my tech friends look over my phone to see if they can find anything. If I'm correct, my phone was probably hacked after I started investigating Zyklon. If they listened in on our conversation or my conversation with the captain, they know all about the two of you and that you were present when Alexander killed himself. I'm calling to warn you to be careful."

"Thanks Jane. I'm guessing you're calling me on a number I don't recognize is you being careful as well."

"You got it. I'll talk to you both later. Bye."

"So, what do you think?" I asked Will after Jane hung up.

"I think we need to be careful," he replied, stating the obvious.

"Beyond that?"

"Fava, I've come to know that look in your eye. You're going to plow ahead, consequences be damned. But without physical copies of the statements or the computer, it becomes more of a situation of your word against that of the Governor of New York slash presidential candidate. Guess who's going to come out ahead in court on that one. And then there's the issue of your physical safety."

"You really think someone would threaten me physically?"

"I wouldn't put it past them, whoever 'them' are. There's a lot riding here."

"So what should I do? I'm at a loss here, Will."

"First thing I think you should do is talk to Richard. He has a right to know the full situation and even pull the plug if he thinks it's necessary. If he's intent on going ahead, I think he should hold off on contacting Kent. If Kent knows about the existence of the evidence, he may seek a court injunction to stop you before you can begin."

Will got out of bed and headed into the other room. I assumed he had to go to the bathroom.

Even though it was after eleven, I felt the need to call Richard immediately. But I didn't feel confident enough to go at him alone. I reached for my phone but before I could dial, Will walked back in.

"Here, use this one. It's a burner phone. Untraceable. If they've bugged Jane's phone they may have done your phone as well."

I dialed.

"Hi, Frank, sorry to call but it's important. I'm checking to see if you fully regrew that pair."

He laughed.

"Oh yeah, huge and ready to go."

"Good. I'm going to conference in Richard."

A few seconds later, Richard Leitz answered. I could tell he'd been asleep.

"Hi, Richard, it's Francine. Sorry to wake you up but there's something that can't wait. I have Frank on the line as well."

"Hi, guys. Go ahead, shoot."

"The evidence—the computer and the hand-written statements—are gone. Disappeared. We think that an NYPD Detective's phone may have been hacked. They know I was at Alexander's suicide, but I don't know if they know that I have photos I took of the statements and the thumb drive copy I have of the computer folder. There's nothing original, nothing that could be entered into evidence in a court of law. If I go forward, we could be sued...or worse."

"That does put it all in a different perspective. Maybe we should rethink what we're doing."

"Richard?"

"Yes, Frank."

"Francine gave a pretty good summary of the situation but she left out one important thing that we have that should tip the scales in favor of proceeding as planned."

"And that is?"

"It's Francine herself. I know you've come to admire her abilities since you've made her a regular part of your show but I've known her since she was an intern out of NYU. We have a reporter who has faced down terrorists, who has brought down a world leader and who has tracked down a serial killer. I have never met anyone with as great instincts as she has. If she says this should be a go, I trust her totally.

"The presidential election is in less than two weeks. If we blink, if we equivocate, we will not only be failing as journalists, we'll be failing as Americans."

There was nothing but silence. If I didn't know any better I'd bet Richard had fallen back asleep.

"Francine?" he asked.

"You give me a mike, a camera and the time, I'll do it."

"I guess it's a go then. I was going to call the Governor tomorrow to invite him to participate and to fill him in on what we were going to talk about. Instead, I'm going to call him to invite him to attend but I'm going to be vague about what the subject will be. Since they probably suspect that you may have this info, I doubt he'll turn me down.

"Frank, is your studio available Sunday morning?"

"Yes, why?"

"I think that if the Governor is anywhere on the same floor that Francine is giving her fireside chat, he's going to demand that he be allowed to barge in to the studio and offer an immediate rebuttal. What I'm thinking is that he be invited to my floor and have him sit patiently in the green room on my floor while Francine begins her spiel six floors below. Francine, you think you can say all you have to in ten minutes?"

"Yes, I can do that."

"Good, this should make for great television. I'll greet him when he arrives for makeup. I'll tell him you're running late and probably will be joining us in progress. I'll also tell him that I've got some usual news stuff to run through and then bring him in after the first break. We'll put him in the Green Room, of course with the TV running. I'll be in my studio opening the show. I'll run through the blah blah stuff and then introduce you. You'll start doing your thing. The Governor will be in an uproar and rush out to the receptionist to demand he be let in right that moment. I have just the person who can handle him.

"She'll walk him over to my studio. He'll burst in and see only me sitting there. We'll have a back and forth for a few minutes when I'll reveal to him that you're six floors below. I'm going to have a couple of my staff holding all the elevators on other floors. It's Sunday morning so that shouldn't be an issue. After a few minutes of waiting, we'll impatiently head for the stairs. We'll rush down the stairs only to find that the door onto your floor is locked and need a card to access but somehow I'll have forgotten my access card. I'll call to my assistant to come down with one. Then we'll rush down to your studio.

"By the time we get there, Francine will have about finished her talk. We'll sit down at that point and we can start our debate. Of course, he'll be all sweaty and out of breath."

"You're enjoying this way too much, Richard."

"You're probably right, but it's a fun scenario to go through, isn't it? Odds are, nothing of the sort will happen but we'll find ourselves out of jobs once this is done. But it will be worth it. Let's talk over the next couple of days on the details. I think you should get out of town until Sunday, for your own safety."

"You're kidding, right?"

"I don't think he's kidding in the least," said Frank. "You can stay in my cabin up in the Adirondacks."

"Sounds like I'm in witness protection," I joked.

"You are." This time it was Will who chimed in.

29

Will and I packed up the kids first thing the next morning and we headed up the Thruway. Four and a half hours later we pulled into the driveway leading up to Frank's cabin, a cute 2-bedroom yellow bungalow behind which was a small pond.

Albert had sulked the entire trip up. He was going to miss his soccer game and several other school activities. When he saw the lake, however, his eyes lit up.

"Dad, can we go fishing? I've never been before."

"I was counting on it. There are some fishing poles and a rowboat in the shed. We'll have to dig for our own worms, I'm afraid."

"Cool. What about you, Fava? You want to go fishing, too?"

"I'd love to, but maybe I'll fish with you from the shore. I'm not much into small boats. And I've got to stay back and watch Stella and Rosa when you men are out catching our dinner."

He laughed.

"One more thing. When we fish together you have to put the bait on the hooks. I am not touching those things."

"Right, you're a girl."

"You better believe I am, big man. Now, why don't help your father bring our stuff in and select your bedroom."

"I get to pick?"

"You sure do."

He ran into the house, forgetting to help Will. I was hoping that both bedrooms were substantially the same. Otherwise, Will and I could be shoehorned into a tiny single bed. I thought it important to give Albert this decision to make, especially after him wanting to include me in the fishing.

Over the course of the next couple of days, I spoke with Richard, Frank and Detective Kelly a number of times. I kept telling them that I thought they were all being crazy hiding me away like this. I do live with an FBI Special Agent, I argued. They all agreed that it was better safe than sorry.

Rather than worry about getting to the city on time Sunday morning, Emma came up on Saturday afternoon to stay with the kids. After dinner, Will and I headed down to stay at a hotel not far from the office. I joked that I didn't particularly want to stay at l'Hôtel. Will responded that I was sick.

I arrived at the studio a full two and a half hours ahead of the broadcast to prep. Frank was there waiting.

"Nervous?"

"A little."

"You'll do fine. Just be your usual self."

"Thanks."

As he was leaving I called out to him.

"Nice pair, by the way."

Without turning around, he responded.

"Yup, big, brassy and proud."

I'm not usually one for making demands but this time I did make one stipulation. Jonas was to be my cameraman. There was a bit of a union kerfuffle in kicking the usual cameraman off his camera, but Frank smoothed everything over and my demand was met. I'd been through so much with Jonas in the past that I had to have him there for this. If I faltered at all, I needed his smiling face to look at me and get me back on track.

I also asked Heather to be there. I didn't have any real duties for her except perhaps as a gofer, but she'd been a key part of all this and deserved to be there.

Jonas later confided how nervous he was. He was used to his shoulder-held camera but not the studio camera. I hadn't even thought about that when I made my demand. But he didn't say anything until after we were done. If I wanted him that much, he certainly was not going to disappoint. He had spent all day Saturday getting himself acquainted with this model until its operation became second nature to him. 'A camera is a camera,' he nonchalantly claimed, but I knew and appreciated the extra effort he put in to learn the ins and outs of the equipment.

The time came and I assumed my seat. A PA clipped the mike to my blouse and helped me with my earpiece. We went through a sound check and Jonas made a couple light checks and some technical adjustments. We were ready to go.

Richard had April Cantrell, the director for *Issues & Answers*, up with him in his studio while I had Krishna Sidhadda, the show's assistant director, down with me in our studio. Krishna quieted everybody and with his hand indicated five, four, three, two, one.

Richard appeared on the monitor.

"Good morning and welcome to this week's edition of *Issues & Answers*. Today, with the national election less than a week and a half away, we have presidential candidate Governor Peter Kent with us but before we bring the Governor on, I'd like my colleague and friend, Francine Vega, to make a statement. Francine, the floor is yours."

The viewer was switched over to me. Despite the different background color scheme, I doubt many of our audience realized we were not in the same studio.

"Thank you, Richard, and good morning everyone.

"Over a decade ago I became acquainted with a beautiful young woman, Wendy Smith. I never got a chance to meet Wendy because she had been brutally murdered just one day earlier. This was a young woman who had devoted a year of her life to helping others in the Peace Corps. When she was killed, she was busy planning her wedding. She had a full life ahead of her that was snatched away from her... and from us.

"The manner in which she was killed—being exposed to the infamous gas Zyklon B used by the Nazis in extermination camps—and the note left at the scene of her murder soon linked her to two previous murders— Frieda Horzapfel in New York and Vincent Prieto in Chicago—and then to three subsequent murders—Maurice Frankl in Paris, France, Lawrence Heinz in Austin, Texas and Hilda Chandler in Norfolk, Virginia. The serial killer was dubbed the Zyklon Killer by the media.

"The notes left with these victims provided the reason and twisted justification for their murders. Their crimes? They were descended from a group of Nazi war criminals known collectively as the *Munich 7* who evaded justice after the war. The murder of these innocent people was justified with the perverted premise that, if future generations' SS officers believed that punishment may be exacted on their progeny, they may think twice about committing their crimes in the first place.

"Earlier this year, the State of Texas announced that they had executed Aaron Kaplow, the Zyklon Killer, for the murder of Lawrence Heinz but today I am here to announce that Aaron Kaplow was not the Zyklon Killer. He was framed and was the seventh victim of the killer. The state executed an innocent man.

"I know this because I knew the actual Zyklon Killer. I had been acquainted with him for over a decade, although I didn't even suspect him of being the killer until he confessed to me just before he committed suicide last Monday. I would like to now read the statement prepared by Alexander Kent, the Zyklon Killer, before he took his own life.

"I, Alexander Kent, leave this testament and confession of my own free will. I, Alexander Kent, am the Zyklon Killer.

"I began my crusade on January 7, 2001, when Frieda Horzapfel, the daughter of a Nazi SS officer, called to blackmail my father, threatening to tell the world that his father, my grandfather, was former Nazi *Obersturmbannführer* Hans Georg Steiner, not the Maximilian Kent I had always heard about. If we did not pay $50,000, this would jeopardize my father's run for Governor of the State of New York.

"Whether it was similar to Henry II's 'Will no one rid me of this meddlesome priest?' or whether my father's request was more direct, I knew what I had to do. I tracked her down, not to kill her but to scare her. It was then that I learned Frieda and I were members of an exclusive club. We were both descended from *Munich 7*, Nazi war criminals that escaped after the war. She had the names and addresses of five other descendants, people she was also looking to blackmail. She started with us not only because of my father's fame but because my grandfather was the most venal of them all. The more she talked, the clearer my realization became: I was the spawn of pure evil. I needed to wipe the evil of the *Munich 7* from the earth and I had to do it in a way that sent a message that future evil would not be tolerated. I knew just what to do.

"Growing up, in the shed at the back of the house there was a box of my grandfather's prized possessions. I was given strict orders not to touch it, so of course I looked. Among things like medals he had received and other memorabilia were eight canisters labeled Zyklon B. Luckily, I was a boy at the time and I wasn't strong enough to open any of the canisters but what I did was go to the school library the next day and looked up the chemical. I became aware of how it was used to kill millions.

"We kept those canisters. Mementos my grandfather wanted to keep of his past? I don't know. Remembering that we had them, years later I went back to my childhood home and grabbed one. It would be a perfect way to send a message while punishing the guilty. Though the canisters were old, they still had enough potency to kill one person.

"After killing Frieda Horzapfel, I went and told my father what I had done. Like any good parent, his first concern was to protect his son. In fact, my father supported and protected me after each killing. When I told him how guilty I was for framing Aaron Kaplow for my crimes, his advice was not to say anything. He knew that I framed Kaplow even before the man was executed. Father knew best."

At that moment, Governor Kent followed by Richard burst into the studio.

"Lies!" he shouted.

"Good morning, Governor," I calmly responded. "Won't you have a seat?"

"How dare you dishonor my son's memory so shortly after his death with these lies? He was not the Zyklon Killer!"

"Governor, I was there when he took his life. He confessed to me. These are the words he penned."

"You lie!"

"Governor, how can you sleep at night knowing that if you stopped your son after the first murder, Wendy Smith would still be alive. Vincent Prieto would still be alive. Maurice Frankl would still be alive. Lawrence Heinz would still be alive. Hilda Chandler would still be alive."

"You lie! That man in Texas was the killer."

"Aaron Kaplow and my friend Alan Westbrook were the two people he admitted to having some regrets about murdering."

"Those were not his words."

"Yes, they were. The police have them right now in evidence."

"You lie!"

"Governor," Richard interjected, "we have NYPD Detective Jane Kelly standing by."

Jane's face then appeared on the giant monitor to my left.

"Good morning, Detective Kelly. I take it you've been listening to Ms. Vega's account of Alexander Kent's suicide and the statement he left behind, which she has been reading?"

"Yes, her account is correct. I entered the written statement into evidence myself. He also left detailed accounts of each killing"

"There are no statements like this! Produce them now before you debase the memory of my son more than you already have. These accounts are all made up. I happen to know that Francine Vega wanted a romantic liaison with Alexander for years but he rebuffed her. For all we know, in a fit of the wounded pride of a jilted lover, she produced these statements herself and forced my son to sign them. She is well aware of all the details of the Zyklon Killer. She could have developed that computer file."

Richard went in for the kill.

"I don't recall anybody saying anything about a computer file, Governor. For the viewers out there, the computer file to which the Governor is referring is an exhaustive record of each killing, providing details that only the killer would know. Isn't that correct, Detective?"

"Yes, it is."

"I also don't believe it is public knowledge that your son signed his statement. Isn't that true, Detective?"

"You're correct, Richard. There were only seven people who knew about the signed statements and the computer file. Myself, my captain, Francine, FBI Special Agent Will Allen, you and two officers from the precinct's evidence room."

"And none of these individuals are known to have released this information to the public, correct?"

"That is correct."

"Governor, how do you happen to have this knowledge?"

"I...I just knew my son. He'd sign them, if they existed."

"And a computer file? Again, that wasn't common knowledge."

"My son was computer savvy. It would only make sense."

"I see."

"Richard," Kelly interjected, "I've been given information that the statements and the computer have been removed from evidence. We are investigating one of the officers who is seen on video entering the vault late at night just after he received a $10,000 deposit into his bank account and whether there is any connection to the evidence's disappearance."

"You wouldn't know anything about this, would you Governor?"

"You bastards! How dare you even think I had anything to do with such a thing! You'll be hearing from my lawyers!"

With that, he got up to storm out. Before he reached the door, I called out to him.

"Governor, you may be interested to know what your son's final words were. 'Tell my father that I love him but I can't live with this evil coursing through my veins, and neither should he. Tell him I'm sorry.' "

The Governor hesitated only a second but then continued his trip out the door. Richard allowed for a dramatic pause as the camera focused on the closed door and then returned back to him as Richard addressed the viewers.

"We'll break now for a few messages. When we come back, we'll discuss what just transpired here. In summary, we have evidence that the State of Texas did not execute the Zyklon Killer; that the Zyklon Killer was in fact Alexander Kent, son and campaign manager of presidential candidate Governor Peter Kent; that the Governor is actually the son of escaped Nazi war criminal Hans Georg Steiner; that Alexander Kent killed his victims, all of whom were descendants of fellow Nazi SS officers, in a perverted attempt to stop future butchers from emerging; and that he killed his victims with the full knowledge of his father, who did nothing to stop his son from killing again. Peter Kent was also aware that the State of Texas was about to execute an innocent man, but he kept quiet. He let the execution proceed. That is an awful lot to digest. Hopefully we can make some sense of it when we get back."

I was practically in tears when we went to commercial break. I told the truth, which is what everyone from my mother on said I should always do. Why, then, did I feel so terrible? Was the Governor correct? Did I just besmirch the memory of his son, a man who had just killed himself? And for what? Ratings?

Richard sensed my angst.

"Do you remember the first time we met?"

I nodded.

"I told you how impressed I was that you stood up to the Prime Minister of Israel, even after he ordered you to be killed?"

"Yes."

"You told me you couldn't understand the fuss. You were just doing your job. Well, that's all your doing here. You bring the truth to the American people. You dive in and investigate and separate out the facts from the bullshit. You do your job. No more, no less."

"This feels different."

"Why? Because the guy is running for president? Because you were friends with the Killer? I know you're into this 'sins of the father shouldn't be visited crap' but knowing that a candidate's father was a brutal Nazi is relevant stuff for the public to know. To borrow another time-worn saw, they need to make a determination whether 'the apple has fallen far from the tree.' You've uncovered something for them. Now, we're back on in twenty seconds. If you don't feel you can go on, I'll understand."

"No, Richard. I'll finish the show."

I sat up straighter in my chair, took a deep breath and prepared myself as the director counted down. Richard led us back into the show. We were the only two in the studio but three others would be joining us via video feed.

"Welcome back. Joining Francine and me are three other regular contributors to our show, presidential historian David S. Ballard, syndicated columnist Patricia Wentworth and Michael Przewski, a former FBI analyst and expert in evaluating forensic evidence. Welcome to the three of you to what has proven to be an interesting morning thus far. I look forward to your insights on today's revelations and what it could mean to the presidential race but before we proceed I've just been handed a note that Lansing Miller, the Attorney General for the State of Texas, is on the line. Good morning Mr. Attorney General."

The angry voice of the Attorney General was piped into the studio. He laid into us for shoddy journalism, for not giving the State of Texas the courtesy of advance warning and the opportunity to comment and reply, for unsubstantiated and biased reporting, for disparaging the justice system of the State of Texas, in which Aaron Kaplow was convicted and sentenced by a jury of his peers. He rattled off a half dozen other things. Richard just let him rant until he tired himself out. Finally, he responded.

"Sir, we've just reported the facts. I've personally gone through the computer file left by Alexander Kent. If you would like, we could go through what he described, point by point and victim by victim. As he noted in his statement, the details presented in this file are those that would only be known by the killer himself and by law enforcement officials."

"Lies! As Governor Kent postulated, it is more likely that Ms. Vega fabricated this so-called evidence after his son spurned her advances."

"That's pretty lame, Mr. Attorney General. I do hope you're not resorting to use sexual biases to attack a female journalist. What's a more likely scenario is that you were had. You were played by Alexander Kent who used you to exact revenge on a mortal enemy, Colonel Jacob Lawson."

"Who the hell is Colonel Jacob Lawson?"

"Really, General, you don't know who Colonel Jacob Lawson was? You should be better prepared when you come on TV like this. Let me invite our panel into this conversation and I'll start with Francine who will explain who Colonel Jacob Lawson was, how Alexander knew him and how framing Aaron Kaplow was a perfect revenge against this man. Lawson was someone your investigators definitely should have known about. Francine?"

I went through the Lawson/Kaplow/Kent relationship and sequence of events. Eventually, the Attorney General simply shouted 'Lies!' and hung up the phone. The four of us then proceeded with our discussion of all that had been revealed and our conjectures of what this could mean for the presidential race.

After the show ended, Richard and I sat there, emotionally exhausted.

"To think I almost chickened out of this. Wow, that was great television. We are going to be hearing from whole batteries of lawyers— including being raked over the coals by our own lawyers for not discussing this with them before we aired—over the coming weeks, but it was worth it. I bet our ratings increased by the minute as this show progressed. Thanks, Francine."

"Richard, have you ever witnessed someone commit suicide?"

"No, I can't say I ever have."

"I don't recommend it. Will suggested that I sit down with one of the agency shrinks. I waved him off but maybe it's not such a bad idea after all."

"It probably would be a good idea. I have a bunch of post-show things I have to take care of. You gonna be okay?"

"Yeah, I guess so." And that was an accurate response. Part of me felt exhilarated, part of me exhausted, part scared and part terrified. I didn't know which part held sway.

30

The effects of our show were instantaneous. New polls were conducted that evening and what had been an insurmountable twenty-eight-point lead shrank overnight to four points. A different poll had it down to three. In other words, the race was now nearly a statistical tie. That was another thing weighing on me. I could be personally responsible for an incompetent person—someone who didn't really want the job—becoming President of the United States.

Analysis of the polls indicated that people weren't bothered by the Kent's Nazi lineage. The Governor had never shown any fascist proclivities in his public life. It was his knowledge of—and almost complicity in—his son's murders that was dooming his prospects. It was his inaction knowing that an innocent man was about to be executed that bothered people. The Governor's prospects got even worse as my journalistic colleagues dug into Alexander Kent's life. They found a history of emotional problems throughout his life that were continually glossed over and covered up by his father. One high school teacher said that Alexander was extremely smart and mastered everything he tackled but his temperament could be "mercurial". The teacher was nervous for his safety one time after reprimanding his student.

Many respondents to the poll still thought The Governor to be 'more qualified' to be president that was The Reverend. However, they now trusted McKenzie more. The prevailing attitude was that there must be other skeletons in Kent's closet that he had hidden thus far that would only come out after he was elected. The general population may not agree with McKenzie but they now trusted him more. You knew where he came from.

Kent was entirely on the defensive now. He spent much of his time attacking me and the yellow journalism I represented. While many people in the general population had little use for the media, especially us in the broadcast sector, they generally seemed to have a favorable image of me. Much of that had to do with Richard and his dogged defense of me, which continued into the following week. Detective Kelly faced some criticism and there was even talk of an official reprimand. When she became a frequent guest on the evening news and put forward a good face for the NYPD, that talk died down. She also helped my cause with her methodical and factual explanations. Her no-nonsense, practical approach was appealing.

The election was two days away when Reverend McKenzie called me. The race was truly a statistical tie at this point and he had even pulled into a slight lead in two battleground states.

"Hi, Reverend. To what do owe the pleasure of this call?"

"I'm not sure. Maybe I just wanted to hear a familiar unfriendly voice."

I laughed.

"C'mon, have I really been that bad?"

"I didn't say it was a bad thing. I'm also not sure whether I'm calling to thank you or damn you. Because of you, I may not end up a well-deserved footnote in the history books. I'll leave it to you and other great minds whether that's good or bad."

"It's one of those things that only time will tell. If it's any consolation, while there's probably not a single issue I agree with you on and will continue to tell you so, I have come around on you as a person. You just needed to do some growing up from when I first met you. I think you've done just that."

"Let me think about that for a few days to decide whether I've been insulted or not."

"Good luck on Tuesday...and afterward, sir."

"Good luck to us all. Oh, one thing I wanted to let you know that I've already decided who I'm going to ask to be my Press Secretary if I win."

"I do hope you're not saying it would be me."

"No, the quid pro quo accusations themselves would mire my administration in a scandal from the get go. The person I'm going to ask is Katrina Turow. I'll need someone smart who will tell me like it is."

"If the rest of your choices are as wise as this one, I don't have any worries about a McKenzie Administration."

"Thanks, Francine. I'll be in touch, regardless of how things go."

Normally, on election night I would be at the office with Frank and all my reporter and news staff colleagues, gathered around numerous monitors with different networks on so we could get each result as it trickled in. This night was different. I wanted to be home, with my family, with not a single electronic device on. I wanted to go to bed not knowing who the new President would be. Even the following morning, I wouldn't actively seek out the news. I would find out who won, eventually.

I invited Jonas over for dinner. Albert had been asking about him, wondering if they could have a Twister rematch. I knew it would be difficult for Jonas. He still walked with somewhat of limp and there were parts of him that were permanently damaged from the blast, but there are certain things you can't explain to a ten year-old boy without breaking his heart. So when I told Jonas about the request for a rematch, he readily agreed.

We went home that night and I hugged Will and my kids longer and tighter than I ever had. We would have a wonderful evening, away from politics, away from killing, away from the news. It was just what I wanted; it was just what I needed.

View other Black Rose Writing titles at www.blackrosewriting.com/books
and use promo code **PRINT** to receive a **20% discount** when purchasing.

BLACK ROSE
writing™

www.ingramcontent.com/pod-product-compliance
Lightning Source LLC
Chambersburg PA
CBHW010444100726

47904CB00008B/2473